ENJOY THE DEVILISH TOUCH OF THESE THREE BESTSELLING AUTHORS

ANNE STUART

"Anne Stuart delivers exciting stuff…."
—Jayne Ann Krentz

"Anne Stuart is an expert craftsman."
—*Romantic Times*

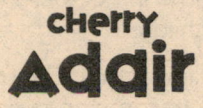

CHERRY ADAIR

"One of the reigning queens
of romantic adventure."
—*Romantic Times*

"Adair's captivating storytelling
sizzles with tension."
—*The Romance Readers Connection*

MURIEL JENSEN

"Muriel Jensen has a flair for
blending humor and romance."
—*Romantic Times*

"Muriel Jensen has a definite skill for
penning heartwarming, humorous tales
destined to remain favorites…."
—*Romantic Times*

Anne Stuart has written over sixty novels in her more than twenty-five years as a writer. She has won every major award in the business, including three RITA® Awards from Romance Writers of America, as well as their Lifetime Achievement Award. Anne's books continue to make national and chain bestseller lists, and she has been quoted in *People, USA TODAY* and *Vogue*. When she's not writing or traveling around the country speaking to various writers' groups, she can be found at her home in northern Vermont with her husband and two children.

USA TODAY bestselling author **Cherry Adair** took nearly ten years to become an overnight success. Before deciding to channel her creativity into writing hot, steamy love scenes and nail-chewing, action-packed suspense full-time, Cherry owned an interior design business. She lives in western Washington dreaming up ways to torture her characters to make them find love. In addition to being a multiple RITA® Award finalist and having one of her books voted one of the Romance Writers of America's Top Ten Favorite Books of the Year, Cherry has won dozens of awards for her action-adventure novels.

Muriel Jensen is the award-winning author of over seventy books that tug at readers' hearts. She has won a Reviewer's Choice Award and a Career Achievement Award from *Romantic Times* magazine, as well as a sales award from Waldenbooks. Muriel is best loved for her books about family, a subject she knows well, as she has three children and eight grandchildren. A native of Massachusetts, Muriel now lives with her husband in Oregon.

Date with a Devil

ANNE Stuart
cherry Adair
muriel Jensen

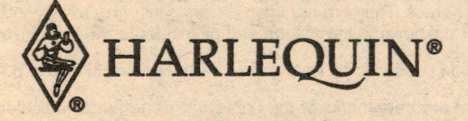

HARLEQUIN®

TORONTO • NEW YORK • LONDON
AMSTERDAM • PARIS • SYDNEY • HAMBURG
STOCKHOLM • ATHENS • TOKYO • MILAN • MADRID
PRAGUE • WARSAW • BUDAPEST • AUCKLAND

ISBN 0-373-83597-3

DATE WITH A DEVIL

Copyright © 2004 by Harlequin Books S.A.

The publisher acknowledges the copyright holders of the individual works as follows:

BLIND DATE FROM HELL
Copyright © 2003 by Anne Stuart

DANCE WITH THE DEVIL
Copyright © 2003 by Cherry Wilkinson

HAL AND DAMNATION
Copyright © 2003 by Muriel Jensen

This edition published by arrangement with Harlequin Books S.A.

® and TM are trademarks of the publisher. Trademarks indicated with ® are registered in the United States Patent and Trademark Office, the Canadian Trade Marks Office and in other countries.

Visit us at www.eHarlequin.com

Printed in U.S.A.

CONTENTS

BLIND DATE FROM HELL

Anne Stuart

CHAPTER ONE

GIDEON RAN HIS FINGERS over the piano keys, his mind only half on his task. As far as hell went, he'd been in worse ones. The three hundred and forty-seventh level wasn't bad at all, and his assignments weren't particularly onerous. He spent his time at the piano, letting his long fingers dance over the pure ivory keys, and if there were screams of torment from his fellow damned, he couldn't hear them.

It wasn't the first place he'd landed after his unfortunate demise at the hands of someone's angry boyfriend. For some reason there'd always been a piano for him, and the heat had varied from suffocating to mildly tropical. Here on the three hundred and forty-seventh level it was practically balmy.

Ralph wasn't a bad host, all things considered. Right now he was looking more like a Wall Street shark than a ruler of a level of hell, but in the end Gideon wasn't certain if there was that great a difference between the two.

Then again, he wasn't certain of anything, including his years on earth. He knew why he was in hell, though. He'd had an insatiable craving for women. He'd adored them, all of them, the tall, the short, the plump, the scrawny, old and young, sweet and sour. He just liked women. Which would probably have been fine, but he'd loved sex as well, and made it his goal to be the most inventive, astonishing lover. Maybe that wouldn't have damned him either, except it had been his own pride and pleasure that had driven him, not altruistic feelings toward the women he'd bedded. He'd wanted them so blissed-out that any man who followed him would never measure up. And that had added up to a lot of men with inadequacy complexes, since he had never stayed with a woman for long.

No, he'd signed his own contract with hell early on, whether he'd known it or not. Married, single, involved or even a holy nun, it had made no difference to him who the woman was. It was little wonder that sooner or later some jealous lover had caught up with him.

He could remember the pain of the knife carving into him, but he couldn't remember the place, the time or the man who'd done it. It could have been seventeenth century Venice—there was every possibility he could have been Casanova himself. Or it could have been the courts of Salzburg. The only thing that remained in his memory and in his hands was the piano, and when he tried to guess what kind of life he'd lived, he liked the idea of being a womanizing piano prodigy, like Liszt. Except when he played Liszt from memory he played it badly. Almost as badly as he played Chopin.

For all he knew he could have been a child of the twentieth century. Or the twenty-first—time had no place on the three hundred and forty-seventh level of hell. At least playing piano was better than shoveling coal into the vast boilers that ran the pits of eternal damnation.

There were times when he wondered if there even was a heaven. The bureaucracy of hell was so varied, obtuse and complex that even after eons, maybe centuries, Gideon had no notion of how it was organized. Every time he thought he was coming a little closer to understanding, he'd be whisked off to another level, his mind wiped clean of everything, only his fingers still remembering what they could do with the keys of a piano.

As far as imps of Satan went, Ralph wasn't bad. He had a snarky sense of humor but a real affection for Gideon's music, and he tended to leave him mostly alone. Except for the unexpected summons that had materialized on top of the piano. A summons Gideon knew better than to ignore.

He made his way through the dingy corridors, humming beneath his breath. He was reasonably content where he was, despite or maybe because of the total lack of women. There was no one to tempt him into his old ways, and celibacy had its own charms. And if the three hundred and forty-seventh level had an unfortunate resemblance to a decrepit military school dormitory he was hardly in a position to expect white palaces and cloudless vistas. He was in hell, after all, and deservedly so.

Ralph had a vain streak and a weakness for theatricality. The first time Gideon had met him he'd been sitting on a white throne, surrounded by androgynous creatures draped all over him, and it had reminded him of some bad biblical epic. Today he was in an office on a lower floor of the dormitory, a battered steel desk in front of him, the curtains closed, lights off so that the room was flooded with darkness. Gideon could barely make out his form from behind the desk.

"Nice hair," he said dryly. Despite the darkness, he couldn't miss Ralph's unexpected spiky mane of orange and blue hair that fell over one side of his face—he changed his hair almost as often as he changed his face and body. Only his eyes remained constant, watchful.

"I like variety," he said with a faint Russian accent. He changed his accents just as often, delighting in how long it took Gideon to identify his latest choice. But he didn't seem in a playful mood today.

"Have a seat," he added, not moving out of the darkness.

"Mind if I turn on a light?"

"Yes."

Gideon hooked his foot around the steel leg of the office chair and pulled it under him, stretching back to survey his... He never could quite figure out what Ralph was. His boss? His friend? His mentor? His god?

"Fiend from hell pretty much covers it," Ralph said out loud.

"I hate it when you read my mind," Gideon said.

"I'm devastated." Ralph's Russian-tinged voice was unmoved. "I have a job for you."

"And I would accept this because...?"

Long silence. "Well, because I can pretty much make you," he said. "But this will work much better if you're willing. There's a time element involved."

Gideon just waited.

"And why is that, you ask?" Ralph continued,

ignoring his silence. "I have a bit of a medical emergency, and you're the one best suited to take care of it."

"I know nothing about medicine."

"Antibiotics don't work in hell, Gideon. Ask Dr. Crippen. And if I don't get this little problem taken care of, and soon, I'm going to end up blind. And a blind devil is a pissed-off devil, and no one likes a pissed-off devil."

Gideon resisted the impulse to inform him that no one liked any kind of devil. "Going blind, eh? I told you you should have women here. The hairy palms should have tipped you off."

He half expected Ralph to fling a lightning bolt at him or at least the jar of pencils on the desk, but he simply laughed. "You see, that's why you're exactly the man I need. Your thoughts immediately go to sex. And that's what I need—a sexual professional."

"I'm not having sex with you, Ralph," Gideon said flatly.

"You should be so lucky!" Ralph scoffed. "I need you to have sex with a woman. A beautiful woman. Think you can manage it?"

"Last time I looked this was a boys-only hell, boss. Where am I going to find a woman?"

Ralph rose, moving around the desk into the

murky light. He leaned down, shoving the brightly colored hair away from his face, to expose an eye swollen shut, pink and crusted.

"That's thoroughly disgusting," Gideon drawled. "So you've got pink eye. Or a sty. Whatever. I don't see what I can do to help. Get Crippen back in."

"I told you, Crippen can't help. This is beyond his expertise. But not yours."

Ralph didn't usually beat around the bush for so long. Gideon decided to shut up and wait until Ralph came out with what he wanted. He had little enough leverage when it came to Ralph, but he would use any that he had.

Ralph sat back on the edge of the desk, letting the fluorescent hair drop back over his face. "'A woman's chastity is a sty in the devil's eye,' he said glumly. "Haven't you ever heard that saying? Didn't you ever watch any Ingmar Bergman movies?"

Gideon laughed, unable to help himself. "Can't say that I did. And you underestimate me. I'm good, but not good enough to nail all the virgins in the world before you go blind."

"Not all the virgins. Just one particular one. Seduce her, and my eye clears up, and you get to move up another level. You've been stuck on the three hundred and forty-seventh level for too long. Aren't you ready to move on?''

"And miss your charming company?"

"Oh, trust me, my boy. I'll always be with you," Ralph said with an annoying chuckle.

"So how did you manage to narrow it down to one particular virgin? Think of all the nuns, lesbians, spinsters…''

"They're all in a state of annoying purity because they should be. Sam is an affront to nature."

"You want me to make love to a man? I suppose I could, just to get out of here, but I'm not sure…''

"Sam's a woman. In fact, she's known as Samantha. No last name, like Madonna or Cher."

"The Virgin Mother doesn't need a last name, and who the hell is Cher?"

"Not the holy mother, you innocent. Madonna's something else entirely. As is Samantha, though on a completely different level. She's a model. You know what that is?"

He closed his eyes and the knowledge came. "Of course I do. Which means she's tall and blond and pretty and brainless."

"Not quite. But you'll have to come to your own conclusions. She lives in L.A., shares the house with another girl, and has somehow managed to keep her beautiful body pristine and untouched no matter who has tried. She's resisted the best-looking men in Hollywood, the most powerful politicians, the dreamiest of artists, the richest of businessmen. She's totally impervious to the male sex. And that's where you come in. No one can resist you. Gideon, Gideon, he's our man—if he can't do it, no one can.''

''Why don't you just send someone to rape her? If you're so convinced her chastity is making you blind, why waste time with niceties? Five minutes in a dark alley should take care of the problem.''

Ralph frowned at him. ''Are you offering your services? Personally I have nothing against rape or even murder—I am an imp of Satan, after all. But I thought you were a bit too squeamish for that sort of thing. I thought seduction was more in your line of expertise.''

Gideon sighed. ''It is. I'm just not in the mood. Send someone else.''

''After all these years? Get in the mood! I've made all the arrangements, and no one's even going to question it. The infection's already spreading to the other eye, and I don't have a whole lot of time to screw around. Neither do you. Get to it.''

''I haven't said I agreed to do it yet...'' Gideon began, but the words were caught in a gust of wind, torn into the bright blue California sky.

HE WAS DRIVING TOO FAST—funny, he hadn't even known he could drive. That probably ruled out the notion that he might have been Mozart. He was driving an elegant, low-slung car in heavy traffic, and it felt like he was looking up the ass of every SUV and truck that surrounded him. The exhaust was thick in the air, but the traffic was moving fast enough to blow it past him, and anything was better than the faintly sulphuric tang of hell.

"You'll love her, buddy."

He wasn't alone. He glanced over at the man sprawled in the passenger seat. He was tall, well built, well dressed, with thick blond hair, a chiseled jaw, teeth so straight and white they looked unnatural and hands the size of hams. He'd have a two octave reach with those hands, Gideon thought absently. Though with those thick fingers, he'd probably play like he was wearing boxing gloves.

"I'm sure I will," he murmured, glancing at his reflection in the rearview mirror. He looked the same as he always had, even though it must have been eons since he'd looked in the mirror. Narrow, thoughtful face, dark eyes, strong nose and a mouth that gave away no secrets, only pleasure. It was the same body, dressed in Armani this time. He was about five foot ten, lean and wiry, stronger than he looked. He wore clothes well—he remembered that much. It should endear him to a brainless, virginal model.

"You're a pal to do this, Gideon. I can't get over running into you after all these years," the man continued. Aaron, Gideon realized suddenly. Aaron McAndrews, advertising executive, smart only when it came to his own desires, ruthless and shallow and California handsome. Gideon had never seen him before in his life, but Ralph had worked his magic.

"I wouldn't set up Sam with just anyone," he continued. "You know what they say—blind dates are an invention of the devil. It was all Jasmine could do to talk her into it. But I know I can trust you. After all the time we've known each other, you've never let me down."

He'd known him ninety seconds and counting, Gideon thought, flashing him a cool smile. "Explain to me again, why are we doing this?"

"I don't know really. Because you're new in town and you need a date? It's not usually like me to be so altruistic, I know," he said with a smile, then shrugged. "But once you're seen with Sam your reputation is made. You can have all the chicks you want without lifting a finger. You'd do the same for me, old man."

Gideon smiled faintly. "I live to serve. Where are we going tonight?"

"There's a new restaurant in Hollywood that everyone's raving about. I had to use Sam's name to get a reservation—usually there's a monthlong wait, and Jasmine isn't enough to do the trick. Everybody who's anybody will be there."

"Everybody who's anybody," Gideon repeated, half to himself.

"Just don't think you're going to get anything in the way of the old horizontal rumba. Sam's gotta be a lesbian."

"What makes you say that?"

"She resists everything I've ever thrown at her." There was no missing the disgruntled tone in Aaron's voice. "But don't worry—just being seen with her will land you knee-deep in willing starlets. One date with her will be worth it in the long run, even if she won't put out."

"That sounds like a challenge," Gideon said. He automatically reached into his coat pocket, but there were no cigarettes there. Come to think of it, he didn't want to smoke. He'd had enough smoke for the last innumerable years.

"Don't even think about trying to seduce her, man," Aaron said. "She won't let you touch her."

Gideon simply smiled.

"YOU'RE REALLY expecting me to go out on a blind date?" Sam demanded, standing in front of the mirror in her favorite little red dress, silver-flecked hose on her legs, one platform heel on, one in her hand. Her tawny hair was a wild mane, her makeup had been applied with practiced skill, her honey-colored eyes were enhanced with colored contact lenses, her wide mouth painted a cherry-blossom pink.

"You've gotten this far," Jasmine said. "You aren't going to change your mind, are you?"

"You know what blind dates are, don't you?" Sam said in a dire voice as she pulled the other shoe on, pushing her normally five feet eleven inches to six foot two. "They're an instrument of the devil. They're for masochists and sadists and people who have nothing else in their lives."

"They're for people who are willing to do a favor for a good friend, no matter how unpleasant," Jasmine said softly. "You know how I feel about Aaron. He's losing interest and I have to do something before it's too late and he finds someone else. The only way he'd go out with me is if I fixed you up with his friend."

"And I still don't understand what you see in someone like…"

"Let's not go over that again," Jasmine said in a soft voice. "Love isn't practical, it just is."

Sam smoothed the red silk down over her narrow hips. "I think you can be as practical about love as you are about anything else. Pheromones shouldn't make your brain fly out the window."

"You're a lot more levelheaded than I am, as well as a lot more discreet. I've known you for four years, shared a house with you for two, and I haven't met one of your lovers."

"I keep my life compartmentalized," Sam said. She glanced at herself again in one of the many mirrors that covered the walls of the small, rambling Spanish-style villa. Jasmine had put up those mirrors. Samantha didn't need them—she knew perfectly well what she looked like. A certain combination of bone and muscle and skin, and a symmetry of body and face, that for some reason the American public found particularly pleasing. It was nothing more than a trick, a disguise, but even Jasmine didn't seem to realize it.

"So tell me about my date," she said, turning away from the mirror with a resigned sigh. "Is he going to be all over me like the last one?"

"Most of them are, sweetheart," Jasmine said.

Sam looked down at her skimpy designer dress. "Maybe I should wear something with a little more coverage."

"It wouldn't matter. You could wear burlap and

they'd be trying to jump your bones. Don't worry—I've warned Aaron you're doing this as a favor to me and that his friend needs to be on his best behavior."

"Any friend of Aaron probably doesn't know much about good behavior," Sam said. "How do they know each other? Did they go to Cal together?"

"Aaron didn't say. I'm not sure he even remembers. Just that he's known Gideon all his life and that he's a great guy."

"Gideon," Sam said in a doleful voice. "He sounds like a wannabe rock star. He's probably an accountant named George who changed his name and wears a comb-over." She tilted her head thoughtfully. "Actually I might almost prefer that."

"I'll tell Aaron you prefer comb-overs next time we double-date."

"We're not doing this again, Jasmine. I love you, but there are limits, and blind dates are above and beyond the call of duty." The doorbell rang, and Samantha froze. It was too late to run, too late to feign sick, though she would have liked nothing more than to have thrown up all over her unwanted escort for the evening.

"Cheer up, Sam," Jasmine said, heading for the door. "Everyone knows blind dates are from hell."

"Yeah," Sam said gloomily. "I'd rather be at the dentist."

It was too late. Jasmine had opened the door, beaming up into the chiseled face of her beloved. His shadow dwarfed the man beside him, and Sam groaned inwardly. She was going out with a midget. Probably one who tried to compensate for his lack of height by being too aggressive. She couldn't do it, wouldn't do it!

"And this is the famous Samantha," Aaron was saying, introducing her with an infuriating tone of ownership, as if she were a favored toy he was sharing with a friend. "Sam, this is Gideon Hyde."

She lifted her head, drew herself to her full height and looked at him. Not tiny, and if she hadn't deliberately chosen the highest heels she owned, they might be close in height. As it was she could enjoy the sensation of looking down at him, a faintly haughty expression on her face. She didn't hold out her hand.

"Delighted to meet you," she said in a bored voice dripping insincerity.

She didn't get the reaction she was hoping for. He wasn't standing there, openmouthed, awestruck. He simply nodded politely, then returned his attention to the chattering Jasmine, listening courteously.

Sam stood motionless in astonishment. She

wasn't used to being ignored, in particular by a blind date. Not that she'd ever had to go on a blind date before—she was able to say no to anyone—except Jasmine, especially when she cried.

But Gideon Hyde seemed to be totally uninterested in her, and Sam felt an irrational spurt of annoyance deep inside.

"Hey, our reservation is in an hour, and it's going to take at least that long to drive into the city from out here in the boonies," Aaron said in his chummy voice. "Why don't we head out? We've got Gideon's car—a sweet little Mercedes. If you want, you can sit in the back with me, Sam."

And there was another problem. Aaron seemed to have a thing for her, and he expressed it any time he thought Jasmine wasn't paying attention. She could just imagine what an hour-long ride in the cramped back seat of a Mercedes would be like. "I'll sit up front with my…date," she said sweetly. There was no reprimand in her voice, but Gideon turned and looked at her anyway, as if he'd only just remembered why he was here.

"Good idea," he murmured. He had a rich, musical voice, though she couldn't tell what part of the country he came from. She liked his voice, even if she didn't like his presence in her house.

And she was tired of waiting around. The sooner

this date from hell began, the sooner it would be over. "Let's go," she said briskly. "I'm starved." And she walked out the open front door, knowing they wouldn't be far behind.

CHAPTER TWO

SAMANTHA'S LONG LEGS quickly carried her to the car parked in the small yard of her little house, and she climbed into the front seat before her so-called date could open the door for her. She didn't really want to find out whether he would have done it or not. If he held the door for her, it probably meant he was old-fashioned, condescending and searching for a way to look up her skirt. If he didn't, it meant he was self-absorbed and rude. She'd already figured he was rude, but with hours left to this torment, she didn't need to confirm it. Why make this date any harder than she had to?

He drove fast and well down the winding road from her house perched on the hillside. A little too fast, she decided, casting a surreptitious glance over at him, ready to catalogue his flaws. She looked at his hands on the wheel. No rings at all, thank God. He had beautiful hands, with long fingers and narrow palms. She had a weakness for beautiful hands.

He dressed well. He was wearing either Armani

or something custom-made, and she knew clothes well enough to recognize the quality of the dark silk. He wore sunglasses, shielding his eyes, but his cheekbones were high, his face narrow, his mouth revealing nothing.

His hair was the only anomaly for a young Californian on the make. It was long, much longer than was currently fashionable, shiny black and perfectly straight, and he had it tied back with a strip of silk. That hairstyle went out with Steven Seagal, and she wanted to tell him that, except for some reason it looked good on him. Exotic.

She'd slipped her own sunglasses onto her face and slid down in the seat, keeping her legs stretched out in front of her. She was used to men ogling her famous legs, but he seemed far more interested in the car and the road than the famous beauty beside him.

Sam had no illusions about her beauty. It was a fact of life, a gift given her by mischievous gods, and she knew how to use it effectively when she had to, on the days when she was in the limelight. Today should have provided some downtime for her, when she could just hang around the house and play with the dogs, watch TV and read, not have to do a thing with clothes or makeup.

But giving up one day for a friend was not so

great a sacrifice. Especially since her blind date seemed totally impervious to her surface charms.

"Nice car," she said idly, when the silence had grown uncomfortable.

He glanced at her, startled, almost as if he'd forgotten she was there. "Very nice," he agreed in that cool, mysterious voice. "I've never driven one before."

"Is this a rental?"

For a moment it seemed as if he didn't know the answer. "Yes," he said finally.

"You don't live in California?"

"No. I come from a place farther south and a lot hotter." His answer seemed to amuse him.

"San Diego?"

He shook his head. "No place you've ever been."

"Actually I've never been to San Diego, though I'm not sure why. I was supposed to do a photo shoot at the Hotel Del but it got canceled at the last minute." Now why in hell was she talking to him? It wasn't as if she actually wanted to do anything more than get through the next few hours. When forced into a social occasion like this one, she usually made her way through it with a distant, slightly vacant boredom. And yet here she was, prattling away to a mysterious stranger like she actually wanted to.

He didn't say anything, making it abundantly clear that he had no interest in her conversation. She sank back into silence, plotting revenge on the totally preoccupied Jasmine, who was about to break all sorts of decency laws in the back seat, with Aaron's enthusiastic assistance. She closed her eyes, thinking dark thoughts. She'd become and expert at enduring trying situations. She'd once stood for seven hours in the pouring rain on the Spanish Steps in Rome while on a photo shoot, and when the rain let up they sprayed her with hoses. She'd tromped through mud, posed in bathing suits amidst the snow, sat for hour after endless hour, unable to move and mar her perfectly arranged hair and makeup. At least tonight she could move, she could speak, she was neither wet nor freezing. She could just retreat into that quiet place she went to when the rest of the world got too noisy, and her obtuse blind date wouldn't even see.

She should have known they'd end up at Murph's Steak 'n' Grill, the latest, trendiest of restaurants. It was designed to look like a midwestern steakhouse chain, except that most of the steaks came from creatures far more exotic than steer, the waiting list for reservations stretched into next year and prices on the menu would support a third-world country for at least two years.

Her date, and she'd already forgotten his name, pulled up to valet parking. By the time he'd climbed out and Aaron and Jasmine had disentangled themselves, she was tapping her foot on the sidewalk, waiting impatiently.

Hyde, that was his name, she remembered. Gideon Hyde. He came over to her, seemingly unbothered by her deliberate attempt to dwarf him, and she straightened her back to increase the distance. He was probably five foot ten or eleven—her own height, in fact, but he couldn't wear platform heels. He had no choice but to be overshadowed.

It didn't seem to bother him. Aaron had pushed between them, talking a mile a minute, and a slightly mussed Jasmine followed behind, looking slightly sheepish. Sam suppressed an inward sigh. The things she did for her friends.

"Shall we?" Gideon said. If he put his hand on the small of her back, she'd kick him with her lethal shoes, but he wisely did no such thing. Odd, how he managed to sort of usher her into the ultratrendy restaurant without even touching her. She felt oddly protected. Not that she needed protection from anyone. Still, it was a strange, not uncomfortable, sensation.

The noise assaulted her once she stepped inside. She'd long ago learned to ignore the eyes that focused on her when she was in a public place, and tonight was no different. She followed the circuitous route the maitre d' led them, in order to show off their celebrity acquisition to as many guests as possible, before seating them at a far too public table. She considered asking for one out of the limelight, but Aaron had already plopped himself down, leaving Jasmine to fend for herself. He rubbed his hands together in visceral delight.

"This is great, isn't it? Just great!"

Gideon moved around her, and she stiffened, waiting for his touch. Instead he pulled the chair out for Jasmine, and the sweetness of the smile he directed at her was a revelation.

Sam didn't wait for him to pull out her chair. If he didn't she'd have to hit him; if he did she'd have to thank him. Right now she was far too interested in considering other possibilities, such as whether Gideon was really interested in Jasmine and had used this hellish blind date as a simple ruse to get close to her. If so, she could certainly applaud his good taste—Jasmine was worthy of devotion from far better than a lout like Aaron.

Lout. She liked that word—it fit Aaron entirely too well. A boring, shallow lout. Whereas Gideon

Hyde was an enigma, and more interesting than she cared to admit.

He ordered single malt scotch, of course. "I don't drink," she said in a cool, serene tone.

Jasmine didn't blink—if she'd learned one thing it was not to contradict Sam in public. She didn't say a word when Sam closed the huge menu and ordered a salad of mixed baby greens and nothing else. She'd had enough sense to pig out before they left, hoping a quick meal would make the end of the evening come that much faster.

"You don't eat meat?" Gideon said. He still wore his sunglasses, as did half the people in the darkened room, but it annoyed her. "Are you a vegetarian?"

"A vegan. I don't partake of flesh of any sort, but since the menu is unfortunately devoid of tofu I'll have to make do with salad."

"Tofu," Aaron said with a shudder.

"A steak house was probably not the best choice of restaurant then," Gideon said.

There was something behind those dark glasses, something behind that odd, liquid voice that she couldn't quite define. She wondered what he'd do if she pulled the glasses from his narrow, strong nose and threw them across the room.

She was going to do no such thing, of course.

That would require touching him, and she certainly wasn't about to do that. "She'll be fine," Aaron said carelessly. "Models don't eat anything, anyway. Too easy to get fat." He was sitting to one side of her, and he reached out and pinched her thigh with one meaty hand.

She jumped, not expecting it, and glared at him. If Jasmine hadn't been sitting there looking so lovelorn she would have thrown her water glass at him. As it was, the night was still wretchedly young, and she would just as likely have a chance to do it later.

"You don't drink, you don't eat," Gideon said. "Do you have any weaknesses at all?"

"None that concerns you." She cast a suspicious eye at Aaron. "You chose this place, didn't you?"

"Hey, I've been trying to get in here for months. It was only when I used your name that a table magically opened up. Come on, Sam, you'll love it. They serve everything from emu to baby seal, and the chef's an animal lover. He keeps his pet bichon frise with him in the kitchen."

"In case he runs out of meat?" she drawled.

"Ewww," Jasmine said.

"They eat dog in Vietnam," Gideon said.

"Thank God you didn't choose a Vietnamese restaurant," Sam said. "I can't stand dogs, but I'd just as soon not eat one." She picked up her glass of

Pellegrino, tossed her thick mane over her shoulder, and gave Gideon a cool, assessing look. Daring him to say something.

They'd brought him his scotch, and he held it up, a silent, almost mocking toast, before taking a drink. For some reason she watched his mouth, the line of his throat as he swallowed the liquor. For some reason she felt uncomfortably hot. She wondered if the taste lingered in his mouth.

"Would you prefer to go somewhere else, Samantha?" he asked.

She'd always hated the name her mother had saddled her with, and she deliberately used it only for her professional life, to keep her personal and professional worlds separate. "We're here now. We might as well stay," she said. She was treading a fine line between elegant boredom and outright rudeness, and she wasn't quite sure why. She knew how to behave, but Gideon Hyde with his dark glasses and his liquid, silvery voice managed to get under her skin.

He reached over and patted her hand like a pediatrician comforting a fretful child anticipating a shot. "Don't worry—it will all be over soon."

She snatched her hand away as if burned, and put it in her lap under the table. And she gave him her coldest, chilliest smile, one that could freeze the fires of hell itself.

He simply smiled back, unmoved.

YES, SAMANTHA was beautiful. Cold as ice, which should have appealed to Gideon after his endless incarceration in such a hot climate. He genuinely liked women, thought he understood them, but Sam wasn't quite so easy to read. When she looked at him, which was as infrequently as possible, she seemed to view him as a cross between a serial killer and a pervert. As far as he could remember he was neither, but maybe she was psychic.

He didn't think so. He wouldn't put it past Ralph to send a twisted murderer back to earth, just for his own entertainment, but despite the few concrete facts he possessed about himself, Gideon didn't think he was a truly bad man, even if he had ended up in hell.

No, the problem rested with the astonishingly beautiful woman sitting beside him. Her luminous tawny eyes were cool and emotionless, her perfectly tinted lips held only the most dismissing of smiles, except when it came to her friend. Jasmine was vulnerable, sweet and not too bright, and she seemed to incite the only emotions Samantha was capable of feeling, or at least showing. Maybe Ralph was wrong; maybe her sexual orientation was toward other women. That wouldn't stop him from seducing her, but Ralph had assured him she was neither gay nor frigid. She just hadn't found the right man.

She had now, whether she was willing to accept it or not. She was a challenge, no doubt about that, and he didn't know how much time he actually had for the project. He supposed it was possible he could manage to get her in bed tonight, but that would require superhuman effort.

Come to think of it, he wasn't human, was he? He wasn't quite sure what he was. And after all this time, he wasn't even sure he wanted to make love to one of the most beautiful women he'd ever seen.

She picked at her salad, like someone nibbling on sautéed worms. She sipped at her water, her magnificent eyes downcast. She was a little too thin for his tastes, he thought, then corrected himself. No one had ever been too thin or too plump for him. He was looking for excuses.

Maybe he just didn't like following orders. For the first time in what might be centuries he had something under his control. And despite the cost, he might very well simply refuse to cooperate. It would certainly be with Samantha's cold-blooded blessing.

Was this night never going to end? He ate the

rarest, bloodiest beef steak he could get, partly to annoy her, partly because it might be the last great steak he'd ever get. And it was so wonderful he almost forgot why he was there.

Bored, he thought. He needed something to liven things up, or he wasn't going to get within an inch of Samantha's long, luscious legs. Just a small distraction to shake things up...

It wasn't a large explosion, though the kitchen door slammed open with a gust of smoke and flames. The sprinkler system came on, and he wasn't sure whether all the overdressed guests were screaming because of the danger from the fire or because their clothes were being ruined by the water pouring from the ceiling. They were racing toward the exits with all the calm of a cattle stampede as thick, dense smoke filled the room. Aaron had bolted at the first sign of danger, Jasmine was standing frozen in shock, Samantha was already in motion.

He had to get them out of there. He'd already figured out that Samantha didn't like to be touched, but Jasmine was another matter. He put his arm around her waist and started toward the door, knowing Samantha was more than capable of finding her way on her own. And she would have if her ridiculous kiss-my-ass shoes hadn't collapsed under her, sending her sprawling.

Personal space be damned. He reached down and hauled her up, dragging her from the chaos that had been one of the L.A. area's most exclusive restaurant just a few short minutes ago. And he'd been complaining about being bored.

The three of them stumbled out into the night air, followed by waves of billowy smoke. The drenched diners were coughing and crying, including Jasmine, but Samantha simply pulled her arm free, fastening her fierce gaze on a sheepish looking Aaron.

"You cowardly son of a—" she started, when an anguished howl broke through her incipient tirade.

"My Choux-fleur!" someone cried. Samantha whirled around, tottering slightly on her ridiculous shoes, and honed in on the chef.

"You can get more cauliflower," she snapped.

"No! Choux-fleur is my bichon frise. He was asleep on his little bed when the explosion happened. I must go back…"

He was immediately restrained by a group of firefighters. "You left your dog in there?" she demanded.

"Mon petit Choux-fleur!" he was moaning.

Gideon felt a hand on his arm, and he turned to see Samantha holding on to him as she slipped off first one shoe, then the other, bringing her down to his height. It was odd to be looking directly into her eyes, but she wasn't paying attention. She thrust the shoes and her ridiculous swan-shaped purse into his hands. "Take care of these for me," she said. And a moment later she was sprinting across the littered sidewalk, back into the smoky restaurant before anyone could stop her.

He immediately started after her. Mortality wasn't much of an issue for him, and he'd been in hotter places, but by this time the firefighters had managed to push everyone back.

"My date went back inside," he said helplessly, still clutching her stupid shoes and purse.

"Don't worry, buddy," a cop standing nearby said. "The guys have gone in after her. If she's still in one piece they'll get her out okay. Does your girlfriend have a death wish or something? She do crazy shit like this a lot?"

"I don't know. She was a blind date."

The cop's laugh was unsentimental. "If it was a blind date you're probably better off if she doesn't come out."

Gideon stared at him, then blinked as Ralph's face looked back at him from beneath the cop's hat. His bad eye was in the shadow, and his grin was far too cheerful. "Better get to it, old man," he said, clapping Gideon on the shoulder. "You don't want to disappoint me, now do you? Especially when I went to all that trouble to alleviate your boredom?"

"You set the fire?"

Ralph shrugged. "Nothing so pedestrian. I arranged it. And she'll be coming out in a minute or two, you just wait. I'm not about to let anything happen to her. My eyesight is precious to me."

"You're a conscienceless bastard."

"Of course I am, Gideon," he said. "What would you expect from hell? Now, stop wasting time."

A second later Gideon was staring into a different face, an older policeman. "You okay, buddy?" he said, looking worried. "You blanked out on me for a second. Did you hit your head?"

Gideon shook himself, mentally cursing Ralph. "My girlfriend just ran back into the restaurant," he said. "You have to let me go in…"

"That her?"

Gideon looked up. Samantha had reemerged, her tawny mane wet and bedraggled, her face and arms and endless legs streaked with soot, a squirming white bundle of fur in her arms, trying to lick some of the dirt away.

And then the chef rushed over, tears of gratitude pouring down his face as he tried to take the dog out of Samantha's arms. The dog snapped at him, and a moment later the three of them had disappeared into the crowded night, leaving Gideon standing alone still clutching the most ridiculous pair of shoes he'd ever seen and a crystal-studded purse shaped like a swan.

"Hey, man, can you give us a ride home?" Aaron loomed up beside him, a shaken Jasmine in tow. Aaron didn't even have a spot of soot or water on him—clearly he'd saved his sorry ass before the sprinkler system had even been activated.

"I need to find Samantha."

"Don't worry about her," Jasmine said. "She's gone to the animal emergency room with the chef. She'll find her own way home."

There was nothing he could say. He simply nodded, tucking the shoes under his arm and slipping the tiny jeweled purse into his pocket. By the time he arrived at Aaron's house he'd come to a decision, one he'd been flirting with all night. Ralph wasn't going to have his way, no matter what the cost.

"Sorry about the date, old man," Aaron said, climbing out of the car and waiting for Jasmine to follow. "I did my best, but Samantha's a cold bitch. If you want me to set you up with someone a little friendlier just let me know. How long are you going to be in town?"

"Not long," he said, expecting Ralph to haul his

ass back to hell the moment he refused to play along.

"Jasmine and I are spending the weekend at my place in the mountains, but I'll give you a call when I get back, okay? You'll still be at the same place?"

"I expect so," he said calmly. Still in hell, where he presumably belonged.

He just wished he could remember why.

CHAPTER THREE

"FORGET IT."

Gideon blinked. A second ago he'd been about to climb back into the gorgeous Mercedes on a warm California night. Now he was back in the stifling confines of the three hundred and forty-seventh level of hell, with Ralph sprawled on a wooden bench, peering at him from beneath luxurious black curls that could only be a wig. The last time he'd seen him he'd been an able-bodied policeman. He'd morphed into Captain Hook, with an elegant frock coat, a gold hook in place of a hand, a carved ivory peg leg, and an embroidered eye patch.

"Not Captain Hook," Ralph said with a trace of irritation, reading his mind again. "He had both eyes and both legs, if I remember my classics correctly. But we're not talking about literature, we're talking about my eye. I'm not taking no for an answer."

Gideon glanced down at his own clothes. He was in jeans and a T-shirt—the silk suit long gone, but for some reason he reached for his nonexistent pocket, for the swan purse he'd tucked there. Gone as well, and the thought was oddly troubling.

"You can't make me."

"You sound like a teenager. I can make you do anything I want," Ralph said. "All I have to do is threaten you with another millennium in this place as opposed to a chance of moving on, and you'll do exactly as I say. Besides, what have you got to lose? She's gorgeous, and you love women. Are you afraid you can't get her? Afraid to fail?"

Afraid to win, he thought absently.

"Sentimental crap," Ralph said, reading him. "You'll screw her senseless, my eye will be healed, you'll move on to someplace with a little more air conditioning, and she'll move on to someone like Aaron who'll marry her, give her babies, cheat on her and leave her for a younger woman the moment her looks start to fade."

"You're so sure of that?"

"Hell, no. The future isn't preordained—I thought you knew that. There are all sorts of possibilities. The only thing that isn't negotiable is whether or not you'll seduce her. And she's got to like it."

"I wouldn't think that would make any difference in whether your eye will heal or not."

"It doesn't. I just want your work cut out for you. Giving a virgin an orgasm is a tough job, but you're the man to do it."

"And if I say no?"

"I told you, not an option."

Gideon kept his mind deliberately blank, looking around the tiny, heat-filled space. "So why am I back here?"

"What do you think this is, summer camp? You're not on furlough, you're on a mission. When you're not working you come back here, not to that hotel suite."

Gideon only raised an eyebrow. "You want my cooperation, Ralph? Then maybe you'll have to give a little more than vague promises. I get to stay up there until the job is done, or no deal."

Ralph scratched his head with the golden hook, and the long black wig shifted slightly. "You're annoying, you know that? I could always make a trade, get someone a little more cooperative in your place."

"Why don't you?"

"You've already made some progress. She likes you, even if she's not sure why. Besides, I prefer to work with what I have. You've got forty-eight hours, Gideon. Get her, and get her good, or you'll find you didn't even know what hell could be like. I'll be watching."

"Voyeur," Gideon said.

"Don't try my patience, boy."

"I'll do..." Gideon's words trailed off. He was standing on a balcony, looking out over the sprawling city of Los Angeles. Looking toward the hills, where Samantha's house was nestled. Ralph had sent him back, but that didn't mean he wasn't listening to every thought, watching every movement.

He summoned up the most insulting mental picture he could imagine, just for Ralph's benefit, and then laughed. It was a cool night, the silk was soft against his skin, and the swan-shaped purse was in his pocket. The shoes were on a low table behind him, and he picked one up, running his fingers along the high arch, the ridiculously high heel. He couldn't figure out how a woman could walk in those things, much less run. Or why a woman who hated dogs would run back into a burning restaurant to rescue one.

He'd find out soon enough. In the meantime he was going to strip off his silk suit, slide naked beneath the silk sheets that he was sure would be on the huge bed in his hotel room and sleep without dreams.

And he wouldn't even break a sweat.

IT WAS A HOT, lazy afternoon. It had taken Sam forever to scrub the soot and smoke from her hair and skin, and she'd slept late, only dragging herself out of bed at Rags's insistence. Dogs were a pain in the butt, she thought fondly, leading the partially blind, totally deaf springer spaniel out to the backyard, where he immediately began leaping around like a puppy instead of the twelve-year-old elder states man that he was. Whether they were tiny little yapsters like Choux-fleur or huge goofy dumbbells, she loved them all. Right now she only had Rags in residence, but she was expecting two rescued King Charles spaniels in the next week or so, and she was looking forward to it.

She hadn't slept well. For some reason she kept dreaming of her annoying blind date. Not that there was any other kind of blind date, but what's-his-name was more insidious than most. Or less forgettable, which made him dangerous. And she knew perfectly well what his name was. Gideon Hyde. She just wished she didn't.

She liked him. She wasn't sure why—maybe it was his kindness to Jasmine. Maybe it was the way he didn't let her borderline rudeness bother him. Maybe because he didn't fall at her feet or try to paw her. Maybe she was just obsessed by his mouth. It didn't matter—she wouldn't be seeing him again.

No doubt, he'd have learned his lesson the hard way last night—that just because a woman possessed certain physical attributes didn't mean she'd be an agreeable companion. Not to mention that she'd ditched him at the last minute. Plus a pair of designer shoes and her Judith Leiber purse. She'd always liked that purse, too. The swan appealed to her sense of humor. And it was going to be a pain to replace a couple of its contents.

She worked out for her allotted hour, hating every moment of it, then rewarded herself with a huge roast beef sandwich and a bottle of Sapporo beer. She had a real weakness for beer, one she couldn't indulge too often, and she was working her way around the world. She'd gone through German, Danish and Mexican beers, and she was two weeks into Japanese beers. So far she liked them the best, but there were dozens of countries left to go.

She was wearing cutoffs, a well-worn white ASPCA T-shirt without a bra underneath and her hair was yanked back in a loose ponytail as she settled on the grass beneath the jacaranda tree. She didn't bother with her contacts—her sunglasses had prescription lenses and it was a bright day. Rags came over and plopped down beside her, putting his head on her lap. He could smell the roast beef, but he'd always been too much of a gentleman to beg, and she wasn't about to tempt him.

It was a beautiful day, and she had nothing to do, and even if she did, her car was in the shop. She didn't need to worry about anything, not even Jasmine. And she'd managed to dump her unwanted date the night before, so why wasn't she feeling more peaceful?

She took another drink of the icy beer, savoring it. She only allowed herself one a week—beer was fattening and for as long as her fifteen minutes of fame lasted she intended to respect the tool that had given it to her—her body.

She heard the car pull into her long driveway, and she breathed a sigh of relief. Jasmine was back early. She'd probably be crying—Aaron was a pig and a beast and Jasmine was a fool to love him, but all the reasoning in the world wouldn't make any difference. Thank God she wasn't plagued by any romantic weaknesses.

"I'm out back!" she called, taking another bite out of her sandwich. "Come and tell me how your night went. Was Mr. Tall, Dark and Brooding pissed off that I dumped him?" And then she stopped, horrified, as Mr. Tall, Dark and Brooding himself came around the corner of the house.

"Not particularly," he said. He still had his dark

glasses on, but today he was wearing black pants and a black silk shirt. No gold chains, and only a couple of buttons undone. She found she wanted to see more of his chest and had no idea why.

Fortunately Sam was incapable of blushing. She tilted her head sideways, observing him. "You'd make a good model," she said. "You wear clothes well."

"I'm not bad without them," he replied in his calm, liquid voice. "You left your shoes and purse behind. I figured you weren't being Cinderella, but by the time I dropped Jasmine off she was too involved with Aaron to pay much attention, or I would have given them to her."

"Rather than use them as an excuse to see me again?"

"I didn't get the impression you were swept away by my charms, but you can always disabuse me of the notion." He set the shoes down on the chair by the pool, placing the swan purse on top of them. "You hate dogs, do you? And I suppose Sapporo suddenly started making nonalcoholic beer, and that's roast beef-colored tofu on your sandwich?"

She should have been annoyed. "You're just lucky Rags is blind and deaf. He hates men. He was abused as a puppy and he gets very aggressive when men come near."

"Does he? Sounds like his owner." Without waiting to be asked he sat down in one of the French wrought-iron chairs by the pool. As luck would have it Rags suddenly realized someone was there, and he lifted his head, sniffing, and a quiet growl started in his throat as he lumbered to his feet.

She grabbed for him, but he slipped past her, heading toward Gideon with unnatural accuracy, given his cloudy eyesight. Sam closed her eyes, waiting for the inevitable snapping and growling. Rags wouldn't actually bite him, but he could make enough noise to scare the devil. Well, she'd warned him.

To her astonishment the incipient growl ended. She opened her eyes to see Rags slobbering happily beneath Gideon's beautiful hands.

"He seems to like me well enough. Another lie?"

Sam shook her head. "He's never let another man near him. That's very odd."

"Maybe he has better instincts than his mistress."

She took another drink of beer. "Okay, I'm sorry. I just don't happen to like blind dates."

"Or men?"

"I like men just fine. In their place," she added with a trace of wickedness.

"And where is that? As far away as possible?"

"Depends on the man," she said. "Do you want a beer?"

"I want…"

The ring of the cell phone stopped him midsentence. She picked it up, crossing her bare legs and leaning forward.

It was Jasmine, sobbing. "Sam!" she wailed on the other end.

"What's wrong?"

"Aaron and I had a fight. He left me up here, all alone!"

"Where are you?"

"Up in the mountains. The house in Santa Ina—you remember. You came here for the Fourth of July. I'm all alone here and I don't think he's coming back!"

"Jerk!" Sam muttered.

"What?" Jasmine exclaimed.

"Aaron, not you," Sam clarified. "I'll come and get you. Just calm down, and I'll be there as soon as I can."

"You don't have a car. It's in the shop, remember?" Jasmine started sobbing even harder.

Sam glanced over at Gideon. He was concentrating on scratching Rags's head as it lolled blissfully against his leg. "I'll borrow one," she said. "Give me three hours and I'll come get you. Okay?"

"Okay," Jasmine's voice was watery. "But come soon."

Sam disconnected, rising to her feet with one fluid movement. "I need your car," she said flatly.

"Forget it. You're not getting it. Not without me."

"If you think I'm going to sleep with you just to borrow your car…"

He laughed. "Who said anything about sleeping with me? Since it's a rental, I don't want anyone else driving it. If you need to go someplace, I'll drive you."

She couldn't blush, but she could mentally kick herself. Why in hell had she said something like that? She had no idea whether Gideon Hyde wanted to get her in bed or not. Most men did, but she'd already discovered that Gideon wasn't most men. He was far more interesting. Dangerously so.

"I need to drive up to a cabin in the mountains near Santa Ina and pick up Jasmine. Apparently she had a fight with Aaron and he left her there."

"All right," he said. "Let's go." He rose, and he was her height. She needed her shoes on again. She needed her hair and her makeup and her uncomfortable clothes.

"Give me a minute to change."

"I thought we were in a hurry."

She looked at him. It was an odd sensation—he was picture-perfect, she was the slob. "Let me see your eyes," she said abruptly.

"You want to see if I'm on drugs?"

"No. I want to see whether I can trust you."

He reached up and took the dark glasses off, looking directly into her eyes, and for a moment her heart stopped. His eyes were so dark they were almost black, and they were slightly tilted, exotic-looking, deep and unfathomable. And all she could do was look into them wordlessly, falling into some deep, velvet tunnel.

"Now you," he said, keeping her trapped in the watchfulness of his gaze.

"This isn't strip poker."

"Take them off." His deep, liquid voice was almost hypnotic, and she took off her sunglasses.

"I'm not wearing my contacts," she said. "You'll be a blur." But she could see him quite clearly. See his eyes, feel them. It was almost physical and totally unnerving. Her skin felt hot, prickly, and she wanted...

She didn't know what she wanted. She put her glasses back on hurriedly and stepped away. "Satisfied?"

"Not yet. What about the dog? Will he be all right alone?"

No man had ever expressed concern about any of her dogs. "He'll be fine. My housekeeper is coming over later to feed him—if I'm not here she'll just take him home with her. He's used to her."

"Then let's go."

"I need shoes."

He smiled. Another danger—with his dark, unreadable eyes and that half smile he was disturbingly attractive. And she didn't want to be attracted to him. "You could wear the ones I brought back. Unless they've already served their purpose."

"What do you mean?"

"They put me in my place. I think you can comfortably get away with flats now. I know you're above me."

She almost put the damned shoes on just to spite him. She had a pair of well-worn sandals by the pool—she shoved her feet in them instead.

"Purse?" she said. He tossed the tiny jeweled swan to her, and she caught it. It held nothing but a hundred dollars cash, her driver's license and her ATM card, but it would do. "I'm ready," she said, not sure if she was.

The black Mercedes was parked in her driveway, the same car he'd driven the night before, of course. "I don't suppose you'd change your mind about letting me drive?"

"Not in this lifetime. Do I open the door for you or will you hit me?"

He'd managed to surprise her again. Had he read her mind last night? Impossible. "I can open my own doors."

"Then what's stopping you? Get in."

She hesitated for a moment longer. For some reason she kept thinking it was the point of no return. Once she stepped into that car her life would be changed forever.

And then she shook away the odd superstitious thought and climbed in. Jasmine needed her. This was no time for her to give in to her overindulgent imagination.

This wasn't the river Styx, and he wasn't Charon, taking her down into hell. She wasn't Persephone, she wasn't Cinderella, she wasn't anyone but Sam going to rescue a friend, forced into the company of a fascinating stranger.

She'd survive. She always did.

CHAPTER FOUR

SO MAYBE REFUSING to do Ralph's bidding was the dumbest idea he'd ever had in his entire life, both before and after death. She'd been beautiful and desirable with her go-to-hell shoes and her perfect hair. In cutoffs and a T-shirt, and with her hair yanked back in a ponytail, and no makeup, she was close to irresistible. She wasn't wearing a bra, and he sent a silent thank-you in Ralph's direction for that benefit. No, he probably wasn't going to be able to resist her. He'd just have to hope her will was stronger than his.

She had the prettiest eyes. Pretty wasn't a word most people would have used when they thought of Samantha—striking, gorgeous, beautiful were even too mild. But when she took off her dark glasses and looked at him, without the artificial shield of contact lenses, she'd looked vulnerable and almost…sweet. So sweet that he knew if he touched her he'd hurt her. So sweet that he knew he was going to have to try.

He glanced over at her in the passenger seat. She was clutching that ridiculous little purse in her beautiful hands, and he tried to wrench his mind away from what those hands could do, what those long, smooth legs would feel like wrapped around him.

"Why the swan?"

"I collect purses."

"But the swan wasn't just a random choice, was it?"

She looked at him. "No."

"So were you too tall and gangly as a child and always felt like an ugly duckling and now you identify with the swan?"

"You're not nearly as smart as you think you are," she shot back. "I'm a swan who'd rather be a duckling. But you take what you're handed and deal with it."

"Ah, poor baby. It's a curse being beautiful," he said lightly.

She stared at him. "Go to hell."

He laughed, resisting the impulse to say, *Been there, done that.* "Sorry. I'm not being suitably reverential."

She pushed her sunglasses up on her forehead to look at him, and once more he got the full force of her eyes. "I don't have the right nature to be beautiful," she said. "But I also don't like to waste things. I was given a certain gift, and I'll nurture it and sell it for as long as I can. When it's over I'll take my money and move as far away from L.A. as I can.''

"And what will you do then?"

"Anything I damned please. So what do you do? I expect you're in advertising like Aaron.''

"You really don't like me much, do you?'' he said.

"You really haven't given me any reason to like you, have you?'' she countered.

He racked his brain, but his mouth was already coming up with an answer. "I play piano.''

"For a living?'' She sounded dubious.

He shrugged. "I write music. Soundtracks, some stuff for television. It keeps me relatively solvent.'' It sounded oddly right even as he made it up on the spot.

"And you do all this someplace farther south and a lot hotter?''

He'd forgotten he'd said that. She must have been paying closer attention than he realized. "No, that's just where I came from. Right now I live on a small island in Puget Sound. Fortunately I get to work long-distance.'' He changed the subject. "So you don't like being a model?''

For a moment he thought she was going to blow

him off. But instead she put the sunglasses back on, and he could see a little of the tension leave her body. "It has its good points," she said. "I make a great deal of money and I get to play dress-up. I was always into fantasy when I was a kid, probably because I was an only child. So now I get to dress up like a thousand different women and pretend I'm them, and then I get to go home and be me."

"And who do you prefer?"

"Me," she said with absolute certainty.

"So do I."

"What?"

"Prefer you to the thousand different women. When you're not trying to scare the hell out of me."

"I don't think anyone could," she said, sounding slightly aggrieved. "So why did you agree to bring me up here? Surely you must have better things to do if you're just in L.A. on a visit."

"Nothing better to do. Besides, I like you."

He'd really managed to astonish her. "You *like* me?" she echoed. "Men don't like me. They want to sleep with me, use me, fall in love with me, but they don't like me."

"Oh, I want to sleep with you. But then, I only sleep with women I like."

She looked uncomfortable, but she was the one

who'd brought up the subject. "Isn't it better to sleep with women you love?" she asked.

"Maybe. But it's a little soon for me to be in love with you. If you want I can make the effort..."

She laughed then. "You're being ridiculous. Besides, I know why you really agreed to drive all this way with me."

"Do you?"

"I'm more observant than you think. You have a thing for Jasmine. I watched you with her last night—you were paying far more attention to her than you were to me."

"You made it clear you could take care of yourself. Did it bother you?"

"Not at all. I love Jasmine, and you'd definitely be an improvement over Aaron. The two of you might..."

He'd been driving fast on the secondary road, and he hit the brakes a little too hard, so that the tires spun as they slid to a stop on the shoulder. "I don't have a thing for Jasmine," he said firmly. "I have a thing for you." And because he couldn't wait any longer he caught her face in one hand and kissed her, unbuckling his seat belt with the other hand.

Her mouth was cool, shocked beneath his, and she slid back against the leather seat as he leaned over her, letting him kiss her but not contributing in any way. He felt a moment's grievance—her total passivity was enough to cool any man's desire. No wonder she'd managed to stay a virgin for so long.

But he had no intention of starting the car again, of doing anything, until he could get her to kiss him back. It wasn't a matter of obeying Ralph's orders, it wasn't a matter of pride. He just had a sudden, desperate need for her to kiss him.

He put his tongue against her lips, tasting them, then pulled back, looking into the opaque darkness of her sunglasses. "You don't like kissing?"

"Not much," she said coolly.

"Then you haven't had the right man kiss you." He put his lips against hers, softly. He made no demands, he was in no hurry, just small, lazy kisses against her soft mouth, clinging for a moment, then releasing, touching her with his tongue, then brushing the side of her mouth.

She wasn't as cool as she had been. He put his mouth against the side of her neck and he could feel her pulse moving fast beneath his tongue. He moved his mouth up again, to her lips, and he pushed her mouth open with his, just a little bit, nudging her, teasing her, as he could tell her breathing was growing more labored. Maybe he was just taking her breath, but he didn't think so. He would have given ten years off his life to touch those small, perfect breasts beneath the thin T-shirt, but then he didn't have any years left. And her mouth was enough for now.

Particularly when he felt her lips move beneath his, just slightly.

He pressed a tiny bit harder. She opened her mouth for him, and he couldn't stand it anymore— he had to use his tongue.

She jumped, and he could almost feel her try to reach for that Zen-like passivity, but he was having none of it. He knew how to kiss, and it had been too damned long since he'd kissed a woman. And he didn't know if he'd ever wanted to kiss a woman as much as he wanted to kiss Sam.

The tiny noise she made was almost enough to make him explode. It was the unmistakable, delectable sound of desire, coming from deep inside her, half a moan, half a growl, and he wondered whether he could manage to get her out of those raggedy cutoffs and into the back seat.

Her hand came up and touched his face, just as he was about to reach for her seat belt. Her skin was cool, her fingers trembled, and the touch was the merest hint of a caress.

It was enough. He drew back, breathing hard, to stare into her opaque sunglasses. "Not Jasmine," he said. And he started the car, pulling out onto the empty road without looking.

SAM TRIED TO SLIDE down further in her seat, but her legs were too long—there was no more room in front of her. She crossed her arms over her chest as she realized in sudden horror that not only was she not wearing a bra, but her nipples were hard and sticking out against the thin cotton.

She wanted to wipe her mouth. No, she wanted to touch her mouth, to see if it felt any different. She kept her arms tightly crossed over her chest, hugging herself, shaken and unsure.

She glanced over at him as he drove down the highway. He didn't look as if he'd spent the past five minutes kissing her into a puddle of mindless need. Unless you looked at his mouth, and she certainly didn't want to be doing that, because she couldn't look at his mouth without wanting to feel it against hers again.

The silence between them was making it even worse. She summoned her coolest voice. "You kiss very well," she said. "You must have had a lot of practice."

He glanced over at her, a faint smile drawing her eyes to his mouth again. "And you haven't had much at all."

She wasn't quite sure how to react to that. "Are you saying you don't like kissing me?"

"Oh, no. I like kissing you very much indeed. You make it very interesting."

He wasn't improving things all that much. "I didn't think kissing was supposed to be merely interesting."

"If you want me to pull over again I can demonstrate just how intense interesting can be."

"No!" She sounded panicked, and she didn't care.

"All right," he said calmly. "We can play later."

"We cannot!"

"Not if you don't want to."

"I don't! Ever!"

"Never?" he murmured.

He couldn't know. No one could really know—most people thought she had a secret lesbian lover stashed somewhere, or else they thought she was so kinky her sex life was clouded in mystery. No one knew that not only did she not have a lover, but that the only thing deviant about her sex life was that she was still a virgin.

No one would believe her if she told them. And why should she? She had no intention of having sex with anyone right now, and when she decided to she planned to have plenty of time to get to know the guy first and give him advance warning that she hadn't done it before. The last thing she was going to do was hop into bed with a stranger she'd known less than twenty-four hours.

Even if, inexplicably, she wanted to.

None of this made any sense. She liked big, capable men, not slender, elegant ones. She needed a long time to get comfortable with a man, and this man put her in a strange, restless state that was unnerving. That made her wonder what his skin would feel like against hers.

She had nothing against sex, premarital or otherwise. She'd come close a couple of times, years ago, but in the end had backed out, much to the disgust of the boys involved. By the third time she decided not to let it get to that point, not unless she was absolutely certain, and she hadn't even been tempted in God knew how long.

She wasn't tempted now—that would be insane. It was just that he knew how to kiss. But it was just a talent like any other, like playing the piano or painting or playing tennis. One that improved with practice. He must have kissed a lot of women to be that good, and she didn't need to start having feelings for a man who used women like that.

But if he kissed that well, what would sex be like with him? Anyone who could put that much sensuality into the touching of mouths would likely be quite extraordinary when it came to actual intercourse.

But then again, she didn't know what ordinary intercourse was like, so why bother fantasizing about anything else?

She pushed her sunglasses up on her forehead and squinted into the bright afternoon. She was moderately nearsighted—she could do without her glasses but it made life more complicated. The leaves overhead dissolved into a gentle blur of green against the blue sky, and the highway stretched out as a gray expanse in front of them. She glanced at her companion, but he was close enough that she could see him clearly. Far too clearly.

She'd been in various stages of dress and undress with some of the most beautiful men in the world, both gay and straight, and she'd never been so fascinated by someone's face and body. His skin was a faintly golden color, not really tanned, more a natural pigment, and his long black hair was silky straight against his neck. He had high cheekbones, a narrow nose and the most beautiful mouth she'd ever kissed. But beauty had never been that valuable a commodity as far as she was concerned. She knew just how ephemeral it could be, and how utterly random, a simple combination of genes and luck. It was

ridiculous to be swept away by an accident of nature. She thought of all the men who'd wanted her
over the years, simply because she looked the way
she did. She'd never understood it. But she couldn't
keep from looking at Gideon. Wondering what it
would be like to...

"It's going to rain," he said. He must have felt
her eyes on him. A faint smile played around his
mouth.

"It never rains in California," she said firmly.
"Besides, there isn't a cloud in the sky."

He said nothing as the first bolt of lightning split
the sky, followed by earthshaking thunder. He'd
turned the windshield wipers on before the first tor-
rent slapped the window, and he slowed his dangerous pace just slightly.

The weather wasn't improving things. The darkness and heavy rain made the interior of the car feel
smaller, closer, more intimate, and intimacy was the
last thing she needed from the stranger beside her.
Who didn't feel like a stranger at all.

"Did you do that?" she asked suspiciously,
knowing how ridiculous it sounded.

"Do what? Control the weather? I get enough
rain up in Washington that I wouldn't be looking
for more." It was coming down in sheets of water,
washing across the road.

"It's dangerous when it rains down here. All the oil on the road gets very slick."

"I have no intention of getting into an accident. We're on a rescue mission, remember? What good would we do Jasmine if we ended up in a ditch?"

She bit her lip to keep silent. Never in her life had she been jealous of another woman, but even bringing up Jasmine's name might encourage him to...to try to prove his lack of interest. And she didn't want that to be the reason he kissed her.

She didn't want him to have any reason at all to kiss her, she reminded herself. None at all.

"You never did tell me where you disappeared to last night," he said after a while.

"I went to the Animal Emergency Center with the chef. He was almost as traumatized as poor Choux-fleur, and he needed moral support."

"And since you hate dogs you decided to go with him."

"I don't hate dogs," she admitted. "I usually have five or six roaming around the place. I'm part of a rescue network."

"In your spare time?"

"Hey, standing around and looking beautiful isn't that onerous a job," she said in a flippant voice. "And we already agreed that I drink alcohol, eat red meat, like dogs and have a thousand other sins."

"Do you? Name one."

"I get easily irritated by strange men asking me rude questions."

"I'm not that strange." Another bolt of lightning snaked down from the sky, uncomfortably close. "You want to tell me exactly where we're going?"

"It's a glorified cabin up in the mountains. Aaron uses it for sex."

"Really? When did you have sex with Aaron?"

"I didn't!" She shivered at the very thought of his meaty, thick-fingered hands touching her. "I came up with Jasmine for a Fourth of July picnic last year."

"And you still remember the way?"

"I've got a good sense of direction. I'm not about to get lost with you in the back end of beyond."

He said nothing. It was dark in the interior of the car, and he'd taken off his sunglasses, but his eyes were trained on the road ahead. Which was just as well—his eyes were almost as unnerving as his mouth.

The rain was beating down in a steady rhythm and the hum of the tires on the wet road vibrated beneath her. She could feel her eyelids begin to droop, and she tried to force herself into alertness. But she'd had a long, long night, and Rags had woken her early this morning, and right now all she wanted to do was sink down further in the soft cocoon of darkness and sleep.

"Go ahead," he murmured. "This stuff is going to slow us down—we won't get there for another couple of hours. You may as well sleep."

She wanted to ask him how he knew how long it would take them to get to the cabin. How he knew how long it would rain. But she was too tired to summon the effort, too tired to keep her arms clasped so tightly around her body. "All right," she said sleepily, leaning her head against the door. "I hope I don't snore."

"Don't you know? One of your lovers would have told you if you did."

One of her lovers. She wasn't so sleepy that she was going to let the truth slip. He wouldn't believe her anyway. "My lovers have all been much too polite to say anything." She yawned, snuggling down lower in the seat.

"Glad to hear it. There's nothing more desirable in a lover than proper manners."

She should have responded, but she was on the verge of sleep. Knowing she'd dream of dangerous kisses.

CHAPTER FIVE

"IT DOESN'T LOOK like anyone's home. That, or I took a wrong turn somewhere."

Sam woke with a start. Gideon had pulled the Mercedes to a stop, and the headlights speared through the darkness and the driving rain to illuminate the outlines of a sprawling log cabin.

"This is the right place," she said, opening the car door. She sprinted through the heavy rain, thoroughly drenched by the time she made it the short distance to the house. The door was unlocked, and the headlights provided enough illumination for her to find the light switch. She pushed it, but the cavernous house remained dark.

"The power's off," she called over her shoulder, but Gideon was already directly behind her, the car still running.

"Well, find Jasmine and let's get the hell out of here," he said. "The road was beginning to wash out, and this place looks like it's at a dead end."

"It is." The headlights provided enough light for

her to see the notepad propped on the wooden counter.

"Hell and damnation," she said, scanning Jasmine's scrawl. "We're too late. She's gone. Apparently she patched it up with Aaron and the two of them are off to Cancun to get married!" She dropped the note back down on the counter. "How could she be so gullible?"

"At the moment that's the least of our worries. Let's get out of here as well. We'll get dinner on the way back, and this time you can eat all the steak and drink all the beer you want."

"That's what you think," she said. "This perfect body requires upkeep. I can only afford one beer a week and I've met my quota. And steak is fattening."

"Perfect body, eh? That's a matter of opinion. You could use some fattening up, if you ask me."

"You sure know the way to a girl's heart," she drawled. "And I don't remember asking you. This body is a tool, nothing more, and I keep it in good working order."

"Nothing more than a tool? Where does pleasure factor in?"

"I limit it. Pleasure's too fattening. There'll be time enough when my fifteen minutes of fame is over."

"I wasn't talking about food. Sex isn't fattening."

It was too shadowy for him to appreciate the full force of her glare, so she made do with ignoring his comment. "We can argue about dinner once we're on the road again," she said, suppressing a shiver. The room was cold.

"We weren't talking about food," he said, following her out into the rain.

He turned on the heat full-blast in the car before putting it in reverse and heading back down the narrow road, deftly avoiding potholes. Waves of blessed warmth enveloped her, almost enough to stop her shivering, when the car slammed to a halt.

"What's wrong?" she demanded, though she immediately saw for herself. The road ahead of them was covered with wide expanse of rushing water.

"We're not going anywhere."

She stared at what had once been the road. "Why can't you be like everyone else in Los Angeles and drive a huge SUV?" she asked bitterly.

"I wouldn't drive through that in anything less than a tank," he said, putting the car in reverse. "And neither should you. Don't you know you shouldn't drive though water like that? You never know what's underneath. I'm not about to get you killed."

"Aren't you worried about your own skin?"

He smiled his enigmatic smile. "Not particularly."

"You think you have some kind of guardian angel keeping you safe?"

He laughed then. "You could say so. His name's Ralph."

"Who would name their guardian angel Ralph?"

He pulled back in front of the house, not answering. "You stay in the car while I try to find some candles."

She wasn't in the best of moods. The thought of spending the night in Aaron's rustic love pad with Gideon Hyde was filling her with an odd foreboding that seemed centered in the pit of her stomach. "I don't think so," she said, leaping out ahead of him.

By the time he'd followed her into the house she'd managed to go through most of the drawers beneath the hardwood counter, and she'd come up with nothing. He followed her into the kitchen area, silhouetted by the headlights still shining in the windows. The whole thing felt odd, otherworldly. Especially when the lights from the car went off, plunging them into darkness.

"Damn," his disembodied voice floated in her direction in the darkness. "I thought the delay on the lights would last a little bit longer. Have you found any candles?''

His voice was coming closer, and she panicked, trying to move past him, away from him, only to collide against his hard body.

His hands caught her arms, and in the darkness she froze, close enough to feel the heat coming from his skin, close enough to feel his breath on her face.

She could feel her heart beating in the darkness, feel the blood pulsing in her veins, throbbing. It had to be fear rushing through her body, and yet she knew she had nothing to be afraid of. He wasn't going to hurt her.

She broke away, stumbling back, and he let her go without a word. ''I can't believe Aaron wouldn't have candles all over the place,'' she said nervously, feeling her way out of the kitchen area, away from her. ''This is his little love nest—last time I was here the place was equipped for seduction.'' The moment the words were out of her mouth she could have kicked herself. All she could think about was sex.

''Then maybe we're looking in the wrong place,'' he said calmly. She heard the snick of a lighter, and a small flame appeared in his hand. ''Why don't we look over by the living area?''

''Do you smoke?''

"Not anymore," he said, that note of amusement in his voice, the one she found both annoying and appealing. At that point she wasn't sure whether she liked him or should put him in the jerk category with most of the men she'd dated. No, he was beyond that point. Whatever she felt for him was a great deal more complicated. And she wasn't in the mood for complications.

He found the candles before she did, a veritable treasure trove on every available surface in the living area. By the time he'd lit every one the center of the room was filled with warm light, though the corners were still shrouded in darkness.

"There," he said, turning back to look at her. "All equipped for seduction."

"I don't think so," she said sharply.

"You're cold. Much as I hate to suggest it, you should probably find something dry to put on while I start a fire. There's a lot to be said for the wet T-shirt look, but you're shivering."

She looked down at her body in horror. Even in the dim light she could see her small breasts outlined quite clearly against the thin wet cotton. She might as well be wearing nothing at all.

She followed her first instinct, crossing her arms over her chest. Her second, totally insane, impulse had been to drag the shirt over her head and toss it to him. It wouldn't have given him much more of a view than he'd already gotten though the thin wet cotton, and the thought of his shocked reaction was definitely appealing. She hadn't a trace of real modesty, not after the years of modeling, but stripping in front of an interested male was a different matter altogether.

And he was interested, there was no doubt about that. Not after the bone-shaking kiss in the car. He hadn't lied—it wasn't Jasmine he wanted.

She grabbed one of the scented pillar candles. "I'll see if there's anything upstairs. Knowing Aaron, he probably keeps a Victoria's Secret line for his guests."

"Promises, promises," he murmured.

Most of the glass-and-cedar cabin was the large downstairs room, but there was a loft bedroom upstairs. It was pitch-black and icy cold, but still a fairly simple matter to find one of Aaron's oversize T-shirts and a pair of drawstring gym shorts. She left her wet clothes on the floor for Aaron—he could fantasize about them next time he came back.

And he would be back, without Jasmine. That relationship had been doomed from the beginning, but nothing Sam had said had been able to make Jasmine see the truth.

By the time she came back downstairs Gideon

had managed to get a blazing fire going in the huge fieldstone fireplace, and the added light cast a soft glow around the room.

"Did you try the telephone?" she asked, moving into the warmth.

"Not working. And there's no signal for my cell phone. Face it, Sam, we're trapped for the night."

She didn't like him calling her Sam. It made him a friend, and she needed him to be a stranger. "And tomorrow?"

"If the road's still washed out and no one comes, we'll hike out in the daylight. The rain can't keep on forever."

"Let's hope not," she muttered. "It's late—we may as well try to get some sleep. There's a bedroom upstairs if you want to use it."

"Is that an offer?"

"In your dreams."

He'd unfastened his black shirt, pulling it free from his pants, and she stared at his chest for a moment. He had smooth, beautiful skin, lit golden by the firelight, with dark, flat nipples, a narrow waist, framed by the black silk.

She yanked her eyes upward. "There are extra T-shirts upstairs if you're cold."

"Do I look cold? I come from a very hot climate—I'll take all the coolness I can find."

"Seattle has a hot climate?"

"Before Seattle. As a matter of fact this fire is too hot for me."

"Then for heaven's sake why did you start it?"

"Because, for heaven's sake, you were freezing," he replied, mimicking her. "Where are you sleeping?"

"Not with you."

"I don't recall asking," he said calmly. He moved from the fire, and his beautiful chest was no longer illuminated. He had a brandy snifter in one hand, and he held it out to her. "There's no food in this place, but his liquor cabinet is well stocked. This is for you."

She made no effort to take it. "I told you, I already had my weekly limit..."

He simply reached down and picked up her wrist, placing the snifter in her hand. He was right, his skin was warm, almost hot, against her cool flesh. "You missed dinner. You'll manage." Too close again, and she could feel her blood stir once more. Treacherous, inexplicable.

But he stepped back without touching her again, and she forced her breathing back to normal. She even took a sip of the brandy, feeling a pleasant burn as it slid down her throat. It made her feel warm. Reckless.

"I'll sleep down here," she said. "The sofa is a futon. Aaron likes to be prepared for all eventualities. You can sleep wherever you want."

An unfortunate choice of words, as she waited for him to say he wanted to sleep with her. But, of course, he didn't want to. Or at least that's what he'd said. Or had he simply said he hadn't asked her...yet?

He didn't say anything, simply picked up his own glass of brandy and sat back down in front of the fire, his skin reflecting the golden glow.

She pulled the futon flat, tossing a couple of throw pillows at the head. "I'd offer to help with that but I know what you'd say." He sipped at his brandy. "But if there's anything you want from me you have only to ask."

On a cold day in hell, she thought, but kept it to herself. She should have brought a blanket down from the bedroom, but she hadn't thought to, and the sooner she closed her eyes and shut everything out, the safer she'd feel. Besides, the fire was kicking out heat—it would fill the room eventually, and at least she wasn't shivering any longer.

She made a noncommittal noise and stretched out on the futon. She wasn't going to think about it. Think about him. Think about the strange knot in her stomach, her tingling skin, his smooth, golden chest. She wasn't going to think about his mouth, on hers. She was just going to sleep, and with any luck she'd snore.

She let out a deep sigh, trying to drain the tension from her body. And as she drifted into sleep, her hand drifted to her mouth, and her fingers touched her lips, touched his kiss, as she slept.

"WELL?"

Gideon looked up from his contemplation of the fire. He wasn't sure why he was so fascinated by it—he'd been surrounded by flames and fire for as long as he could remember.

He turned and looked at Ralph. Perched on the end of the futon, right by Sam's sleeping head, he was wearing a flame-red bishop's outfit and thick-framed glasses. The right one was blacked out, and he had spiky blond hair and all sorts of interesting piercings.

"What do you mean?" Gideon replied, trying to keep his attention on his nemesis. Ralph's appearance never failed to astonish, but in truth he was safer looking at him than at Sam's sleeping figure.

"You're here, she's just lying there. Go for it."

"So much for romance," Gideon murmured.
"No."

"What do you mean, no?"

"I mean I'm not going to do it."

"Don't be ridiculous. Don't tell me she's not your type—all women are your type."

"I've changed my ways. Time in hell will do that to a man. I've decided to embrace celibacy."

"You'll decide to embrace Sam, and fast."

"Make me," he said simply.

The purpled rage in Ralph's face didn't go particularly well with the red outfit. "What's your problem? Don't pretend you don't want her—I know you do. Do it. Jump her bones."

"Sorry, you'll have to find someone else. It should be easy enough—just make her fall in love with the next man who comes by and he'll take care of it."

"If it were that simple I wouldn't have needed you in the first place. I can play games with the weather, set things on fire, that sort of stuff. But I have no power to affect people's emotions. That's what you're for."

"Sorry." He held out his wrists as though for handcuffs. "Take me back to prison, Warden. I'm not making love to her."

"Oh, for pete's sake!" Ralph said, and Gideon had to smile at the mild epithet. "I know what you've done! You've gone and fallen in love with her, haven't you? Of all the stupid things! When you were alive you seduced every woman you wanted and you never once fell in love, and now you're screwing everything up. Why did you have to go and do such a damned stupid thing right now, when I'm counting on you?''

He considered denying it, then shrugged. "Maybe you're right," he said after a moment. "Just your bad luck. You can send me down to the four hundred and sixty-eighth level of hell if you want, but you can't get me to hurt her. Send her someone to fall in love with.''

"I did." Ralph said morosely. "I didn't mean to—you were just supposed to get rid of her virginity. It's a nasty trick if you ask me. I don't need you two falling in love, I just need you going at it like rabbits.'' He cast an accusing glance skyward. "You did this, didn't You? Always messing with my fun.''

"What are you saying?''

"I'm saying she's in love with you. It happens that fast sometimes. Probably because she's taken so long to do it, she was ripe for the right man.'' He cast a curious glance at Gideon from his one good eye. "Ripe," he said again. "Just waiting, lying there, those long, gorgeous legs, that mouth...''

"Forget it. I'm not falling for your blandishments.''

Ralph sighed. "No, I suppose not. But she's a different matter." He reached over to shake her, but his hand passed right through her, and she didn't move. "Damn," he muttered.

Gideon laughed. "Tough luck. May as well give it up. She's immune to anything you want to try, thank God."

"Thank God," Ralph echoed grumpily. "You've got another twelve hours."

"I don't need another twelve hours, Ralph. Take me back now. I've had enough."

Ralph's grumpy expression vanished. "We'll see about that." And he was gone.

Gideon leaned back in the rocker, staring into the fire, as Sam slept on, oblivious to any devil sitting at her head. He wouldn't have thought he was capable of such restraint. Ralph might not be able to influence emotions, but he was a master at messing with people's minds. Gideon wasn't about to fall for it. Sam was no more in love with him than she was with Aaron. She found him more an annoyance than anything else, and she was having a fine time putting him in his place.

Except for when he'd kissed her. It had probably shocked the hell out of her, but that was nothing compared to how he'd felt. Kissing her had been more profoundly sexual than any encounter he'd ever had.

He'd make it through twelve more hours, no problem. She'd sleep through most of them, and the rest of the time they'd be slogging their way down this mountain to civilization.

Was he in love with her? It didn't seem possible, and yet it seemed so right. One more flame to add to the fires of eternal damnation. Of course he'd fall in love the moment he couldn't do anything about it.

He looked over at her, the face scrubbed free of makeup, the tangled hair spread out over the futon, the long legs. He wasn't going to sleep—he was too hot in every sense of the word. He could spend all night looking at her, but that might be pushing it. He rocked back, staring into the fire, and considered the nature of eternal damnation.

CHAPTER SIX

SHE DREAMED OF HIS HANDS on her body. She dreamed of his mouth on her, of him inside her. She dreamed the devil sat at the end of the futon and told him to sleep with her. She dreamed he told him no.

She shifted restlessly, hot and cold at the same time, waking with the dreams still moving through her head, her body. She needed him. It made no sense at all, but she needed him, wanted him.

She'd always assumed that the time would come when she'd want to make love with someone. That sooner or later the right man would show up, court her, maybe even marry her before they finally went to bed together.

And now, here she was, ready before she wanted to be, half in love with a stranger, all against her better judgment, her common sense.

But her brain had nothing to do with it. And her body, though demanding, was still marginally involved.

It was her heart that wanted him, a stranger, to lie with her. And for the first time in her life she was going to ignore her brain.

She opened her eyes. The rain was still falling heavily outside, and she wondered briefly how secure this house was. Mudslides were common enough in this kind of weather. Maybe the house would slide away with them in it. Maybe it would get buried beneath a deluge of mud. Maybe she didn't care.

He was still awake, staring into the fire. The room was warm now, and the flames had died down. He'd blown out some of the candles, and she could see the firelight reflected on his smooth skin, his flat stomach. She closed her eyes, trying to shut him out.

"You're a stranger," she whispered. "I don't know anything about you."

He didn't turn to look at her. "Go back to sleep, Sam."

She pushed up from the mattress, shoving her hair away from her face. She'd had men—good men who'd loved her—begged to sleep with her, and she'd sent them away. She'd resisted good men and bad boys, charmers and bullies, big men, small men, strong men, weak men.

But if Gideon moved from his seat in the rocking chair she wouldn't resist him.

He wasn't moving. Maybe she'd fallen half in love with the one man who didn't want her.

She sat up, back on her heels, watching the firelight play across his face, shining in his dark eyes, sending shafts of gold through his straight black hair.

Finally he turned to look at her, and there was an expression of distant sorrow on his narrow, beautiful face. Why sorrow?

"This isn't a good idea," he said.

"What isn't?"

But he'd risen from the chair, and he was coming toward her, slowly, the black silk shirt fluttering around his body. She was in the middle of the bed, out of reach, but he simply knelt down on the edge of the bed and cupped her face with his hands. "Not a good idea at all," he whispered, and he kissed her.

The first kiss hadn't been a fluke. The moment his mouth touched hers she felt her body come alive. He moved closer to her on the bed, his body almost touching hers, but he did nothing but kiss her, his hands on her face, as her body burned for him.

And for a moment it was enough. She closed her eyes and kissed him back, drifting into a dark, warm space with his mouth, his tongue.

She hadn't even realized that she'd reached up her hands to his shoulders, his hard shoulders beneath the slippery silk shirt. And she was clutching at it, holding on to it, on to him, as he kissed her. As they kissed.

And then he pulled back, and caught her hand in his, and she could see the tension running through him. Feel the heavy beating of his heart, counterpoint to hers.

"Am I doing this wrong?" she said. "I've never done it before."

He didn't seem surprised. "Don't do this now, Sam. Wait until you fall in love with someone."

She didn't know where the words came from. "I did," she said, and kissed him.

He'd turned her hands in his, holding them, but now he placed them back on his shoulders, and a shudder danced through his body. She didn't know what it meant, and then she didn't care, as he reached for the hem of her T-shirt and began to pull it off, then tossed it over the side of the bed.

For the first time in her adult life she felt modest. She took her body for granted, but he'd said it wasn't perfect, and she suddenly felt unsure.

"My breasts are too small," she said, but he simply laughed in her mouth, putting his arm around her waist and pulling her up against him. Her virgin skin against the golden heat of his chest.

His skin was more like silk than the shirt, and she found herself pushing the piece of clothing off his shoulders, down his arms, in love with the texture of his flesh, the scent of him, the taste of him. And she wanted to taste more, everything, all of him.

He eased her back onto the futon—she wasn't even sure how—and he pulled the baggy shorts down her legs. Leaving her in nothing but her black lace panties. And then those were gone before she could even get used to the idea, and he'd settled himself on top of her, the cloth of his pants between them.

He kissed the side of her neck, and she trembled. He bit her earlobe, and she moaned. He put his mouth on one small breast and she cried out as his tongue flicked against her nipple, then sucked, and she could feel her body burning.

She threaded her fingers through his thick, silky hair as it fell around her, and she brought it to her face, breathing in the scent of it.

Something was pressing hard against her stomach, and she moved her hand down, thinking it was his belt buckle, but he'd gotten rid of his belt, and the top button of his pants was unbuttoned. She started to pull her hand away in sudden nervousness but he caught her wrist in a hard grip, dragging her hand back to press against him.

Now was the time to panic. Now was the time to change her mind, before it was too late. And he'd let her—she had no doubt of that. He wouldn't even call her the names other men had—he'd simply move away from her, back to his chair by the fire.

And she didn't think she could stand that. She touched him through the soft fabric, letting her fingers press against him, and he seemed to jerk against her hand, growing harder. And she realized she was actually going to do this. Nothing could make her change her mind.

She liked the feel of him. She slid her hand down along his length, and he groaned, falling back against the futon. She leaned over him, letting her other hand move up his flat stomach. His nipples were dark circles against his golden flesh, and she leaned down and put her tongue against one, feeling it pebbled and hard against her mouth.

He made a choking noise, and he took her hand away from him, holding it for a moment before he pushed it inside his pants. So that she felt his erection, hot and heavy against her skin.

She lifted her mouth from his nipple. "Unzip your pants," she said, before putting her mouth against him once more, sucking at his skin, hungry.

He freed himself, and a moment later he'd kicked his pants off entirely. Now that she'd asked him to, she wasn't sure that she was ready for him to be naked, but it was no longer an option. He felt silken smooth and iron hard beneath her hand, and she moved down, wanting to taste him, wanting to take him in her mouth.

She barely managed to put her mouth on him before he pulled her away. "No," he said in a rough voice. "It's been too long. It'll be over..." He grew suddenly still. "Unless you change your mind. Because you don't have to do anything you don't want to do."

She looked at him from beneath her curtain of heavy hair. "Do you want me to...kiss you there?"

A spasm of what almost looked like pain crossed his face. "Not this time," he said. "Later. After you're used to all this."

She didn't know why the thought should make her happy, but it did. "All right," she said, moving up to kiss his mouth.

He moved her down on the bed, leaning over her, letting his hand brush against her stomach. She knew where he was going, and instinctively she tensed, as his fingers trailed downward.

"We don't have to do this." He leaned over and whispered against her ear. "As a matter of fact, we shouldn't be doing this. Tell me no."

She turned her head to kiss his mouth. "Yes," she said.

His hand touched her thigh. "I don't know what you've heard, but it doesn't work with your legs together. I'm not going to hurt you."

She relaxed, and he slid his hand between her legs, touching her. She choked, tensing up again, but he was too strong.

"Tell me no," he said again, touching her.

"Yes," she said, as he slid his long fingers inside her, so that she arched her back in sudden, surprised pleasure.

A pleasure that was turning darker, deeper. He knew just how to touch her, where, when to be gentle, when to be slightly rough, and her breath was coming in shallow pants, her body shivering, but this time not with cold.

She should have known, but it hit her with no warning, a sudden spasm of such intense pleasure that she cried out, followed by another, and then another, and then an endless stream of such intensity that it left her shaken, breathless, so lost that she didn't even notice when he'd pulled away from her, no longer touching her.

And then she realized he was moving away from her, off the bed. "That's enough," he said in a shaken voice.

She moved faster, reaching for him, and they fell back in a tangle of limbs. Then he was on top of her, between her legs, hard and pressing against her, and with a groan he was pushing inside her, the feel of him such a powerful claiming that she wanted more. She wanted to explode all over again, with him inside her. She wanted everything.

But he'd stopped, and she realized he must have reached the absurd barrier of her virginity, still intact after all these years. She could see the spasm of anguish cross his face, as he tried to control himself. "I'm going to hurt you," he said in a raw voice.

"Do it," she said. And arched her hips, enough to break through the last trace of control that he had.

He drove in deep, tearing through her, but the pain was nothing compared to the joy of having him inside her. He dropped his head on her shoulder, panting, not moving. "It'll be better in a minute," he said.

She reached up and took his face in her hands. She'd never felt so strong, so powerful, so complete. "It's better already," she said, stroking his face. "Your turn, Gideon. Tell me no."

He took a deep, shuddering breath. "Yes," he said, moving, slowly, back and forth, teasing her. Teasing himself. "Yes," he said, kissing her mouth, rocking slowly against her. "Yes," he said, moving faster, and she brought her legs up around his hips, pulling him deeper.

And then there was no thought, only feeling, as they moved together, bodies slick with sweat, glowing in the firelight, faster, harder, and when she thought she couldn't bear any more he put his hand between their bodies, touching her, hard.

"Yes," he said against her mouth, as she convulsed around him. From a distance she could feel him go rigid in her arms, and then all connection to reality splintered, disappeared into the flames of the night.

SHE WAS ASLEEP the moment he moved away from her, an expression of bliss on her face. In the firelight he could see the salty traces of tears on her face, and he reached out and touched the still-damp trail they'd made. He hadn't even known she'd cried.

He stared down at her for a moment. He always preferred women who fell asleep—it made it easy to escape without that awkward morning-after crap. He could escape now—just walk away into the rain-swept night.

Where the hell was Ralph when he needed him? Gideon had done his duty, against his will. No, that was wrong. He'd wanted nothing more than to touch her since...

It hadn't been at first sight. Her elegant, distant beauty wasn't a particular turn-on for him. It was the vulnerability in her pale eyes. It was stubbornness he often saw on her mouth. The way she carried her body, as if it wasn't even a part of her. He liked the way she told him to go to hell. He liked the way she fell apart when he kissed her. He liked that she was still fighting it, fighting what she wanted, even when she was going to take it.

She didn't stir when he climbed off the futon. There was a quilt in one corner of the room—he got it and draped it over her body, taking a moment to look at her. She was entirely relaxed—probably more relaxed than she'd ever been in her entire life, he thought. He was still faintly amazed at how responsive she'd been. He couldn't credit himself with making her come. His sexual experience and technique was impressive, or Ralph wouldn't have sent him on this task, but if it had simply been up to him it might have taken all night.

And he wouldn't have minded.

Would she respond that way to anyone else? There would be others now, there was no question of that. Once she found out what it was like she'd have a healthier attitude. She'd find her body was good for other things besides striking haughty poses.

But not with him. She might think she was in love with him, and he still blamed Ralph for that despite the devil's protests of relative innocence, but once Gideon vanished she'd move on, sadder but wiser. Ready for a real man, not something like him.

He had no idea what he was. A ghost, a spirit, a nasty trick of fate played on a tenderhearted beauty?

It didn't matter. Soon he'd be nothing more than a memory, and after a while, maybe not even that.

He tucked the quilt around her carefully, but she didn't stir, exhausted. He pulled on his clothes, about to go back to his seat by the fire, when the sudden crack of thunder startled him. Maybe his time here was over already.

He stumbled out into the rainy night, barefoot. The rain was pouring down in sheets, soaking him, but he didn't care. He tilted back his head to stare into the midnight sky. And then he cried out, a voice of pain from deep inside him. "It's done!"

There was no answer. No responding crack of thunder, no supernatural voices. Nothing but the storm all around him. He fell to his knees, and for the first time in his memory, and maybe in his entire misspent life, Gideon Hyde began to cry.

IT WAS LIGHT when Sam opened her eyes. She lay still on the futon, awash with a strange sense of well-being tinged with foreboding, as she tried to orient herself. She was at Aaron's cabin. Lying naked beneath a thin covering. Not just naked. Seduced. Deliciously, gloriously seduced by a man she barely knew.

Love at first sight didn't exist. It grew out of friendship, a slow, natural progression, so the confused emotions that were busy assaulting her had nothing to do with love. They couldn't.

But Sam made a point of never to lying to anyone, particularly herself. And no matter how irrational, insane, or unbelievable it was, the fact remained that she had done the impossible. Fallen in love with a mysterious stranger. And after all these years she'd acted upon it.

She could hear the sound of the shower running. She was achy, sticky, a thorough, sated mess. And he would be standing naked in the shower, letting the hot water run over that golden body of his. And maybe she needed to find out if last night had been an act of insanity, a total aberration, or not.

The shower in Aaron's master bath was huge, a tiled mini-room with built-in seats and jets of water coming from golden pipes in all four corners. Gideon stood in the middle, head back, eyes closed, letting the water run over his body like a lover's caress. A lover's tongue. A lover's tears.

She stepped inside the steamy room and closed the glass door behind her, and he opened his eyes, looking at her with an expression that was almost wary.

Yet he wanted her. There was no disguising that fact, not with both of them naked in the steamy shower. And then she stopped thinking about it, moved up to him and put her arms around his neck, so that the water slid over both of them. His mouth was wet and hungry against hers. And she moved closer still, wanting to sink into his body.

He broke the kiss, holding her face in one hand, but his arm was around her waist, holding her up against his body. "This is a bad idea," he said.

She smiled into his eyes. "You're the gloomiest lover I've ever had."

"I'm the only lover you've ever had."

"True enough," she conceded. "And I want to make up for lost time." She ran her hand down his stomach to touch him. "And don't tell me you aren't willing to further my education."

"You've gotten pretty saucy all of a sudden."

"I've always been a saucy wench," she said, leaning forward and nibbling on his lower lip. He had glorious lips.

"I don't think…"

"Good," she said. "I have no intention of thinking either."

The tile was hard against her back as he pushed her up against it, and then he was inside her, supporting her with his hands and the wall as she wrapped her legs around his narrow hips and took him in, shivering in pleasure as the hot water rained down on them.

This time she made noise. She couldn't help it— her tiny cries and weak moans bounded against the tile walls, echoing through the steamy enclosure.

She was surrounded by heat and steam and pleasure noises. And Gideon, around her, inside her, taking her to places she hadn't even known existed, and when he came inside her his own choked cry joined hers as she shattered.

Through a haze of slowly fading contractions she could feel him shaking, and he pulled free, lowering her down onto the tile seat. She collapsed against the wall as the water poured over them, and he sank to his knees in front of her, his arms around her hips, his head in her lap, holding tight.

She managed to find enough energy to lift her hand, to stroke his wet black hair away from his face. His eyes were closed, and if she'd had more energy she would have leaned over and kissed him. But there was something infinitely trusting about his pose, and she liked him like that, his head in her lap, completely and totally hers. At least for now.

CHAPTER SEVEN

HE LEFT HER ALONE in the shower. When she caught his hand, tried to stop him he muttered the word "coffee" and she let him go, sinking back against the tile as the hot water continued to stream down over her. She could fall asleep like this, she thought, her face turned up into the steamy mist. She could just sit here forever, or until he came back to her and...

The water turned to ice with no warning, and she let out a screech, practically ripping the door off the shower in her haste to get out of the chilly spray. She half expected Gideon to come check on her after her outburst, so she opened the door to the bathroom, calling out, "I'm okay." He didn't answer, but she figured he was concentrating on the coffee, something she couldn't help but approve of.

She dried herself languidly, glancing at her reflection in the steamed-over mirror. She stared at the naked body that had always served her so well. It didn't look any different, and yet it felt completely changed. She was connected to it now. It was more than just legs and breasts and stomach and hips, blended in a pleasing manner that sold products well and created a fantasy. It was hers in a way that could belong to no others.

Except for Gideon.

Her clothes were neatly folded on the sink, though the black lace panties were missing. She'd gone without underwear in the past—she could do it again. She pulled on the shorts and the T-shirt and went in search of coffee and Gideon.

It wasn't until she reached the deserted, spotless kitchen area that she realized she hadn't smelled coffee. There was no sign of any. The great room had been picked up—the futon was back together, the quilt folded in one corner, the candles put back, the brandy snifters washed and put away.

But no coffee. And no Gideon.

She heard the sound of a car driving up, and relief washed over her. He must have gone to check on the road. Hardly flattering that he was in such a hurry to get out of there, but it was better than vanishing without a word. She went to the door and flung it open, ready to tease him about the coffee, when she saw the taxi. And no sign of the Mercedes.

"You Miss Samantha?" the taxi driver asked,

climbing out. "Dispatch sent me to bring you back to Los Angeles. You ready to go?"

"Where's Gideon?"

The man shook his head, pulling his cap lower on his thinning gray hair and rubbing his eye. "Dunno who you're talking about. I got orders to take you to L.A., and that's what I'm planning to do. It's already been taken care of—I get paid whether you come with me or not. It's up to you."

She felt like a candle dying in the wind, the light fading inside her. She closed the door behind her without a backward glance. "I'm ready," she said, heading for the back seat of the yellow cab.

She sat still and quiet in the center of the back seat, the seat belt tight around her, her long legs crowded behind the front seat. Her driver was a chatty soul—he went on about the weather, the condition of the roads, the politics in the state of California, his recent eye infection, his opinion of the world in general, and Sam let the unending words wash over her, replying with a suitable "hmm" when prompted.

He was gone. Vanished, as if he'd never existed, disappeared in a puff of smoke like a magician.

This was the best thing that could possibly happen, she told herself. Last night had been an aberration, a moment of total insanity. But it was daylight now, he was gone, and she was Sam again. Practical, levelheaded, loyal Sam.

With one major difference. She really should be grateful to him. As the years had passed and she had lived in celibate comfort she'd begun to wonder if there was something wrong with her. Was she frigid? Missing the ability to fall in love? Her untouched state had become a liability, a dark, dirty secret she didn't want anyone to discover, as embarrassing as kinky tastes. In the end it was a kinky taste not to want love, and she was glad she was finally past it. She was grateful, truly she was. She was calm, serene and grateful.

And she was going to track him down and kill him.

How dare he just abandon her, drive away without a word, a note, just disappear like that? No matter how inexperienced she was, she couldn't have been that bad. If she'd had any idea how wonderful making love could be she would have tried this a lot sooner.

Except that there was no one else she'd wanted to do it with. And no one she wanted in her future. She wanted only Gideon Hyde, with his golden skin and his beautiful mouth.

It was a good thing he'd run out on her. She didn't believe in love at first sight, or any kind of love at all that wasn't built from knowledge and familiarity. She knew nothing about Gideon Hyde— he was a stranger, and smart women didn't fall in love with strangers.

And right now she was feeling dumb as mud, because no matter what she tried to tell herself, she'd fallen in love with a mystery. For all she knew he could hate animals and vote Republican.

But Rags had liked him. Rags, who snapped and growled at any man who'd ever come near her, had slobbered happily over Gideon, totally entranced.

And in the end, she trusted Rags more than she trusted herself. If he was good enough for her dog, he was good enough for her.

She shut her eyes, closing out the endless voice of her driver. So he'd run away. She had long legs— she could run faster. And she wasn't about to give up without a fight.

"HAD A GOOD TIME?"

Gideon blinked. He'd been searching for the coffee, certain that a man with a stocked liquor cabinet would have to have coffee stashed somewhere. Now he was standing in the middle of what looked like a deserted car factory. Ralph had given up his bishop's outfit—he was now dressed in drag, with heavy makeup, long reddish curls and lace everywhere.

"Very pretty," Gideon murmured.

"Don't avoid the subject!" Ralph said. "I want to know if you had a good time during your…what should we call it? Shore leave? Did you get lucky?"

Cursing at him was a waste of time—Ralph thrived on negativity. "Don't you know? I assumed you were happily watching the whole thing."

"I'm surprised that the thought of me watching didn't affect your performance."

"Believe it or not, Ralph, I wasn't even thinking of you at the time. Why am I here? I thought I had twelve more hours."

"Six at this point. But you accomplished your mission, didn't you? My eye cleared up and all is well."

"You didn't give me a chance to say goodbye. She'll think I used her and abandoned her without a word."

"And why should you care? Oh, I forgot, you fell in love with her. Disgusting, really. I would have thought you were past such sappy emotions."

"I should have said goodbye. Or something."

Ralph chuckled. "Like telling her that you love her? You really think that's a good idea? Won't a clean break be easier on her in the long run? Not for you, of course, but since there's no future for a woman like that and a dead man I don't suppose it matters. You may as well enjoy yourself while you can. Love 'em and leave 'em, that always was your style.''

"Has anyone ever tried to kill you, Ralph?''

"Waste of time, dear boy. But they've tried. I can be…irritating. We're getting off the subject. You want your final six hours? I can arrange it.''

Gideon closed his eyes for a moment. He could see her, sprawled out on the futon, sound asleep, looking as well-loved as he could have managed. He could smell the scent of her skin, taste her breasts. And he'd give ten years off his life to touch her again.

But his life was already over. And going back would only make it harder on her.

"No,'' he said. "I'm not going back.''

"And why is that?''

"Because she's better off without me. As you said, there's no future. And I don't mind. I don't remember why I got sent here in the first place, but after last night I don't care. The best thing I could have done for her was keep my hands off her, and in the end I couldn't, even to spite you. I hurt her, and she didn't deserve that. If you think that falling in love with someone means you hurt them, then yes, I probably am in love with her. And the damnable thing is, it feels like it's the first time.''

"Hey, this is the three hundred and forty-seventh level of hell and I'm in charge. Of course I think falling in love equals hurt and pain. You done me proud, boy. And for what it's worth, no, you were never in love before. You may have slept with hundreds of women, but you were never in love.''

"Hundreds?" Gideon echoed, bemused.

"And you don't remember any of them,'' Ralph said in his chummy voice. "So now we've come to your final choice.''

"My final choice? I didn't know I ever had any choice at all.''

"I told you, I can't control emotions, and I have no power over free will. Terrible idea, free will was. Look how it's backfired.''

"What choice, Ralph?"

"You're finished on this level. Done your time, my boy. Passed all the tests. I do believe you're ready to graduate.''

"To the three hundred and forty-eighth level? What's it got, a little more air-conditioning?''

"Not exactly. Here's the choice. You can go back for a few days, screw Sam out of your system for good, and then move to the next level. Or you can choose to let her find someone new. He's already waiting in the wings, and thanks to you she's finally ready to notice. The veterinarian at the animal shelter is young, handsome, good and kind…''

"And noble as hell. He sounds revolting," Gideon muttered.

"You sound jealous. He'd make her very happy. It's up to you. Reward for a job well done. You can have another week in bed with her, or let her have a happy life."

"Who says she wouldn't have a happy life even if I did get my extra week?"

"True enough. Free will and all that."

In the end it wasn't a choice at all. "Send her her damned Prince Charming," he growled. "Just don't make me watch."

Ralph beamed at him. "You really do love her."

"One more torment of the damned. I'm going to forget all this, right? Everything else I've ever been through is a blur—I don't have to remember her, do I?"

"And miss her? But isn't hell about everlasting torment? Want to change your mind?"

He shook his head. "I'll do the right thing for once in my life. I just hope it annoys the hell out of you."

Ralph snapped his fingers, and the old garage disappeared. They were standing on the edge of a cliff, and Ralph was dressed like a biker, with dark hair slicked back. "Take a look," he said, nodding toward the cliff. "See where you're headed."

Gideon moved toward the edge, expecting God knew what. There were wisps of fleecy clouds, and beneath, quite clearly, he could see Sam's house.

He stepped back from the edge. "No!"

"The thing is, Gideon, there isn't any three hundred and forty-eighth level of hell. The three hundred and forty-seventh is the highest level, and you just graduated. You get to go back and start all over again. Just try not to screw up this time."

"What are you talking about?"

"Time to live again."

Gideon stared at him, uncomprehending. "Shouldn't we be looking up, not down?"

"Heaven and hell all kind of blend together. Kiss the bride for me."

"I'm not going back. Not to Sam. I don't deserve—"

"Oh, cut the martyred crap and get out of here," Ralph said, putting his hands on Gideon's shoulders. With one swift shove he was gone, tumbling down through the clouds, the feel of Ralph's hands still burning into his skin.

RALPH STEPPED BACK from the precipice, a satisfied smile on his face. He gave himself a little shake, and the biker's leathers transformed into soft white. He stretched, and behind him a pair of huge white wings unfurled, cramped from being tucked away for so long.

"I always love it when one of my boys graduates," Ralph said softly. And then he was gone as well.

HE HAD NO IDEA how he'd gotten there, and he wasn't even sure where he'd just been. Bits of memory danced in and out of his brain before they drifted away like fleecy clouds. He was in Sam's garden, standing by her swimming pool.

He heard a faint, warning growl, and he turned. Sam's ancient dog was there, looking at him through rheumy eyes.

He didn't know what day it was, or what time. He'd guess it was late afternoon, but he didn't know how long it had been since he'd last seen her. A vague memory danced through his brain—was she going to marry a vet?—and then vanished again. How long had he been gone? And where had he been?

Rags stopped growling abruptly and bounded over to him, full of affectionate doggy greetings. Gideon knelt down and rubbed his head. "How you doing, old boy? You still my friend? What about your mistress? Is she ready to cut my throat?''

"Maybe." Her voice came from directly behind him. He turned to face her, slowly, warily, not sure what he was afraid of.

She was dressed in her armor—designer clothes, shoes that would make her a good three inches taller than he was, flawless makeup, artfully arranged hair and a cool expression of disdain on her distant, beautiful face.

"Where did you go?"

He didn't know the answer to that one. "You got back from the cabin all right?"

"The taxi you arranged picked me up right after I realized I'd been abandoned. Where did you go?"

He racked his brain for an answer, but his mouth was already taking care of things. "I had an appointment. The reason I came down to L.A. in the first place, as a matter of fact."

"And you couldn't take a moment to tell me you were leaving?" Her voice matched her cool, flawless exterior. She was standing there, every man's perfect dream, and all he wanted to do was strip the clothes off her and mess up her hair. But he didn't move.

"It was a deal to do the soundtrack for a big budget movie. I figured I need to be gainfully employed for the next year—there aren't many modeling jobs on Maclean Island." The words were coming and making sense. He could even see his house up there, and the doubts were dissolving and blowing away. He could see her at the house, even though she'd never been there. She'd like it, he knew she would. It was a big, rambling place, only half-finished, with plenty of room for dogs. And children.

She was still looking at him warily. "And why should the presence or absence of modeling jobs matter?"

"You shouldn't have to give it up if you don't want to."

"I'm ready to," she said flatly. "So what do you suggest I do on your island?"

"Anything you damned please," he said, echoing her words from the first night they met. Strangely, he felt a burning pain in his shoulders, and the black T-shirt rubbed against them uncomfortably.

She was standing with her back against the crystal-blue water of the swimming pool, and the mouth that could be sweet and vulnerable curved in a haughty smile. "And what makes you think I'd want to leave everything and move up there?"

"More room for dogs?" he suggested. "And

look at it this way—if you come home with me
you'll never have to have a blind date again.''

"I've sworn off them anyway," she said.

"Come back with me," he said urgently. Not
knowing why, only knowing that he couldn't live
without her.

"Why?"

"Because I'm in love with you. And I think
you're in love with me."

"I met you two days ago."

"I didn't say it made sense. I just said it was
true."

She was so close he could reach out and touch
the icy perfection of her. "I'll think about it," she
said after a moment. "I'm late for a photo shoot.
And then I'm meeting Jasmine for coffee. She's still
shaken up about running out on Aaron at the altar—
smart girl. Go on back to your hotel and call me in
a few days."

Her hands were shaking. Beneath her haughty de-
meanor her hands were shaking, and he knew if he
took the sunglasses off her perfect nose he'd see the
truth in her vulnerable eyes. He wanted to kiss her,
needed to kiss her, and she needed him. It was that
simple.

He moved toward her, and she stood her ground,
watching his approach. If she tried to back away,

and if she moved to either side he could reach out and stop her. He still wasn't certain that was the thing to do, wouldn't be until he saw her eyes.

But she didn't move. He reached up and took the sunglasses away, and there it was again. Her eyes, staring into his, her defenses stripped bare. And he knew that the rest of her needed to be stripped bare as well.

"I need to leave," she said, her voice shaky.

And he reached out and pushed her perfect body into the swimming pool, jumping in after her.

She surfaced, spluttered, her makeup running down her face, her hair soaked, her designer outfit ruined as she treaded water in her high heels. She glared at him. And then she laughed.

She dove at him, pushing him under the blessed coolness of the water. When they surfaced she'd managed to pull his T-shirt over his head. Her ruined silk dress was floating nearby, and he was kissing her. She was kissing him back, her body wrapped around his. She broke the kiss for a moment, pushing him away. Just a little bit away. "You're lucky my dog likes you," she said. "I trust his judgment better than my own."

"Trust *me*," he said, kissing her again. And as they sank beneath the cool blue water, she did.

THE HEAT on his shoulders woke him up, burning into his flesh. He was lying on his stomach, and he wasn't alone. He turned his head, and Sam was lying next to him, her tawny hair cropped short, a sleepy smile on her face. He could hear the water nearby, and he knew they were home. On his island. Their island.

Sam put her hand on his mouth, touching it gently, and he saw the ring on her finger.

"I had a nightmare," he said, not moving. "I dreamed you married a veterinarian."

"It would save a lot on bills," she said sleepily. "But I prefer a husband who plays the piano. Oh, what those hands can do," she said, smiling again. "What are you doing awake so early? I thought you'd be sleeping until noon."

"What time is it?"

"Just after eight." She rolled over on her back, and he saw the faint swell of her belly beneath the pale blue sheet that covered her. "You'd better get all the sleep you can. In five months you're not going to have the chance."

"Come here!" He caught her arm and pulled, and she rolled against him, then sat back, the sheet falling around her waist. She was most definitely, gloriously pregnant, and he wondered why he was surprised. And even as he thought it, the surprise vanished, as if he'd always known it.

"You know what my favorite part of your body is?" she said, leaning over and kissing the small of his back.

"Yes."

She slapped his butt. "Mind out of the gutter, Hyde," she said. She kissed the nape of his neck, and his shoulders tingled. He could remember hands on his shoulders, shoving him. Strong, burning hands.

Another dream, because Sam was kissing his shoulders slowly, first one, then the other. "Your tattoos," she said dreamily against his skin. She put her hands on him, exactly where the phantom hands had rested. "Though I think you have delusions of grandeur to get a pair of angel's wings tattooed on your shoulders."

It didn't even surprise him. The past was fading rapidly, like fog dissolving in the light of day, and only here and now remained. "Maybe a fallen angel," he said, turning over and pulling her down to his mouth.

"Just the way I like them," she said, kissing him before pulling away.

He reached up and ruffled her short hair. "Just

because we're awake doesn't mean we have to get up."

"And what will Ralph do?"

"Ralph?"

"He's a very old dog, and he's been sitting there patiently, waiting for one of us to get up and let him out, for ages now."

He turned. The old dog sat there, tongue hanging out, a big doggy grin on his face as he waited for them. "Has that always been his name?" he asked, momentarily disoriented.

"Of course it has, silly," she said, leaning over to kiss him before pulling away.

"Ralph," he echoed in a meditative voice. "You know, sometimes I think I knew Ralph in another lifetime," he said, throwing back the covers and climbing out of bed.

"He's definitely an old soul," Sam agreed. "I just hope dogs end up in the same heaven as people do. I want to find him waiting for me when I die."

Gideon looked down at him for a moment. "He'll be waiting," he said.

And they headed out into the early morning sunrise, with Ralph bounding happily along beside them.

DANCE WITH THE DEVIL

Cherry Adair

CHAPTER ONE

MIA ROSSI paused in the doorway of her town house, a long-stemmed yellow rose in her hand. Narrowed-eyed, she looked down at the black limo purring at the curb, a plume of white exhaust billowing from it into the wintry night air.

Her blind date had correctly guessed her favorite color of rose, but apparently couldn't be bothered to walk the six steps to her front door. Instead, he'd dispatched his driver.

He was either working hard to flaunt the appearance of status or he was too lazy—or disinterested—to walk twenty feet. Either way, it didn't bode well for the evening.

The driver, who'd handed her the rose with a flourish and a self-conscious half smile, turned to look up as Mia hesitated to follow his down the stairs. "Ms. Rossi?"

The car just missed the pool of pale yellow light cast from a nearby streetlamp. The windows were tinted darkly enough to be impenetrable. Davis

Sloan hadn't sounded either mysterious or sinister the half-dozen times Mia had spoken to him on the phone. He'd sounded sexy, straightforward and amusing. His French accent had been subtle, yet intriguing—enough so that Mia had agreed to yet another one of her mother's fix-ups. But now she wondered exactly what she'd gotten herself into.

Her mom, God help Mia, labored under the misconception that her only daughter desperately needed to work things out with Jack. And, as if to prove how right Jack Ryan had been for her, her mother provided a string of blind dates for comparison.

Sallye Rossi worked for the Federal Attorney's office here in DC, and tended to fix her up with men she met at work. And while Mia didn't have anything against attorneys per se, the idea of dating one still made her nervous. Not as nervous, say, as dating a cop, but nervous nevertheless. Attorneys had a way of asking questions she'd much rather not answer, although in her line of work—*ex* line of work—sleeping with a criminal attorney might just have its advantages.

Just in case a miracle occurred tonight, she'd shaved her legs, and put on her most seductive thong underwear and matching sheer black demi-bra underneath her little black dress. She'd never slept with a man on a first date in her life. But this was an emergency. She needed medicinal sex to get rid of the *memory* of Jack Ryan.

Mia shivered in the icy February night air. She refused to think about Jack. Not tonight. Not a breath of wind stirred, and the moon hid behind a thick cloud cover. She had high hopes for this blind date. The long-sleeved, bias-cut silk dress was conservative enough that if her instincts were wrong she wouldn't feel as though she was sending out any mixed signals.

She'd promised her mother, and herself, she'd accept these blind dates with an open mind. She'd been on a dozen or more blind dates in the eight months since she and Jack had broken up, and generally speaking, she'd been pretty fortunate. None of them had been run-screaming-into-the-hills atrocious. In fact, some had even been quite pleasant. *Pleasant* being the operative word.

Not one of them had that special... She reined in *that* thought. None of them had rung her chimes. Until Davis. She'd been intrigued by him over the course of the past two weeks. He'd been everything Jack was *not*. For one thing he'd been open about his past. Of course it had been late at night, and he'd sounded exhausted when he'd called and woken her. Mia had lain there in the dark, and lis-

tened as he'd talked with disarming candor about
his childhood. It hadn't been pretty. But he was neither bitter nor did he dwell on it. He'd been raised
in a series of foster homes. He'd grown up never
knowing his parents and getting into more than his
fair share of trouble. But he'd put himself through
college and made something of the boy who hadn't
had much of a future.

Mia admired him for that. Some of his stories had
brought empathetic tears to her eyes. She hadn't
wanted him to know she was crying for that lonely
child, and had changed the subject happily when
he'd moved on to something else.

He'd faced the odds and become the man he
wanted to be with no one's help but his own. And
he'd been open enough to share that part of his past
with her. Jack had always said, *"Don't live in the
past, darling. It's today that counts."* Jack hadn't
cared enough to let her in. Davis Sloan did. A pleasant change.

She was relieved to be out of the cloak-and-
dagger business. Both professionally and socially.

Mia had known Jack for two years and the only
information she had on him was his name and age.
Jack Ryan. Thirty-four. Worked for the same alpha-
bet soup acronym, government agency that she had.
Big whoop. Jack had clearly taken a vow of silence

long before they'd met. Too bad he hadn't taken a vow of celibacy as well. They'd been like smoke and lightning together. Like a pair of minks... *Damn it*. Mia shut off the memory with a mental steel door. Locked it. Barred it. And painted it with mental invisible ink. A girl liked to know a little more about her lover than just his name and age.

Jack Ryan was her past. Perhaps Davis Sloan was her future.

Too bad he had to get a demerit before the evening even began.

With a small niggle of misgiving, Mia closed the door and followed the driver down to the sidewalk. She touched the slight lump of the .22 in her purse. She'd never shot anyone in her life, but there was always a first time. A girl had to be prepared. It was odd, if not downright rude, for her date not to come to the front door himself. Of course there may be a perfectly good explanation—

"Did Mr. Sloan break a leg?" Lord, was he missing his legs? A paraplegic? Oh God. If he'd told her about his childhood, wouldn't he have mentioned if he were disabled?

Mia felt a flush ride her cheeks. That was something that hadn't occurred to her. Davis Sloan had sounded so...vital on the phone. Not that it would make any difference if he was handicapped, but it would've been a good thing to know up front.

The driver, bundled in a heavy wool overcoat, paused as he reached for the handle of the rear door. He frowned as he answered, "He's fighting fit as far as I can tell." He opened the door for her.

If Mia hadn't been pondering another possible excuse for his rudeness, she would've noticed the absence of the interior light as she slid into the back seat. The door snicked closed behind her.

The supple leather felt warm under her, indicating Davis had been sitting on her side of the car. Had he watched her come down the stairs from her apartment? Had he liked what he'd seen?

In the thick darkness, Mia jumped at the unexpected touch of his hand on hers. A bolt of white-hot lightning shot up her arm and sent a buzz zinging through her. Hot damn! A good start after all.

The limo slid away from the curb and picked up speed. "You look stunning," a husky voice said out of the darkness.

That voice.

Oh no, oh no, oh freaking *no!* "Damn it to hell, Jack!" Tethered to him or not, Mia threw the rose at him and lunged for the door.

Damn. Damn. Damn! She'd recognize Jack Ryan if she were blindfolded in a pitch-dark room.

Something cool and hard brushed the wrist he was holding. She tugged harder. "What the hell do you…" A metallic click cut her off midrant.

Handcuffs?

The bastard.

She remembered then that Jack had eyes like a cat. She could practically *feel* his gaze on her exposed skin. Nerve endings she'd almost forgotten she had prickled back to life with a vengeance. "You son of a bitch. Unlock these things this instant."

"Hear me out, Mia. Just give me five." There was a faint threat of menace in his tone despite the conciliatory words.

Mia bristled. "I already wasted five *months* of my time. Thanks, but no thanks." With her right hand, she fumbled in her small clutch beside her, searching for her cell phone. Or the .22. At the moment, she didn't care which she found first. The fact that she'd automatically packed the .22 for this particular blind date should've given her a clue. A psychic premonition?

"Darling, you're not going to call the cops." Jack's warm hand brushed hers as he shifted his long legs more comfortably in his seat. He was too close. Too familiar. Too damn annoying for Mia to even glance his way. Not that it would've helped.

The inside of the limo was as dark as a crypt. She could feel him though. Hot. His body had always been like a furnace. He was sitting too close. Much too close.

She grabbed the phone, lucky for him, and hit number two speed dial on her phone. There was no number one anymore. Jack damn-him-to-hell-for-breaking-her-heart Ryan had filled that slot, and she'd erased him finally. Once and for all.

"Worse," she snapped. She didn't bother trying to tug her hand free. The s.o.b. had her left wrist handcuffed to his right, both hands resting in *her* lap. His palm felt hot on her thigh, but she refused to give in to the immediate chemical reaction of once again being touched by him. She pretended, to both of them, that she didn't notice.

"I'm calling your partner in crime— Sallye? No, you're no longer *Mom* to me. You are so busted. How could you?" Mia glared at Jack in a darkness that even the faint streetlights flashing barely penetrated.

She tugged uselessly at her shackled wrist. "My blind date has me handcuffed to his wrist, you traitor." Mia rolled her eyes. "No, Mother, that is *not* sweet, nor is it romantic. Yes, I know how you feel about J— No, I don't want to listen to why he— If you'd stop interrupting, I *would* make sense."

Beside her, Jack was stupid enough to chuckle. Mia yanked at the cuffs, the chain jangled and he shut up.

Oh Lord, she didn't stand a chance between Steamroller Sallye Rossi and Jack The Pitbull Ryan. "No, I will not tell him that." Mia snorted when her mother yelled, "Tell Jack I still love him."

"Love you too, Sallye," Jack yelled back.

Mia jerked at the cuffs on her wrist again and cut her mother off in the middle of the love fest. It was hell on wheels having her mother and the man she'd dumped still like each other. Where was the motherly concern? Where was the loyalty? Where was the key to these silver bracelets?

"You low-down, no good, lying, son of a—" she said bitterly. "Stop the car this instant."

She sensed his feral smile. "Not a chance."

Mia yanked hard at their cuffed wrists, wincing as the clasp dug into the tender skin of her inner wrist. "I'm not kidding, Jack. Have your driver turn around. Right. Now."

"Here." Jack pressed something small and round into her hand.

"What's this?" Mia demanded, her fingers automatically closing around the pill. "Planning on drugging me into submission?"

"Nothing's that strong," Jack said under his breath, then more audibly, "Antacid."

"I don't need it." Her stomach burned like the fiery depths of hell. Jack Ryan hell.

"Suit yourself."

"Thank you. Don't mind if I do." Mia glanced out the window, squinting to see better, and slipped the antacid into her mouth to let it melt on her tongue. If he didn't always give her indigestion, he wouldn't have to carry around the remedy.

"Are we really going to the South African ambassador's party, or was that also a lie?"

"I didn't lie to you."

"Right. When was it you changed your name from Jack Ryan to Davis Sloan?"

"Okay," he conceded with a half shrug. "One small lie. Otherwise you never would've talked to me."

"Damn straight. So instead you made up a whole person?"

"I didn't lie."

"You didn't grow up in foster care, Jack," Mia said, tiredly leaning her head back against the plush seat. Jack had always enjoyed the finer things in life. He had a magnificent condo overlooking the city, hot and cold running domestic help and several very nice cars.

Even in something as important as money they'd been opposites. He spent it like water, she hoarded and invested it.

"You grew up in Beverly Hills," she said, her voice flat. "Remember Gloria and Samuel Ryan, your loving, wealthy parents? I got a card from them last Christmas. Won't they be hurt to know you're dismissing them out of hand just so you can make points with a woman?"

"All fabrication. There aren't any parents, Mia. Loving or otherwise."

"Oh, Jack."

"I'm telling you the truth."

"Who sent me that sweet Christmas card? And the flowers for my birthday last year?"

"I did."

Mia stomach knotted when she realized that once again he was all smoke and mirrors. Everyone knew of or about Jack Ryan. If nothing else the fact that his name was that of a fictional action hero was enough to have people talking. Some people jokingly called him *Harrison*. His status as one of DC's eligible bachelors, his wealth, his old money background...all of it was public record. Countless articles had been written about him. He'd even been *People Magazine*'s Bachelor of the Year two years in a row.

"So poor little you grew up in a series of foster homes?" Mia said, annoyed either way. If it was true, she was furious that he'd lied to her before. If it was a lie, she was furious that he was lying to her now. "And just to make it even more poignant, you were arrested at thirteen for breaking and entering and stuck in juvie because there was no one who cared enough to bail you out. And then you worked your way through college and turned your life around? *Right?*"

"Yes."

Mia glared at him in the dark. She must have been getting used to the dim light. She could almost make out his eyes. Narrowed, boring into her with the strength of a power drill.

"All of that was true?"

"I said so, didn't I?"

He *sounded* sincere. Mia didn't know what to make of this information. Or if she should make anything of it at all. Of course, if he'd finally told her some small truths about himself...

No. It was too little too late. "And I'm supposed to believe you?"

He sighed. "Do what you want. You usually do."

"Damn it, Jack, I'm not the bad guy in this."

"Why does there have to be a bad guy?" he demanded. "You used to bug me for information. Now you know why I never told you."

Mia sat back, leaning into the butter-soft leather and staring at him in fascination. "You're saying you never told me the truth because I couldn't take it?"

"Because you wouldn't believe it."

The way I felt about you then, I'd have believed anything and everything you could've told me, Jack. Maybe if you'd tried telling me the truth then— "Well, why would I? All you've ever done is lie to me."

Jack shook his head. "Not always, darling."

His voice caressed her like a mink glove against warm, bare skin.

"You should have told me it was *you* I've been talking to for the past two weeks."

"You should've recognized it was me."

He actually sounded hurt. Mia snorted. Yeah, right. "How could I? You sounded normal and charming."

"I *am* normal and charming."

"No, Jack, you aren't." He wasn't even close to normal. Jack Ryan wasn't just a large man, he was larger than life. He was a flesh-and-blood comic book hero. Thank God she'd managed to dump him, and her job, before one or both of them had killed her.

It hadn't been easy. She'd missed the adrenaline rush.

"I'm charming when I need to be." That voice of his went deeper, darker.

"Believe it or not, that's *not* a positive character trait."

"You never minded before."

There were a lot of things she hadn't minded—or pretended not to mind—because the thought of living without Jack had been unthinkable. Well, that was then, this was now. "This is not amusing. I want to go home."

"You were going to have sex with Sloan, weren't you?"

She sorta kinda had, and the thought that Jack knew her that well made her face hot and her temper rise. "Since you and Sloan are one and the same, I think it's safe to say I've changed my mind."

His other hand slid under their bound wrists before she realized what he was doing. He ran his warm palms over her hip. "You were going to sleep with the guy. Damn it, Mia. How could you?"

"That *guy* was you. Jack, how could you?" She never realized how cold she was until Jack put his hands on her. Then she'd always wanted to curl into the furnacelike heat of him. Not now. Not tonight. Not ever again. She tried to shift out of reach. But it was impossible. Mia gritted her teeth. The limo had to stop sometime.

"You're wearing my lucky thong, aren't you?"

Ah, that thong. They'd both gotten lucky every time she'd worn it.

"No, Jack," Mia said coolly while her blood heated and accelerated through her veins. Could a person die if their internal body temperature went over two hundred degrees? The thin silk over her hipbone where Jack's hand rested heated up as if under a solar blanket. "These are my *unlucky* panties. Get your hand off me."

"Jesus darling, my body's hardly cold and you're ready to sleep with somebody else?"

"It's been eight months."

"Feels like longer."

Yes, it did. "I asked you very nicely to leave me alone. I wish you had."

His fingers tightened briefly on her thigh, as though staking his claim.

"This is business, Mia."

"That makes the subterfuge even worse. And how did you get my mother to help you set me up?"

"I told her your country needed you one more time."

"I quit."

"You've been reinstated for this job."

A flush of interest, even excitement, swept through her, but she squashed it fast. "I don't want to be reinstated. I want to go back home, take a nice warm bath and grab an early night."

"This despite donning your lucky panties?"

Mia sighed. Jack Ryan was like a junkyard dog with a bone. He was the most annoyingly persistent man she'd ever had the misfortune of falling in l— of ever knowing. "What do you want, Jackson?"

The car crossed the bridge and turned onto a traffic-clogged avenue. A couple in a red sports car pulled up beside them at the light. As the dark-haired girl leaned her head on her boyfriend's shoulder, he wrapped a beefy arm about her and dropped a kiss on her waiting mouth. The car behind them honked a split second after the light changed. She and Jack had been like that once. They hadn't been able to keep their hands off each other. One time a bum in the park had yelled at them to get a room for Chrissake.

But that was a long time ago.

"I don't work for Uncle Sam anymore, Jack, remember? I'm a translator." She worked for Dysart International Bank. A nice quiet, uneventful job. Jack didn't need to know that she was bored out of her ever-loving mind every day from 9:00 a.m. to 5:00 p.m. And lonely from 5:05 p.m. to 8:55 a.m. She was just starting to kick the lethal Jack Ryan habit.

She'd gone cold turkey, and had been doing just fine, thank you very much, without him.

"Yeah, I know," he said, sliding his thumb back and forth on her thigh in an absentminded and annoying caress. "But I—*we*—need you for this job, Mia. You're the best. Nobody can—"

"Too bad." Mia shoved at his marauding hand. It didn't budge. Fine. Stroke away. It didn't affect her in the slightest anymore. She relaxed against the plush leather seat. Outside she projected calm, inside mooshy, adrenaline racing. With annoyance, she reminded herself. "My cat-burgling, safecracking days are over," she told him flatly.

"You're back in, darling, whether you like it or not. Orders from the top. We go in, get the disk and leave. You'll be back home in no time. Tops."

"What disk?" Mia demanded. Hell, she couldn't even keep herself from asking. She felt the familiar rush of anticipation. Damn it. Damn *him*. She had to remind herself that it wasn't *Jack* who needed her tonight. This was for her country, she had to remind herself. She felt the zing of energy she'd always felt when she was embarking on a gray ops

assignment. As partners, she and Jack had been un-
beatable.

"You ready to listen?"

No. Mia sighed. "Brief me. And make it…brief."

CHAPTER TWO

JACK UNLOCKED THE CUFFS as the limo pulled up in front of the embassy. They'd been to several parties here in the past. Knowing the layout of the house made tonight's job that much easier. *Too* easy, Mia thought suspiciously, shooting Jack a glance.

The disk they were there to retrieve was probably in the safe in the library. First floor, and just beyond the downstairs bathrooms. They'd never heisted anything from here before, but they'd certainly scoped out what was where. Just in case.

Their job description was—*had been*—gray ops retrieval. If something needed to be copied, or replaced, Jack and Mia were sent in to do the job. If specific information was required, Jack could set up a program to trap key strokes and send the info back to the agency's computers without the user being any the wiser.

While Mia's nimble fingers could open just about anything locked, Jack's expertise was anything computer related. He was brilliant. He could ferret around to his heart's content, change, tweak or copy without leaving a whisper of a fingerprint, not a breath of evidence that he'd tromped all over their hard drive.

But this job was nothing that intrusive or complicated. In this case they were to retrieve a disk with the names and addresses of the people funding the arms race in one of the ever name changing nations north of South Africa.

It was suspected that not only were there thousands of wealthy individuals contributing, but also a good number of American corporations. And of course millions of dollars in funding was being funneled to the cause from certain weapons manufacturers who benefited from the continuing war.

American weapons were killing thousands of American soldiers sent there to protect the nation's citizens from the bad guys. Anyone possessing the list of contributors was in the position to halt the war. Or escalate it.

They were there to retrieve the disk.

Piece of cake, Mia thought as she waited for Jack to round the car to her side and then for the driver to pull away to a predesignated spot in case they had to make a hasty departure.

And she *would* be hasty. She'd be in and out in ten minutes or less.

And this blind date from hell would be over.

Ten minutes with Jack, using their usual cover, was about all she'd be able to take.

With any luck at all, tonight wouldn't even be a blip in her memory this time tomorrow.

She took a deep breath of cold night air. It hadn't snowed in the past couple of days, and gray sludge was banked against the shrubs lining the driveway. She'd be home before the arrival of the predicted snow flurries.

"Still don't bother to wear a coat. Stubborn woman." He didn't remove his own thick, black wool overcoat because he knew from experience she'd never wear it. Not even for the few minutes it took to traverse the driveway and climb the front steps.

She was allergic to wool, wouldn't wear fur and hated to be in anything bulky in case she needed to run like hell. "I'm warm-blooded." She made a grab for the wrought-iron banister as her foot slipped on the ice-crusted sidewalk.

Jack rested his hand on the small of her back to steady her. The heat of his touch sizzled right through the flimsy fabric of her dress and just for one, tiny, ridiculously small, infinitesimal, eensy moment, she enjoyed the feel of his hand on her again.

God help her.

"Hot-blooded, you mean," Jack murmured in her ear.

He was right. She was hot-blooded. Ordinarily, she could ignore the cold, but somehow she couldn't quite manage to ignore Jack. He was the matchstick to her dynamite. The gas to her flame. The—*oh, stop it,* she thought crossly.

Jack hadn't needed a cover. He *was* a wealthy playboy dilettante who couldn't stand a too bright light shone on his activities. He had an…edge to him that was irresistible. Women dropped at his feet like flies and men were intrigued by just a hint of deep, dark secrets behind his midnight eyes. Men and women alike wanted to stand close to Jack's dangerous flame. He was invited everywhere the rich, famous and powerful of DC gathered.

Jack Ryan had never been the right man for her, Mia reminded herself grimly. No matter what her body told her, he was not the right man for her. He was commitment-phobic for one thing, and for another he had no respect for hard-earned money. And she'd always know that there was something he wasn't telling her. She'd always been waiting for the proverbial shoe to drop.

While she'd never starved, or been homeless, she had a healthy respect for the security of a decent bank balance. Her father had split when she was six. The classic—gone out for cigarettes and never come back. She'd seen just how her mom had struggled to support herself and two kids.

Mia wasn't prepared to jeopardize her own hard-earned savings, or the stability and happiness of her future children, on a man who threw his money away, and kept secrets.

She'd kept her head, and systematically gone about searching for the father of those children for years before she'd met Jack.

And for several months she'd lost what was left of her brain.

She'd worked in intelligence at the agency for five years before they'd agreed to put her in the field. Her first assignment with Jack, heisting a briefcase from a foreign diplomat at Grand Central station, had been a onetime thing.

The job had gone so well, her nimble fingers so quick, the agency had made them a team. Jack had guarded her back and planned the jobs. Mia had been his "hands." Her long, magic fingers could caress open any lock in less time than it took to say Uncle Sam. All those years in the trailer park playing marbles and, later, five card stud had given her dexterity. It had also given her a mistrust of the wealthy, and a healthy respect for her own self-preservation.

They'd never discussed their pasts, Mia had realized when it was all over. They'd both thought their lives had started the first time they'd been intimate. A clean slate, a new start, a fresh beginning. For both of them. Boy, had *she* been wrong.

She was already working at the bank, her cover, when she finally quit the agency. The transition had been relativity painless. Relatively.

Light spilled from the open front door down the snow-cleared steps. The house was enormous, imposing and filled with the crème de la crème of Washington, DC society, many of whom Jack and Mia knew from the round of social events they'd been invited to over the past couple of years. Washington was unlike any other city. Power was the ticket here, not money. A five-term senator had more clout than a five-generation family fortune. Because the Washington power brokers all lived on expense accounts, money had long ago become subservient to position and connection.

The foyer was crowded, filled with the fragrances of expensive hothouse flowers, pricey perfume and the scrumptious smells of the savory hors d'oeuvres waiters carried discreetly through the crowd of party guests.

"I have to use the rest room," Mia told him quietly, stepping away from the warmth of his palm, which was resting possessively on the small of her back. "Will you wai—"

He stepped in closer, divested himself of his overcoat to the coat check girl, and wrapped a muscled, implacable arm about her waist, all without missing a beat. "Not yet. You know the game."

Of course he'd known immediately she wanted to go in after the disk alone. Annoying man. "Just let me get on with this."

"Not on your life. It's too soon and you know it."

"The sooner the better as far as I'm concerned."

"Liar," he said with a knowing smile. "Your blood's pumping. Hot and fast."

"It is not."

"You can't fool me, Mia. You never could." His hand slid up and down her arm and tongues of flame danced on her bare skin. "I know you too well. You *love* the game. The excitement. The danger. That rush of adrenaline that jolts your system."

She really did. Which was just another reason why she'd had to leave the business. Loving the danger was as unhealthy as loving Jack.

"Maybe I've changed."

"Yeah? And maybe I'm a priest."

She laughed in spite of the situation. The very thought of blatantly sexual Jack Ryan being a priest was enough to make a statue break out in a grin.

"It's good to have you back, darling."

She stiffened against his casual assumption and then forced herself to smile at the deputy mayor and his wife as they passed. Jack dipped his head and whispered in her ear and she tried her best not to turn into a gooey puddle. His warm breath fanned her skin and it didn't seem to matter that all he was talking about was business. Her blood pumped and she was suddenly, *acutely* aware of the tiny thong she wore beneath her dress. For an outing with a blind date, it had felt naughty, a little dangerous. For an outing with *Jack,* it was an invitation to disaster.

Deliberately, she shifted away from him, but didn't get far. He stayed glued to her side. She used her elbow to shove him away. Useless of course. The man was as immovable as a mountain.

Her stomach growled.

"Too nervous with anticipation to eat before your date?" he whispered in her ear. "Didn't I always tell you to at least eat a piece of cheese to settle that stomach of yours."

"So suggests the rat." He'd insisted on feeding her soup and half a sandwich before they'd gone out on every job. It occurred to Mia that she hadn't had indigestion since she and Jack had broken up.

"Half an hour of making nice and we can slip away," he assured her.

"As long as it isn't you I have to be nice t— Sandy!" Mia smiled, pleased to see the other woman who was a regular at the most "in" parties in the city. They air kissed exuberantly.

Sandra Kilstrom grabbed Mia's hands and held open her arms, raking her eyes down Mia from head to toe.

Clearly disgusted, she scowled. "Damn it. Tell me you starve from Monday through Friday to keep this body or I'm going to have to kill you."

Mia smiled. "I watch every stingy morsel I put into my mouth and repent at the gym four times a week."

Sandy hugged her. "Oh! It's *so* good to have you back, honey. Everyone has missed you."

Jack tightened his arm about Mia's waist and pulled her close. Damn, the position was so familiar so comfortable, that for several seconds she forgot she was over him. She tried to subtly shift out of reach, but he held her more firmly against him and rubbed his palm up and down her bare arm. "She watches what she eats, and I watch her," Jack told Sandy smoothly.

"God, it's great to see you two back together." The older woman smiled at both of them while sidestepping a couple heading for the dance floor.

"We're n—"

"We're in the way of the dancers," Jack inserted smoothly. Then winking at Sandy, said, "See you later, beautiful. Put me on your dance card for something slow and sexy."

Sandra stood on tiptoes to plant a kiss on Jack's chin—the only place she could reach. "I'm going to hold you to that, Jack Ryan, and hunt you down like the dog you are if you don't come looking for me."

"Too bad I'm a one-woman man," he said, charming as ever. "I'm too crazy about Mia to stray. But if she ever dumps me, you'll be the first to know."

Sandy giggled and Mia mentally rolled her eyes. If he'd loved her maybe, just *maybe* she might have stayed. With or without a commitment from him. But he'd never given her more of himself than she'd needed to know for the next assignment. He'd kept her shut out of his life beyond the bedroom. Jack loved excitement. He loved danger. He loved the chase. She'd wanted hearth and home—*stability*. He thrived on the unknown. And she wanted to wake up to see the same face on the pillow beside her every morning. Basically, she wanted predictable and safe.

They were miles apart in every way that counted.

The fact that she'd *had* predictable and safe for the past eight months and had been bored out of her mind had nothing at all do with anything.

She wasn't the first woman to go all weak-kneed and melt into a puddle of goo over one of his sexy smiles. Jack had that effect on *any* female. Damn it.

Patting his broad chest with her fingertips, Sandy shook her head, "You are such a charming liar, Jack, it's no wonder every woman here adores you."

I don't, Mia thought. She may have learned the hard way, but she did, eventually, *learn.* And when dealing with Jack Ryan, it would pay to remember all those hard-won lessons.

She glanced at him. Tall, dark and dangerous, he was the kind of man who fueled hot sweaty dreams. She should know.

She smiled at Sandy. "Oh honey, you're so sweet to try to make Jack feel better."

"Better about what?" Sandy gave Jack a speculative glance.

Mia playfully punched Jack's arm and managed to get a good pinch in while she was at it. "He's always been a charmer and now that he's losing his hair, well, he's a little self-conscious.''

Jack's attention was on Mia's mouth. Mia paid no attention and leaned into Sandy. ''He's in denial.''

''I'll tell you what I am,'' he said mildly, meeting her gaze with a dangerous glint in his blue eyes and a crocodile smile showing brilliantly white teeth.

''Oh honey…I'm sure Sandy doesn't mind hearing about your…*problems.*''

''There's more?'' Sandy gasped, eyes twinkling.

''No,'' Jack took hold of Mia's arm. ''See you later, beautiful.'' He dragged her off through the crowd. ''What was that about?'' he asked smoothing his thumb up her back in a subtle caress. ''Jealousy?''

She snorted softly. ''Just trying to remind you that we are *not* the couple of the social set anymore.'' She shrugged Jack's hand from around her waist. ''Don't pet me, don't stroke me. We are not together—not now, not ever again. Keep your mind on the job. Got it?''

A muscle in his jaw clenched and his eyes narrowed into slits that shot fire. ''Got it.''

''I'm serious, Jack.''

''So am I, darling. So am I. Want something to eat?''

He wasn't losing his hair. Or his appeal, damn it all to hell. One smile from Jack and she was tempted to forget his lack of commitment. One touch of his arm on any part of her body and she was willing to cancel out a future for the promise of a great here and now.

He still had it. In spades. And she was probably in very deep trouble here. So the best thing to do would be to get the job done and get gone. But meanwhile...

"Yes, I'm hungry. Too bad I'm not in that nice restaurant with the ever so charming Davis Sloan. I should've known better, shouldn't I? Nobody is that sensitive, amusing and in tune with someone other than himself."

"I told you I didn't lie to you. Everything Davis Sloan said came direct from *me*."

He again rested his hand lightly on the small of her back to cross the room to the buffet table.

She wished she could believe him. He'd said so many...*nice* things in the past couple of weeks. She'd actually reached the point where she'd lunged for the phone when it rang, hoping it would be Davis—Jack. But painful experience warned against trusting him again. Although...as she thought about some of the things he'd said, she looked at him a little differently. Had he really been that lonely little boy, growing up knowing no one wanted him? She refused to be swayed by a vulnerability he no longer possessed. "Why Jack? Why bother playing this elaborate game? Why not just call me and say, hey, we need you for a job?"

"You would've said no."

"Exactly my point. Freedom of choice."

"You're the best."

"*Was* the best."

"Still are, darling." He dipped his head and whispered in her ear. "Together we were unstoppable, in every way, and you know it."

Pride and pleasure slid down her spine. Probably not a good sign.

"Anyway," Jack said briskly, "we're here now. Are you going to bitch all night?"

She cocked her head as if giving it some thought. "I might."

He almost smiled. "Fair enough. Do this and you can bitch to your heart's content."

"Gee, thanks. Since when we're finished, you won't be around to hear me."

They were briefly separated by a laughing foursome, but Mia distinctly heard him mutter, "Don't bank on it, sweetheart. Don't bank on it."

Fine. Jack always had his own agenda. Just because she'd once loved his agendas and everything else about him, didn't mean she *still* did. She was immune now. Eight months of celibacy had been just what the doctor ordered. Regular sex with Jack had clouded her mind.

Damned if she didn't miss that cloud sometimes.

"They have that imported smoked salmon you like," he said scanning the long table.

"I don't eat it anymore. Makes me break out." Mia grabbed a gold-rimmed plate and started loading it with roast beef and small mushrooms. The last time she'd eaten salmon Jack had fed it to her between long bouts of insanely acrobatic lovemaking on the beach one hot summer night. Salmon made her break out with regret. Very bad for her mental health.

There were too many people to make a private conversation possible or advisable and they were forced to greet dozens of people while they searched for somewhere to sit. "There?" he asked, indicating a wide window seat just vacated.

"Sure." She wanted a glass of South African wine, maybe two—three would be better. She wanted to be in a well-lit restaurant with Davis Sloan, the man she'd thought she was seeing—*Stop it, Mia. Just get over it.* While Jack's methods sucked, and her mother was going to be blackballed for quite a while, the reason Mia was here was valid.

She was the best.

She'd do this one last job with her old partner and then she'd be done.

There was no need to talk. They'd worked together enough times to know the drill. As much as she didn't want to be here, her natural instincts had come back into sharp focus—almost as if she'd never left the agency. As if she and Ryan were still the best team in undercover work.

The house was overflowing with guests. The doors, conveniently left open wide to dispel the body heat, also made it much easier to do a little second-story work. The converted mansions that comprised Embassy Row dated to the turn of the twentieth century. They were similarly laid out and Mia knew the floor plans as well as she knew her way around the local Hecht's Department store. Tuxedo-clad undercover agents guarded the entrances and exits to the building, mandatory in the terrorist climate of the times. But she knew that the security force was there to keep people out, not monitor people within.

Mia slid her plate onto a half-round table against the wall.

"Ready?"

He gave her a heavy-lidded look. "Always."

CHAPTER THREE

BEING SO WELL CONNECTED proved to be a curse and a blessing. It was easy to maneuver the maze of guests with the comfortable ease of familiarity. However, they couldn't move two feet without being stopped. Everyone wanted to chat.

Jack wasn't the only one to have missed Mia in the past eight months. She was well liked. And God only knew Jack loved to watch her interact with people. Even though her face was the first thing he imagined in the morning, and the last thing he imagined every night, the *reality* of Mia Rossi couldn't be replicated—even in his fertile imagination.

She was the only woman there not wearing a fortune in gems. A serviceable gold-plated watch, and a pair of quarter carat diamond studs she'd bought with her first dividend check, were all she wore with the understated black dress. And she *still* looked more beautiful, more elegant, than any woman in the room.

Jack had bought Mia a fortune in jewelry during

their time together. He'd tried it all. Diamonds, emeralds, gold and silver. Made no difference. She'd returned everything with a smile and a no thank you. She'd refused to accept expensive presents from him. He couldn't, wouldn't give her what she wanted most.

The sound of her musical laughter, the sparkle of amusement in her big brown eyes, the habit she had of absently tucking a short strand of dark hair behind her ear as she listened, head half-cocked, to a long story by the terminally boring senator from Arkansas. Everything about her was achingly familiar, comfortable. And so tempting. He had never felt this kind of completeness with anyone. Even though it felt right, somehow things had gone terribly, terribly wrong for them. Jack mentally cursed. This was not the path his brain should be on. It was too dangerous on too many levels.

Mia Rossi was a complete pain in his ass. Opinionated. Stubborn. Unyielding. And worst of all, *unforgiving.*

She wanted nothing to do with him. Yet he wanted to do everything with her. To her.

Hell.

Beautiful. Courageous. Sexy as hell. He fanned his fingers out on the small of her back and felt a visceral jolt as her skin warmed under his touch and she unconsciously shifted under his hand. She'd always been responsive to the smallest of his touches.

Just as he was responding to the knowledge that under that sleek little dress she wore that amazing thong. The thong he still had dreams about. The thong she'd wear whenever she wanted to drive him crazy.

Man. He had it bad.

It took almost twenty minutes to cruise from one side of the enormous reception room to the other. Jack kept his arm around Mia's slender waist, his hand intimately brushing her hip. Her active little brain might be as annoyed as hell at him, but her lush body responded as it always had. Her skin felt hot beneath his palm, and her eyes held that fiery glint that promised either retribution or mind-blowing sex. Tonight he knew it would be retribution.

There were a few groups of people standing around chatting in the wide corridor, which led to the library cum study and to the rest rooms available to the guests. Jack backed Mia against the inlaid mahogany paneling.

"Wha—"

He leaned into her and crushed his mouth down on hers. He dove into the kiss like a man with heatstroke diving into the cool aqua waters of a swimming pool.

Her mouth tasted achingly familiar. Slick, wet from the wine she'd drunk. God. Mia... Jack wasn't going to waste this. He ignored her nails digging into his forearms through his shirt and jacket. Ignored the strength of her grip. He wrapped his arms around her slender body, leaned into her and drank from her mouth until he was dizzy with want, blazing with need.

He slid one hand up her back to cup the nape of her neck. His other palm slipped down to cup her bottom. She murmured against his marauding lips. Jack wasn't sure if it was a protest or compliance and he was very close to that state where he didn't much care. Knowing Mia, her brain was complaining and her body had already started softening. At least, he hoped so. It wasn't possible to even think that she wasn't feeling this. It was too intense, too encompassing. Too...*huge*.

Acutely aware that people milled around them, Jack kept his attention on Mia's mouth. The feel of her peaked nipples were hidden against his shirt-front, and for his pleasure alone.

Her lips, once soft, were now avid against his. She might believe—hell, he wanted her to believe—that this was all part of his game plan. God only knew they'd done it before. Appeared about to rip each other's clothes off and snuck into a dark library, office or locked room to heist something for Uncle Sam.

For Jack this was far more than a game plan to get them into the privacy of the library. Reluctantly, he eased his mouth from hers, lifting his head to look at her. Her eyes were glazed and slightly unfocused. He brushed moisture from her mouth with the side of his thumb. "Ready?"

"A-absolutely." She straightened away from the wall. When he didn't automatically step back, she scowled and shoved at his chest with her palms.

"Don't push your luck, Ryan," she said in a husky whisper.

If observed from more than three feet away they would appear to be nothing other than two lovers engaged in intimate conversation. He wrapped his arm about her slender waist.

"Let's do it." He guided her toward the closed double doors of the library. "Hope to hell there's no one in here," Jack said in a stage whisper.

Mia, as good as she ever was, played right along. "Oh, honey...do you really think we should?"

Jack shoved open the door with an impatient hand, almost dragged her inside and slammed the door, knowing what everyone on the other side would think.

The second the door closed, Mia turned and twisted the lock.

"You didn't have to paint my tonsils, Jack," she complained. The heavy, dark green velvet drapes were open to the night. Without a doubt, security guards were perambulating on the wide patio beyond the French doors. "Close the drapes and let's just get this over with."

Jack started walking past her to cross the room. He felt eyes on them and used the opportunity to touch her cheek. "I've missed you."

"Good, you're well-practiced then. You won't have a hard time adjusting when you miss me again." The daggers in her eyes met their mark. In fact, her marksmanship was a legend at the agency. Legendarily bad. She couldn't hit a barn door at high noon.

"Let's get this farce on the road." She put a slender hand, palm down on his chest. With the other hand she reached behind her for the long zipper that curved up her back.

He wished it was real and not staged for their unseen audience. "I'll get the drapes."

"Make it snappy." The dress parted revealing slender, creamy pale shoulders. Jack yanked at the drapes, but kept his eyes on the woman pretending to strip.

"Stop ogling. I'm doing this for the benefit of those guys outside, *not* for you," Mia said impatiently. "Hurry up and close the drapes, would you?"

Honest to God, looking at her face anyone would be forgiven for believing she was as hot for him as he was for her. But Jack knew that look in her eyes too well. It wasn't lust—it was blood lust. Big difference.

And he was as hard as a pistol despite knowing that Mia was stripping only for the benefit of the job. "The pull's on the left side."

He used the pull and the heavy drapes slowly slid closed, blocking out the square black eyes of the French doors.

All business now, Mia pulled the dress back up over her shoulders and struggled with the zipper as she moved swiftly to the painting on the far wall. "Just for the record, a Hollywood kiss would have done the job."

"You know I strive for authenticity," he told her, handing her a pair of thin latex gloves from his pocket. He leaned against the door and observed her slender, gloved fingers feel around the perimeter of the painting, studying the frame for any creative security feature.

"Anything?" he asked quietly.

"Hand me my purse."

He dug the small clutch out of his pocket and opened it.

His lips twitched. A .22, a wedge of folded tissues, a credit card, lip gloss, twenty dollars and... "God damn it, Mia!"

She spun around. "What?"

"You have rubbers in here."

She lifted a brow. "And your point is?"

"You have *three* rubbers in here."

"You know, Jack," Mia said mildly, "this is absolutely the perfect time to be discussing the items in my purse—while we're breaking and entering an ambassador's personal safe. Your timing, as usual, is impeccable."

"Davis would've brought his own rubbers."

"As it turns out, Davis—that would be you—can inflate the rubbers and float them to the moon for all I care. Hand me the compact of pressed powder." She shot him a glare. "Please."

She took the everyday object and turned it into a trick of the trade. Jack noted that after loosening some of the face powder, she brought the silver compact close to her lips. His body reacted with more than just admiration as she pursed her mouth and blew the smallest stream of flesh-colored dust around the painting.

"No lasers," she said, more to herself than to him, he was sure. Mia was so focused he doubted she even remembered he was in the room. She yanked a hair from her scalp, rubbed the spot absently, then, on tiptoes, slipped the hair a few inches around and under the painting.

A painting which, Jack thought, was a monstrosity of flowers that looked suspiciously like a woman's vulva.

Mia dropped the strand of hair and slid her finger beneath the bottom edge. He heard a quick but distinct click. Then the painting hinged open to reveal a small, black, older model wall safe trimmed in gold.

"Can you—?"

Mia made a small dismissive noise. "Please. Don't insult me."

Jack, ears tuned to the hum of conversation outside the door, watched as she cocked her head and her nimble fingers moved with precision around the old-fashioned dial.

She twisted the knob to the left, then the right, then left again. "Too bad I don't have my—"

He laid a small black velvet pouch on the credenza in front of her. Her custom-made tools.

Mia shot him a frowning glance. "How'd you ge—"

"Left them on your desk your last day."

The day she'd walked away from both the job she'd loved—and him.

Jack straightened as someone rattled the door handle. Mia reached for her loaded handbag and Jack touched the butt of his own weapon hidden beneath his jacket. He held his breath, and after a few seconds, heard them move off down the corridor.

Mia returned to the safe. They each had their job to do.

"Damn."

"What?"

She frowned. "Got any C4 on you?"

"Oh, Jesus. It's not going to open?"

Mia grinned. "Hell, yeah. It's only a TRTL-30." A burglary performance rating of thirty minutes max to open it by common hand tools or mechanical tools—such as a grinder or drill. Mia had the best tool of all. Excellent hearing and perfect pitch. She could *hear* the internal tumblers as they fell into place. She stepped aside and the door swung open a few inches. "Just kidding, Jack. Geez, where's your sense of humor?"

He wasn't amused, didn't appreciate her moment of levity. "Grab the disk and let's book." Other than seeing Mia tonight, he had a bad feeling about this too simple job. Something didn't feel right, hadn't right from the beginning. Something felt... off.

"No disk in here," Mia said softly, after she riffled through the contents of the safe.

"Be sure." He didn't leave his post at the door. He kept one ear tuned to the party outside the thick doors, the music, the ebb and flow of voices, footsteps moving down the carpeted corridor outside.

She was efficient and methodical. After a few more seconds, she said quietly. "Definitely not here. Upstairs safe?"

"Must be."

"How long have we been in here?" They'd been in some tight spots together in their partnership. They may have redefined passion together, and had an eight-month lapse, but as thieves their association was still magical.

"Long enough," he told her grimly, as she replaced the contents of the safe and shut the door.

He didn't budge as she moved to avoid the swing of the painting, stepping back into him. Her silky dark hair brushed his chin. The smell of her skin made him dizzy with longing.

As soon as the picture was back in place, Mia took a step forward, away from him. "Open the door, Jack. You conned me here to help you do a job. Let's just do it, okay?"

He unlocked the door. This was neither the time nor the place. "I'm going to have to kiss you again."

She sighed and tilted up her face. "Fine. Get it over with."

He bracketed her face, then ran his fingers through her hair to muss it up. She stood still beneath his hands, her eyes hard, her soft mouth grim. When they'd done this before it had been part of the fun of the game. Now it was purely business.

"Not even a spark?" Jack asked, keeping his hands on either side of her face.

"Not a glimmer."

"Liar."

She snorted. "I'm not the one carrying a rifle in my pocket."

He grinned. "Wanna see if it's loaded?"

She kept her expression impassive and shrugged. "Open the door and let's wrap this up."

He opened the door. The noise of the party washed over them, an assault to his senses after being alone in the library with her. They weren't going to be able to emerge from the library and immediately go upstairs. People probably assumed they'd just had wild monkey sex on good old Johannes's desk.

"Dance?" Jack suggested when they reached the reception room.

It would get them across the large space and closer to the stairs. But Mia didn't want to be held by him. Not again. She might be able to fool herself a while longer, but she'd never be able to convince Jack that she wasn't turned on and raring to go—not if he was holding her close on a dance floor.

Mia didn't want to be here. She didn't want to be anywhere near Jack Ryan. He was temptation in a suit. The devil incarnate. The serpent with the apple.

Just call me Eve, she thought, stepping into his arms.

CHAPTER FOUR

JACK FOLDED HER into his arms. Her hair smelled of orange blossoms and nostalgic summer nights. The crowded dance floor worked to his advantage.

He smiled secretly, knowing she wasn't going anywhere. He felt the press of her slender body and the brush of her long legs against his, sanctioned by their status as a hot couple.

She used her elbow, strategically pressed to his midriff, to put a few millimeters of space between them. Their faces were close enough for him to count individual eyelashes. Close enough for him to feel the soft caress of her breath against his throat. His eyes tracked from the small wedge of a frown between her brows to the soft curve of her bare mouth. He'd nibbled off her lipstick and, atypically, she'd forgotten to reapply it.

Tuned into every sensuous move of her body, he tucked her much smaller hand into his and held it between them where he could feel the brush of her breasts against the back of his hand and she could feel the slow, steady beat of his heart.

"God, this feels great," he said easily. He'd danced with her before, countless times. Both in public and in private. The memory of dancing naked with Mia in his arms forced him to bite back a groan.

"Maybe you should cozy up to the notion that I'm not interested," she said with asperity. "It should give the expression 'talk to the hand' new meaning for you."

"Christ, Mia, when did you become so tough?"

She tossed her hair back and smiled up at him, keeping up the pretense of cozy lovebirds even while her tone sharpened to a sword's edge. "Gee, let me think. Could it've been when you refused to make any kind of commitment?"

"I told you—"

"And I told you I didn't care. Don't waste any more of my time rehashing the past Jack. Those days are long gone. I'm here under false pretenses, so don't make it harder than it has to be."

The live band and sensuous music beckoned everyone onto the dance floor, crowding them even closer together. Her thigh brushed his as he turned her out of the way of an exuberant couple. His hand dipped into her cleavage and she shot him a ful-minating glance.

Shafts of desire shot through him causing plea-sure, causing pain. How the hell had they gone so horribly wrong?

She'd loved who she'd *believed* he was. Enough said. If he'd told her the truth, he'd have been a different Jack Ryan in her eyes altogether. He hadn't been willing to take the chance. By the time Jack had known it was time to tell her the truth, it had been too late. Each day had found him falling a little more in love with her, and each day had made the lie harder to admit.

Hell, he'd been too scared to take the risk of los-ing her.

Yet he'd lost her in the end anyway.

While he'd been trying to figure out a way to tell her the truth, while maintaining their relationship, *she'd* read it as a refusal to make a commitment. While Jack had used his nonverbal skills to hold her, Mia had read those messages all wrong.

The truth hadn't hit him until months after she'd told him to go to hell. Mia Rossi hadn't *cared* about his money, his status or his acquisitions. By the time *that* penny had dropped she'd refused to talk to him. Tonight was his shot at making restitution.

And right now Mia's verbal thrashing wasn't

making it easy to keep up the cover of being adoring lovers. And she was being just as uncooperative physically. It wasn't possible for Mia to pull her body any farther away, so she'd gathered herself inside her own skin. Her eyes telegraphed her displeasure while her nipples were hard and peaked against the back of his hand. She was a neon flash of mixed signals. If he was reading her correctly, her brain was resisting, but her body was reacting to his touch as if it was as natural to her as breathing. He hoped the desire he sensed could obliterate her brain's convictions.

He wanted to cup the familiar weight of her breasts in his hands, to feel her bare skin against his fingertips. He wanted to taste her again. Wanted the remembered heat of burying himself deep inside her—

She tugged at their joined hands, drawing his away from where it had been happily nestled against the sweet curve of her breasts. "Spoilsport."

"Opportunist." She smiled, all teeth. "How long do we have to do this?"

"Almost there." He easily replaced their joined hands where his would be happiest and steered her expertly through the throng. They moved well together, in bed and out. Dangerously well.

The slip-slide of silk over Mia's smooth skin

made him ache. He was definitely aroused by her familiar fragrance, the feel of her in his arms. Jack felt sweat in the small of his back from the effort not to grab her into his arms and kiss her with all the feelings he'd been suppressing for the past eight months.

He danced her across the crowded ballroom with the ease and nonchalant grace of Fred Astaire. Mia's jaw ached. Other places ached as well, but she willed herself to ignore all her body parts from the chin down.

He was using the back of his hand and wrist to devastating effect, and the devious devil knew it. His eyes sparkled with the knowledge and with the flash of fire she remembered so well. Just feeling his touch burning into her skin was enough to make her knees weak and her brain forget all about the need for self-preservation. Mia felt like a ripe peach about to burst from her skin. Through the fine Egyptian cotton of his shirt she felt his hot skin beneath her palm. His heart beat a steady, heavy pulse in his broad chest as he manipulated them across the dance floor with sublime confidence and ease.

She had no problem maintaining the rhythm of the dance. Nope. Her failure was in maintaining her hard-won conviction that Jack was part of her past. It seemed cruel that the acceptance that had taken months of tears and tirades to achieve was draining from her as if there was a leak in her spine. She needed to be strong. She needed to be levelheaded and realistic.

Jack could not give her what she wanted. That was the simple truth. It didn't matter how badly she wanted it. Her leopard was never going to change his spots.

So much for her conviction that she was over him! Perhaps a few more decades might make that a reality.

He kept her hand captured between then as he negotiated the other couples dancing around them. Jack was an excellent dancer. As good on the dance floor as he'd been in the bedroom— Damn. Mia closed her eyes to block out her view of his strong jaw and mouth made for sin. But the slide of their bodies, the memory of other dances, other close encounters when their naked skin had been pressed together made her eyes pop open again. Lord, it was hot in here. Hot and close and dangerous as hell.

She wanted to be home with her cat, her three dead houseplants and a large apple-tini, in the worst way.

Honestly, she wanted Jack Ryan all to herself. She wanted cool sheets in a dimly lit room. She wanted to rub herself over his body like a purring cat—

Mia shut off the carnal thoughts as they approached the foot of the stairs leading to the private rooms above.

The last time they'd been here, they'd found a secluded and dark balcony overlooking the grounds. And while a party had gone on two stories beneath them, she and Jack had discovered a whole new use for balcony railings.

"Last time we were here it was summer." He released her with one arm, but kept her tethered to him with the other. "Remember?"

"No."

"Liar." He glanced around casually, and Mia knew he, like herself, was marking everyone's location in the room, possible exits, security personnel and camera locations.

She faked a furtive glance around, then grabbed his hand and started up the stairs. Just pretending to be unbearably hot for Jack made her hot. Actually, hotter was more accurate. If someone shoved a thermometer in her mouth right now, she'd blow the end off. Trying to suppress it was useless. The best she could do was make sure *Jack* wasn't aware of how she felt.

At the top of the stairs, she dropped his hand like

a hot potato and preceded him into the west bedroom wing. Her pace was almost as fast as her er-
ratic heart. She didn't care; she was hoping to walk
off some of her need for Jack.

How could she focus when, with every step, her
aching center pulsed with new need, reminding her
that release was only an arm's reach away? *No,* she
thought. *Be strong. Be brave. Don't give into the
dark side.*

Luck was with them and they didn't pass anyone
else on the upstairs landing. They slipped into the
master suite and closed the door.

"Safe's probably in her closet." Mia strode toward one of the half-closed doors on the far side of
the spacious bedroom, Jack right behind her.

"Bathroom. Wrong door." Mia opened the next
louvered mahogany door. "Jackpot. Oh, man," she
said reverently, "look at her shoes."

"Hard to pack a pair of those under that dress."

"I can afford my own shoes," she told him
mildly, listening to her own tone to be sure she
didn't sound defensive. Forget the spoon. Jack had
been born with a silver serving tray in his mouth.
All that nonsense he'd been sprouting to gain her
sympathy was garbage. No, Jack came from a
wealthy family. And he spent money like it would
dry up tomorrow if every dime wasn't blown today.

She'd been born with a plastic spoon in hers. Disposable. Sallye never had liked doing dishes. They hadn't been poor, exactly, but Sallye's paycheck had only covered the basics, no extras.

Mia had hated watching her mother work two jobs to make ends meet. Hated seeing her mom bent over the bills every month trying to figure out which to pay first. Mia had vowed she and her mom and sister would never have to worry about money again. No more living from paycheck to paycheck.

Mia had money now. Hell, she had fifty percent of every paycheck she'd ever earned stashed in a money market account, slowly multiplying at a pretty decent rate. She hoarded her money, saved and invested it prudently and wisely. She made every penny beg for mercy before she reluctantly spent it. And now that she could, she made sure her mom had a few of those "extras" she'd always lacked before.

Well, up until now. Now that Sallye had sold out her oldest daughter to the man who could tear her heart in two with a flick of his wrist, there was no more Godiva for her.

"I was kidding about the shoes."

"I wasn't," Mia said shortly. "Just look for the safe."

The closet smelled of Chanel and cigarette

smoke. Carpeted in the same thick plush ecru-colored carpeting as the bedroom, it felt close and claustrophobic with the sartorial ghosts of past events hanging from their padded satin hangers. Furs brushed Mia's head as she crouched down low and reached to the back to feel along the wall while Jack did the same on the other side.

Their legs brushed several times, sending electrical charges along each of Mia's nerve endings. She worked faster. Where the hell was the damn safe? Somewhere reasonably convenient because the lady of the house would want easy access to her jewels.

"Got it," Jack said, already standing to push aside the pantsuits hanging in front of the safe.

Mia rose to her feet, keeping a foot of space between them. It was still far too close for comfort. Who knew a walk-in closet could feel so tiny?

She checked out the safe. "It won't take me a moment." She inspected the safe and recognized it wasn't half as secure as the safes in all the convenience stores on all the corners of the world. "Hell, you could've done this by yourself. You didn't need me."

"That's a matter of opinion."

"Would you mind giving me a little room here?" She shoved him back a step with her elbow. "You're breathing down my neck."

In deference to their hostess's silks, the lighting in the closet was soft and muted. There was plenty of light coming through the double doors leading from the bedroom, however. The walk-in closet was a small room with racks of designer clothing, from ceiling to floor and two rods deep, with an automated dry-cleaner-type mechanical rack for finding things quickly. Mia had serious closet envy.

One entire wall was made up of a rainbow of shoes organized by color. It was more than the sight of those hundreds of pairs of Manolo Blahnik's that had Mia's heart picking up speed. Ignoring the effect of Jack's proximity as best she could, she slipped on the thin rubber gloves he handed her and got to work.

Unlike the safe downstairs, this was a Conex. On the safecracking scale of one-to-ten, this was about a three. She concentrated on the far-too-loud sound of the tumblers rotating behind the steel door. That was the chink in the Conex—the tumblers made so much noise that the safe might as well have shouted out the combination.

"How's your love life?"

"Hotter than a pistol thank you very much."

"Is that so?" He looked suspiciously happy about it.

Mia frowned. "You're pleased I'm having hot sex with someone else?"

"Hell, no," Jack said with a grin. "I'm pleased as hell that you feel you have to *lie* about it."

"I'm not ly—"

"Still hunting for a husband?" he taunted. He folded his arms and leaned against the door frame. How appropriate that the louvers in the door painted tiger stripes across his face and body.

"Your source is my loose-lipped mother, who considers it a hunt. I, on the other hand, consider it to be more like holding auditions. I'm sure I'll find what I'm looking for," Mia said. The devil had refused to make a commitment. In a fit of anger, Mia had told him she'd be married this summer—either to him or someone else. She was thirty-two. She wanted to start the rest of her life now, while she still had all her working parts. Pinning Jack down to a commitment had been like trying to hold Jell-O in her fist.

"Did you think Davis was going to be the one?"

"He had potential," she admitted, glancing at him for a split second, just long enough to make sure he knew she was still pissed. "I hope you had fun playing me like that. It was childish, Jack. Beneath you."

He'd used his knowledge of her to create the perfect man. And she *had* fallen for it. Hook, line and sinker.

"The only thing that was a lie was the name."

She shot him a skeptical glance over her shoulder and shook her head, "Sure, you already said that. And I already told you I don't believe it." Damn it, why was this safe so stubborn?

"I wasn't ready for a commitment."

"I noticed."

"We were terrific together, Mia. Admit it."

"Sure we were. Unfortunately you took the low road while I took the high road. And never the twain shall meet."

"Why's it so important to you to get married? The sex was outstanding, we're compatible as hell.... Why blow something that amazing for some pie in the sky license? What does a bit of paper matter anyway?"

She flashed him a quick look over her shoulder. "See Jack? That piece of paper means the world to me. You don't get it? Fine. I'm looking for someone who *will* get it."

"Why isn't it enough to have someone—me—who *wants* to be with you?"

"Because I want forever, not just today."

"You know as well as I do," he said, his voice

a tight cord of need, mingled with frustration, "in our business, there isn't always a forever."

"God, Jack," she said on a sigh as she leaned her forehead on the still closed safe, "*no one* gets a guarantee. An *accountant* could wake up fine and be dead by sunset. What I want is the commitment to *try* for forever."

"Darling…" He trailed one finger down her bare back and Mia shivered from both his touch and the endearment she'd missed for eight long months. "You know I…" His voice trailed off.

She laughed shortly, quietly, heartbreak coloring the sound. "You can't even say it."

"Fine," he snapped. "I'm a dog. What are you going to do? Pick one of your blind dates and ask him to marry you?"

"Why not?"

"Aren't you running out of guys?"

"DC's a big place, I haven't even gotten started. Thanks to urban sprawl, I can work my way from Metro Center out to Crystal City. If that doesn't work, I can head up the 270 corridor all the way to Pennsylvania if necessary. I have time."

"Thought you were getting married this summer?"

"Plenty of time." Mia said shortly. Four, five months should be plenty of time. Plenty of time to get Jack Ryan out of her system, meet a new man and arrange the wedding.

Who was she trying to fool? Herself? Or Jack?

"So you'd choose some as yet unknown blind date over me and amazing sex?"

"See, Jack? That's why you earn the big bucks. Because you're so clever. Now be quiet and let me get this thing open and this night *over* with."

"By all means, go for it."

The last tumbler fell into place and Mia swung the door open. How nice of the lady of the house to be so neat and organized. Her jewelry was in slender black leather cases, each labeled clearly with its contents. Her emeralds had a shelf all their own.

A few papers had been slipped sideways next to the boxes. Mia withdrew them, careful to keep everything in the same order. The disk was tucked into a legal envelope marked Insurance. "Got it. Here." She shoved the disk into his hand. "Thanks for a lovely evening. Don't call me, I'll call you. Bye— Uh-oh!" she whispered. "Someone's coming. Hit the li—"

The small room went charcoal-gray as Jack simultaneously hit the light switch and pulled the double doors shut.

Bars of light sliced across them from the bedroom. While the closet was large, it wouldn't be large enough to hide two adults if someone decided to open the doors.

Mia glared at Jack. "Didn't you lock the door?" she mouthed silently.

Looking through the slats of the door, he nodded, then jerked his head to indicate the man and woman who'd entered the bedroom. The couple, holding onto each other like shipwreck victims in a storm tossed sea, still took the time to relock the door behind them. They had a key.

Mia's eyes widened. A married senator from California and her young—good Lord! *very* young—boyfriend. This couldn't be happening! Surely they weren't going to... Oh crap! They were!

The couple didn't so much flow together as they attacked each other like wild animals, falling onto the velvet bedspread with muffled groans and whimpers of unbridled lust. Arms and legs tangled as they tried to rip off each other's clothes in a frenzy.

No way, Mia thought with growing horror. She took a step back and came up hard against Jack's chest. He caught her by the upper arms, presumably to prevent them from crashing to the floor. His strong fingers dug into her tender skin as the other couple thrashed about on the bed.

Her heartbeat manic, Mia squeezed her eyes shut. Oh no, no, no!

CHAPTER FIVE

THE YOUNG GUY was all hands and speed. Lord, he was pistol-hot and in an all fired hurry. Mia tried not to watch the couple rolling around on the bed. She forced her eyes shut and swallowed hard. Maybe, she told herself, if she kept her eyes tightly closed, and stood very, very still, it would be over in a few minutes. They'd leave and no one would be any the wiser.

Unfortunately the way her luck was running tonight, Boy-toy probably had the staying power of a Don Juan.

In the darkness behind her closed lids the animal panting and half-choked groans from the couple a few feet away made sweat pop out on her brow and her center prickle with empathetic longing. Wasn't it bad enough that she'd been on the razor edge of arousal since she'd realized Jack was her blind date for the evening?

This was not helping matters.

Mia opened one eye a slit. Hell, *they* were so busy

ripping each other's clothes off she could probably dash right past them and make a clean getaway.

She was tempted to do just that as Jack slid strong hands down her arms and she found herself leaning against him weakly. Her legs weren't going to carry her anywhere. Not right now anyway.

She tried to ignore the thrill of excitement swiftly running through her veins, fast and hot, as Jack rocked against her slowly. His erection fitted against her like the missing piece in a jigsaw puzzle. Mia shivered, but shifted out of range. Not that there was a lot of room to maneuver. One wrong move and she and Jack would explode through the doors and end up sprawling out at the foot of the bed with the horny couple.

"Is this shocking your Puritan sensibilities, my sweet, precious darling?" Jack whispered in her ear easily pulling her back to where he wanted her.

It would've been nice if she could form a coherent word. Unfortunately she couldn't even form a coherent *thought*. Mia found that her eyes were open.

She frowned. She shouldn't be watching this. *They* shouldn't be watching this. Everyone would be much happier if *nobody* was watching this, she thought hysterically. Sex wasn't supposed to be a spectator sport. Fortunately, making love *felt* a lot better than it *looked.*

The young stud managed to get the senator's dress off. He was having bit of a problem with her bra however. Impatient, he shoved it up on her chest and bent his head to give it enthusiastic attention.

Mia's nipples ached in response.

No fair.

Her head fell back against Jack's chest. She watched the other couple with an intensity that should've worried her, but somehow didn't.

In the darkness, she and Jack were cradled in a net of silence and shadow. On the bed in front of them, the mindless couple performed like actors on a stage. It was a private moment—for all four of them.

The senator ripped off her stud's shirt. Buttons flew. *Now that was going to be hard to explain downstairs.* Neither of them seemed to care. The older woman's hands looked startlingly white on the young man's smooth, tanned skin. Her long red nails lethal as she scored his skin from nipples to belly. The boy-toy's back arched as the woman went for his belt and zipper with an intensity that she'd never shown on Capitol Hill.

When Don Juan had been divested of all the clothes below his waist, the senator smiled and, with hands and mouth, went to work on what had been revealed. The young man hissed in a breath, threw his head back and moaned tightly.

Everything in Mia went hot and still. That ache that had been haunting her all night suddenly pulsed into life, making her bones shake and quiver. She watched, unable to look away, caught and mesmerized by the actions just a few feet from her. Then Jack covered her breasts with his hands, cupping then squeezing gently. Mia locked her jaw tight to keep from moaning. She pressed her palms over the back of his much larger hands, and pressed down. Showing him wordlessly what she needed.

His fingers tightened on her aching breasts. Rough, greedy. Rubbing, coaxing her nipples to hard painful points. Showing none of the restraint he'd show her moments before.

Thank God. Gentle wouldn't do it now. She wanted more. Needed more. She almost keened with the intensity of sensation as Jack manipulated her nipples through the sheer fabric of bra and silk dress. Her hands dropped to her sides and her head fell back, baring her throat.

He bent his head to kiss the side of her neck, a particularly sensitive spot, and he went right to it. Mia arched her throat to give him better access, and used her own hand to guide his between the layers of fabric so he could touch her bare skin. Her womb clenched as if he was already inside her.

She stifled a moan at the piercingly sweet sensation of Jake's callused fingers caressing her feverish skin. As busy as the other couple were, another sound might alert them to the voyeurs in the closet. Mia bit her lip.

To ease her own heat she ground her bottom against Jack. He was as hard as she'd ever felt him. And furnace hot. A jolt of lust as pure and sharp as white lightning zinged through her from neck to groin. She managed not to scream his name only by sinking her teeth even harder into her lower lip.

Jack had always had the unnerving knack of knowing exactly how to make her shudder and moan while keeping her teetering on the very brink, then drawing back just enough to keep her simmering.

Boil. Simmer. Boil. Simmer. Explode.

His hot breath stirred the fine hairs on her nape, making her shiver. The devil bit the side of her neck. It wasn't a gentle nip either—she felt the sharp edge of his teeth on the tense cords of her throat. The fine tremors became a shudder that shook her whole body. He kissed the sting. Succulent, wet kisses, down the side of her throat, around to her nape. He licked her skin to cool it, then

GET 2 BOOKS FREE!

MIRA

MIRA® Books,
The Brightest
Stars in Fiction,
presents

The Best of the Best ™

Superb collector's editions of the very best books by some of today's best-known authors!

★ **FREE BOOKS!**

★ **FREE GIFT!**

★ **BEST BOOKS!**

To introduce you to "The Best of the Best" we'll send you 2 books ABSOLUTELY FREE!

Get an exciting surprise gift FREE!

"The Best of the Best" brings you the best books by some of today's most popular authors!

We'd like to send you two free books to introduce you to "The Best of the Best™!" Your two books have a combined cover price of $11.98 or more in the U.S. and $13.98 or more in Canada, but they are yours free! We'll even send you a wonderful mystery gift. You can't lose!

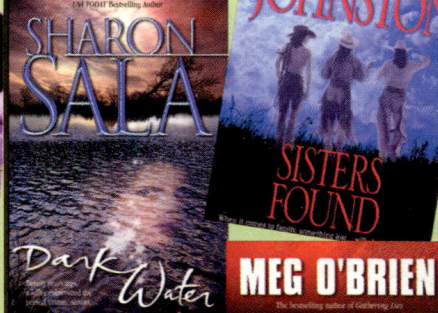

JASMINE CRESSWELL

THE THIRD WIFE

Till death us do part

USA TODAY Bestselling Author

SHARON SALA

Dark Water

New York Times Bestselling Author

JOAN JOHNSTON

SISTERS FOUND

MEG O'BRIEN

The bestselling author of Gathering Lies

Someone has unleashed a vengeful fury

CRIMSON RAIN

Girls Night

"Indulge yourself—*Girls Night* is daring and irresistible."
—Joan Johnston, author of *Sisters Found*

STEF ANN HOLM

ROSEMARY ROGERS

NEW YORK TIMES BESTSELLING AUTHOR

AN HONORABLE MAN

Visit us at
www.mirabooks.com

The **TWO FREE** books we send you will be selected from a variety of the <u>best</u> fiction - from romances to thrillers to family sagas - written by some of today's most popular authors!

FREE BONUS GIFT!

We'll send you a wonderful surprise gift, **absolutely FREE,** just for giving "The Best of the Best" a try! Don't miss out — mail the reply card today!

2 Get **FREE** BOOKS!

Hurry!

Return this card promptly to GET 2 FREE BOOKS & A FREE GIFT!

The Best of the Best ™

Affix
peel-off
MIRA
sticker here

YES! Please send me the 2 FREE "The Best of the Best" books and FREE gift for which I qualify. I understand that I am under no obligation to purchase anything further, as explained on the back and on the opposite page.

385 MDL DRSU   185 MDL DRSQ

FIRST NAME

LAST NAME

ADDRESS

APT.#   CITY

STATE/PROV.   ZIP/POSTAL CODE

Offer limited to one per household and not valid to current subscribers of MIRA or "The Best of the Best." All orders subject to approval. Books received may vary.

The Best of the Best™ — Here's How it Works:

Accepting your 2 free books and gift places you under no obligation to buy anything. You may keep the books and gift and return the shipping statement marked "cancel." If you do not cancel, about a month later we will send you 4 additional books and bill you just $4.74 each in the U.S., or $5.24 each in Canada, plus 25¢ shipping & handling per book and applicable taxes if any.* That's the complete price and — compared to cover prices starting from $5.99 each in the U.S. and $6.99 each in Canada — it's quite a bargain! You may cancel at any time, but if you choose to continue, every month we'll send you 4 more books, which you may either purchase at the discount price or return to us and cancel your subscription.

*Terms and prices subject to change without notice. Sales tax applicable in N.Y. Canadian residents will be charged applicable provincial taxes and GST. Credit or Debit balances in a customer's account(s) may be offset by any other outstanding balance owed by or to the customer.

If offer card is missing write to: The Best of the Best, 3010 Walden Ave., P.O. Box 1867, Buffalo, NY 14240-1867

BUSINESS REPLY MAIL
FIRST-CLASS MAIL   PERMIT NO. 717-003   BUFFALO NY

POSTAGE WILL BE PAID BY ADDRESSEE

THE BEST OF THE BEST
3010 WALDEN AVE
PO BOX 1867
BUFFALO NY 14240-9952

NO POSTAGE
NECESSARY
IF MAILED
IN THE
UNITED STATES

heated her flesh with more sharp hot nibbles. Mia's knees buckled.

Only his strong hands kept her upright. Her entire body throbbed and pulsed. Her goose bumps had goose bumps. Everything inside her turned to churning, seething, hot, molten liquid.

And then his hand left her breast.

Mia scowled in the tiger-striped darkness. She stared out the slits in the closet door at the couple still wrapped up in each other. In the brightly lit bedroom Don Juan had his pants around his hairy ankles and the senator was still busy in the area of his lap. The woman lifted her head—Mia could only see her from the back, thank God—and pulled her lover's face down to hers for a hungry kiss.

Mia's breasts ached fiercely. She fumbled behind her, wanting Jack's hand on her. He grabbed her hands and placed them on her own breasts. Shocked, she felt the hard points of her own aroused nipples. Pressing them hard against her chest helped, but she'd rather have Jack's hands—Oh!

He was bunching her dress up to her waist, his hands skimming up her legs and past the edge of her thigh-highs—and hadn't *that* been a good choice?—to touch bare skin.

"God," he breathed hoarsely against her ear. "Feels just the same."

Mia didn't give a damn if he meant he recognized, by feel, the thong, or if he was referring to her butt cheeks, which he was reverently caressing.

"Hold this," he instructed on an urgent breath, shoving a handful of fabric at her. Mia grabbed a few yards of silk dress and hung on as his hand slid across her belly and down.

She shuddered as his fingers slipped under the edge of her panties to encounter wet heat. He slid two fingers deep inside her, pulling her tightly against him.

Through the slats of the door she watched with glazed eyes as the young stud lay back against the pillow. She felt the steel-hard press of Jack's erection nuzzling against her.

Her muscles clenched and tightened against his hand as he pressed the heel of his palm hard against her aching heat at the same time that he bit the back of her neck.

On the bed, the senator hiked up her skirt past her thighs and clambered onto the mattress. The stud reached for her with a hungry smile.

Please. Please. Please. Mia chanted in her head as Jack's fingers worked her body into a mindless symphony of sensation. He pushed her higher, higher, and still it wasn't enough. She wanted more than his fingers inside her. She wanted him inside her *now*.

The senator flung her leg over her young lover's hip and sank down on him slowly. The guy was panting in earnest now. Mia knew just how he felt. She couldn't look away. Couldn't stop watching.

She let go of the silk fabric and fumbled behind her, forcing a hand between their bodies, struggling to pull down Jack's zipper. An almost impossible task considering how erect he was.

At her touch, he stiffened, his whole body coiled as tight as a spring. Mia kept her gaze fixed on the tableau in front of them, while she diligently worked to free Jack. Don Juan's hands clutched the senator's hips as she moved over him.

Jack finally helped her with the recalcitrant zipper. Mia braced one arm on the doorjamb to keep them both upright, even while bending slightly. Her stomach swirled, her blood pumped. So dangerous. So exciting. So...*frustrating!* This wasn't going to work.

The other couple was moaning and panting. Mia wanted to scream.

Jack's zipper was staggering down. Mia bit back a groan. A little more, more—tooth, by damn metal tooth.

Hurry. Hurry.

Their hands bumped and fumbled together, in too much of a rush to be coordinated.

Hurry!

Finally he put an implacable hand on her back and gently pushed her forward. She went willingly, bracing one arm on the doorjamb, bending enough that he could enter her.

Now, now, now, her mind screamed. She couldn't stop watching the couple on the bed, and while she watched them, Jack slid into her slick heat like a train going through a tunnel at full speed.

Bliss.

He made a low raw, primitive sound as he filled her, moving until she could swear she felt him touch the bottom of her heart. And still, it wasn't enough. She wanted more. Wanted him to be so deep within that he'd never find his way out again. In that wild half second when all she could feel was his length, she knew that that was all she'd ever really need.

He gripped her hips and held her dead still. The sensation of their joining so intense, so sharp, neither dared move.

The couple on the bed didn't have the same problem. Their bodies slick with sweat, their groans melding into one long song of need, their bodies heaved together noisily.

Jack started to move. He kept pace with the couple on the bed. In the shadows, their lower bodies slammed together at fever pitch. Mia's skin felt on fire, her body arched and bucked against Jack's.

She watched the couple in front of her, racing toward the same conclusion she and Jack had nearly reached.

How they remained standing she had no idea.

His breath harsh, he returned his fingers to her slick heat, bringing her close, so close...

"Let go," he whispered in her ear. "Come for me, sweetheart."

Mia didn't have a choice. The climax crashed over her with such force she almost passed out. Her body arched and bucked in unison with Jack's. Her fingers clutched at the doorjamb. In front of her, the couple on the bed reached their climax and the noise covered the soft moan Mia allowed escape from her throat.

She wanted to scream. She wanted to make him stop. She wanted it to last forever.

Too much. She was going to shatter and break apart.

He continued to rock his body into hers. He prolonged her multiple orgasm beyond endurance. Mia's body shuddered and quaked under the onslaught as he let one climax roll into the next and then the next.

She didn't know where his body ended and hers began. Any second now she was going to shatter into a gazillion pieces and, come morning, Mrs. Ambassador would find Mia bits all over her closet.

"Finish," Mia begged.

"I'll never be finished with you," Jack muttered. "Come again."

"N—" *Yes!* Sparklers and rainbows. Shooting stars and fiery waterfalls. Jack could still make Mia's earth move.

She came again, riding that last blast of sensation along with Jack, who finally surrendered and gave himself up to his own climax.

A moment later, she struggled to steal a breath, to regain her equilibrium. He held her, just held her against him, as her rioting nerves settled to a simmer and her brain went back on line.

Jack petted her breasts and stroked the sensitive skin on her belly until she managed to find a little breath and her legs could support her. A shiver ran up her spine as the silk of her dress slithered down her legs.

She blinked. The couple on the bed were dressing. Good old Don Juan had livid red scratches on his chest and his shirt bunched in his hand.

Where was he going to find something to wear— Mia froze.

CHAPTER SIX

"WE'RE IN *HER* CLOSET. Remember?" Jack whispered against her ear, guessing her thoughts. The guy walked by their hiding place and opened the door of the gentleman's closet on the far side of the bathroom door.

He felt the tremors that still shook Mia's body. Good. He pulled her against him and she rested her head weakly against his chest. If they were in bed now, she'd curl into him, her arms and legs tangled with his.

After sex with Mia had always been better than sex with any other woman. He stroked a hand up her arm, then cupped her hot cheek in his hand. She bowed her head and he felt the featherlight kiss she deposited in his palm, all the way to his toes. A shudder of animalistic, male pride wracked his body. It mattered that Mia was satisfied. No, more than satisfied—spent. Shot. Satiated.

He'd risked his future happiness getting Mia to come with him tonight. Sallye, bless her devious romantic heart, had been terrific in setting up this blind date.

Hell, he *had* needed Mia to get into the safe. But there were other operatives at the agency who could've done the job. It was neither difficult, nor dangerous, so any of them would have done. Except none of them was Mia.

Damn it, he ached from missing her. Everything about her. Not just the spectacular sex. He missed her quick, pithy retorts and her bone-deep sense of fair play. He missed how tight she was with money, and how generous she was to those she loved. God. He'd missed the entire Mia Rossi package.

Hell, he even got on great with her mother and her sister, Domino. Family was everything to Mia. That had to count for something.

Life with Mia had been perfect. But perfect scared him. Emotional crap scared him. Anything he wanted as badly as he wanted Mia could be taken away from him in a heartbeat. Every cell he possessed seemed confident that Mia was the one woman designed specifically for him. It was right, it was honest. Correction—she was honest. He was—what? A living lie? A man made up of half-truths and wishful thinking?

Jack tightened his arms about her, feeling the unsteady beat at the base of her throat slow back to normal. They weren't going anywhere until the other couple left the room, but Jack didn't give a damn. Now, for these few quiet, precious moments, he could hold her in his arms. Could inhale the subtle orange blossom scent of her hair, and delight again at the feel of her soft silky hair brushing his chin.

Had she believed him when he'd told her about his real past? Was that dirt-poor screwup someone she could love? And more important, if she could, would she choose to stay? It was a risk he'd been loathe to take the first time around. But this was his last chance to catch the gold ring.

In a few minutes he'd check the all important disk, and then he and Mia would straighten themselves up and go downstairs. They'd have a pleasant dinner, a little dancing, and then he'd take her home. Home to his place. His stomach clenched at the thought of convincing Mia that he truly had been that foster kid before becoming the Jack Ryan she thought she knew. He'd given her a little of the information on the phone when he was pretending to be Davis Sloan—and she'd changed the subject. Jack was tempted— No. He wouldn't lie to her. Not this time.

He'd filled his bedroom with dozens and dozens of the pale yellow roses Mia loved, and had placed groupings of slender white candles around the room. A bottle of her favorite French chardonnay was chilling on ice, and he'd stocked up on chocolate-covered strawberries, hideously expensive and out of season, but one of Mia's favorites. She'd bitch about the expense, but she'd be happy, too.

Jack appreciated the finer things in life. Contrary to his bio, nothing had been handed to him on a plate. He'd had to work hard for what he had. Had to struggle to maintain the lifestyle while he clawed his way to the top of the financial heap. Money was to be spent, and he did. He wasn't going to apologize for enjoying the finer things in life. And he didn't have to divulge his real background if he didn't need to. That part of his life had been buried. Obliterated. Thanks to Uncle Sam. And penny-pinching Mia, who had often gotten on his case at the way he'd spent his money, would've felt a whole lot different if he'd ever admitted that he'd been even poor as a kid. But he hadn't wanted her pity.

There'd never been any reason for him to dig up the corpse of who he'd once been.

Until now.

He glanced at his watch. Barely nine. They'd be home, hopefully in bed, by eleven.

The small closet was warm, redolent with their

lovemaking. He'd never forget this moment. They were on the cusp of something big. Something wonderful.

It was almost a shock to hear someone speaking not three feet from where he and Mia stood.

"Can't we hang around longer?" Don Juan asked in a sulky voice as he came out of the other closet pulling on one of his host's shirts.

"*No*. Hurry up, for heaven's sake! My husband thinks I went out for a smoke!"

"We sure were smokin', weren't we, baby?" He slung a cocky arm around the woman's shoulders.

Before he could dive in for another kiss, she shoved him away. "You forget yourself." She finished buttoning her dress and turned to fix her hair in the mirror over the dressing table. "Go down and warm up the car," she told him without turning around. "I'm ready to leave now."

"Will I see you later?"

"Yes. You'll be driving me and my husband home. Other than that, I'll let you know when it's convenient." She walked over to the window and pulled aside the heavy velvet drape. "Damn. It's started to snow. Go down now. I'll follow in a few minutes."

Jack tracked the guy across the room, watched

him unlock the door, then open and close it. One down, one to go.

"Lunkhead," the woman said in a fond voice as she straightened the bedspread, then fluffed the pillows. With one last tweak to the dust-skirt, she seemed satisfied and she, too, left the room.

Silence throbbed around them for several seconds after the door closed behind her. He used those seconds to hold Mia, but dropped his arms the moment she stepped away.

She pushed open the doors and stepped into the brighter light of the bedroom. "I'll use the bathroom while you check the disk. Then we can split."

"Yeah," he said easily. "Sure." *You're not getting rid of me quite that easily, precious. Hang on, it's going to be one helluva ride.*

At the door to the bathroom she paused to look at him over her shoulder. "What just happened between us, didn't prove—or change—anything."

Jack found that slitty, snake-eyed look of hers sexy as hell. He had it bad. "Then you're deaf, dumb and blind, darling," he told her with silky menace. "That proved *everything.*"

"That's always been your problem, Jack. You honest to God believe that sex is the answer to everything. Purse?" She held out her hand. Jack slapped the small clutch he'd stuffed in his pocket earlier into her palm. "You're too obtuse even to know there's a question."

He walked over and locked the bedroom door again. This time he shoved a chair under it. "I know the question, sweetheart." He turned back to face her across the room. "I'm just not sure you can take the answer."

"Neither am I," she said quietly as she stepped into the bathroom and closed the door behind her.

For a second Mia leaned against the bathroom door without turning on the light. Stupid, stupid, *stupid.* What on earth had she been thinking? Sex with Jack Ryan? In a closet of all places? She shook her head, then pushed herself away from the door and fumbled in the dark for the switch.

Soft, flattering lighting flooded the opulent bathroom. It wasn't particularly flattering to *her.* Her hair stood up like a startled cockatoo, her blush was completely off one cheek, and her mascara had run, making her look like a raccoon. *Most* attractive.

Mia conducted an intense monologue under her breath as she straightened her clothing. First things first. She had to remove her bra and put it on again. How the hell had it been turned inside out while she was wearing it? Her unlucky thong was gone. Better check the floor of the closet. She didn't even remember Jack removing it. She met her own eyes in the mirror as she combed her hair. She *looked* as though she'd had wild, wonderful sex, for God's sake!

"Are you out of your mind?" she asked her reflection. Apparently yes, she was. She'd not only *allowed* Jack to make love to her—but she'd *enjoyed* it. And oh boy, how she'd enjoyed it. Staring at the rumpled woman in the mirror, Mia let her mind drift to those last few moments in the shadows when Mrs. Whozit and her trained stud had been setting the rhythm that she and Jack had followed. To those few shining moments when the whole world had been wrapped around her and buried within her. To the flash of rightness she'd felt as Jack's climax echoed her own.

"Oh, man." She glared at the ceiling and told herself she was the Champion Moron of the Century. "Wonder if there's a trophy?"

She used the facilities, then dug in her small clutch for emergency cosmetics to make herself halfway presentable. Not for *Jack,* of course. She didn't care if she looked like a startled raccoon for Jack. After all, he was the designer of her dishabille. But she did have to exit through the party guests downstairs.

She had to wipe off the smudged mess she'd

made of her lip gloss and reapply it. She realized her hand was shaking.

He made her nuts. Crazy. Insane.

Her body ached. She wanted him again. Worse. She was tempted to take him back on his terms— hell, *any* terms. How was that for pathetic? Or maybe she'd move up her wedding timetable. Get married in spring instead of midsummer. Date more often. Two blind dates a day—maybe three.

She'd find someone—*anyone*—who could light up her insides and make her laugh. Someone like Jack.

There *was* no one like Jack.

There never would be.

Glancing around the bathroom hoping to find another exit, Mia spotted the window. It was a nice big picture window covered in swaths of silky voile— Oh, she was tempted. Climb out of the window, just as she and her sister had done as teenagers when Sallye had grounded them. Nothing to it.

She gave it a moment's consideration. Clambering up onto the side of the tub, she looked outside. Sure they were two stories up, but there was a balcony, sort of. She could probably make the jump down without breaking anything vital.

Nah, it was snowing out there.

Breaking a leg was one thing. Lying in the snow

in agony until someone found her frozen corpse was something else altogether.

She pushed open the bathroom door to find Jack standing in the middle of the room, holding a small, handheld computer. He didn't look anything like a mess. He looked as suave, sophisticated and handsome as he had half an hour ago when they'd slipped into the closet.

Another annoying thing about him, Mia thought sourly. Perhaps she should move to Alaska. Or Siberia. She'd miss her mom and Domino, but on the plus side there'd be no Jack—

"Please tell me that's the disk we were supposed to find," she said as she walked into the room, her brain still playing with possible escape routes. Maybe Tahiti? Bora Bora? Somewhere hot. Yes, somewhere hot and sultry.

Jack was hot and sultry.

Damn.

It all came back to Jack.

"Yeah, this is it." He held up the innocent looking, but highly sophisticated, custom-built PDA to show her the list of names and numbers on the display, then closed it and tucked it into his breast pocket. "In fact, I do believe we have something even more compelling here than we first suspected."

"Good," Mia said briskly. She didn't work for Uncle Sam anymore, but she was happy they had what Jack had come for. Now she was ready, more than ready, to split. "Let's get the hell out of Dodge."

"Mind if I use the bathroom first?" Jack asked laconically.

"Be my guest. I'll go downstairs and say my goodb—"

"Running, Mia?"

That stopped her. "I don't run."

"You always run. You ran the first time we had a minor disagreement. You ran like hell when you realized what we had."

"And what was that?" she asked tightly, forgetting the trivial and zooming in on the crux of the matter. "Interesting sex? A job we could do together?"

"That and a whole hell of a lot more. Let me go in here, and then we can trot downstairs for a little champagne, a waltz or two—"

She folded her arms. "You got what you came for. Leave it at that."

"No, Mia. I didn't get what I came for. Not yet. Stay put. I'll be right back." And he shut the door.

Mia pulled a face at the closed bathroom door. "I do not always run," she told the clothes in the closet as she searched the floor for her thong. "Like any rational woman, I walk away quietly and with dignity when I know things have gone to hell in a handbasket— Where the *hell* is my underwear?"

Maybe Jack had picked it up when she'd gone into the bathroom. She heard the toilet flush and water running. Good. About time. She went over and removed the chair from under the bedroom door handle, then went and stood in the middle of the room to wait for him. Just to show him that she didn't run. "Come on, Jackson! Get the lead out."

"That's my girl, always anxious for me," he said as he stepped out.

Yes, indeedy she was. "Dream on, Romeo. Come on. Let's— Someone's coming again. Good God. This bedroom is like a railway station!"

They heard soft footfalls outside the door and turned as one for the bathroom. The bathroom with an emergency escape route. Too late. As the door started to open, they zipped back into the closet, which was closer.

Trapped again. In a tiny room that was starting to feel *way* too much like home.

If this was another tryst, Mia didn't want to hang around to see what acrobatics these two might have planned. She shot a glance at Jack, and almost laughed out loud at the expression on his face.

Because two men had come into the bedroom.

CHAPTER SEVEN

FORTUNATELY, or unfortunately—depending on how one looked at it—these two weren't lovers. There was no doubt that they were muscle, despite the formal black suits, white shirts and ties they wore. They spoke in rapid Afrikaans, and it was clear to Jack the latest arrivals were in the bedroom searching for someone.

It wasn't going to take the goons long to spring the closet door and find the two someones they were searching for standing there like hookers in church.

Now, how to explain what the hell they were doing in the closet when there was a perfectly good bed not twenty feet away?

Jack grabbed her hand, pushed open the closet door, and walked into the bedroom. "Come on, honey," he told her in a coaxing voice. "Embarrassed or not, these guys were going to find us in there."

It was a toss-up as to who was more surprised by their sudden emergence from the nether regions of the closet—Mia or the two goons who spun around, weapons drawn.

"Whoa!" Jack said, putting up his hands even as he took the step necessary to block Mia's body. The fact that they weren't already bleeding was a good sign. It showed that these guys either wanted information, or they were actually considering his lame excuse. Mia's stunned expression was helping in that department.

The other possibility, he quickly realized, was that they might want to avoid the messy evidence of two bleeding bodies. It couldn't be because they were afraid of someone hearing the shots. There were silencers affixed to the muzzles ensuring that no one outside of this room would hear a thing if they *did* decide to use their weapons.

"What're you two doing in here?" the one on the left demanded in a thick accent. The unibrow was a nice touch for muscle. The Heckler & Kotch USP pistols gripped in their hamlike fists gave Jack pause. These two didn't even have to be good shots to blow him and Mia to kingdom come.

Jack's own custom Smith & Wesson 1911 with its Hogue grip rested comfortably in the small of his back. Mia's .22 was in the purse she held clutched in one hand. They wouldn't even clear leather if these two decided to open fire.

So, since he couldn't shoot his way out of this mess, Jack did what he did best—talked. And hoped to hell Mia would chime in like she always had. They hadn't been called the best team in the business for nothing.

"Come on, guys. A little slap and tickle isn't grounds for getting shot, is it?" he asked easily. The two men stood between them and the exit. Behind Jack and Mia were the three doors. The closet doors, and the one leading into the bathroom.

"Oh," Mia moaned, leaning into Jack even as she pulled her purse, with the gun inside, closer to her shooting hand. She managed to look slightly embarrassed. "Can we get out of here now, Jack? I'm...not really in the mood anymore." She shot him a fulminating glance. "I *told* you we'd get caught."

"Relax, honey. They won't tell."

The second man, greasy yellow hair in a bouffant-on-top-long-on-the-bottom mullet, waved Mia away from Jack. "Stand over there, lady. Keep your hands where we can see them."

"Good grief," Mia said sweetly. "Afraid I'm going to smack you with my little ol' purse?" But she obediently moved a few feet away from Jack and kept her hands up. "My mother always said some day the Sex Police would come. I guess she was right.''

Jack noticed with approval that she'd managed to unsnap the little pearl clip on the small purse for easy access to her weapon. Hell, she could reach inside and fire right through her purse. The hell with pulling it out.

''That's up to these two guys, darling. Well, fellas, what do you say? Now that you've caught us in flagrante delicto, may we go?''

Both men kept a wary eye on Jack, clearly believing Mia to be no trouble. Jack resisted smiling. Mia in a temper was a sight to behold. They had absolutely no idea that she was the really dangerous part of this team. He kept his expression bland, and mildly respectful. These guys were obviously low on the food chain. He didn't want to do anything to set them off.

''Gimme the disk.''

''Disk?'' Mia asked, feigning puzzlement.

Unibrow waved his H&K at Jack. ''The disk you took outta the safe in the wardrobe.'' He waved his weapon wildly in the direction of the closet behind them.

How the hell did they know that *anything* had been removed from the safe? Jack wondered. While he and Mia had been voyeurs had someone been watching *them?* Not that that little detail mattered right now.

Jack shrugged and said, "Didn't see a safe in there, pal. We just dashed in there to avoid being caught in an embarrassing position. Hey, man, can we put our hands down now? This is—"

He saw the punch coming and moved his head in time to avoid it, at the same time he brought his raised hands down in a neat chop to the guy's gun hand.

The gun stayed clenched in the meaty fist, and the guy swayed but didn't fall. Jack sharply jerked up his knee, knocking out a few of UniBrow's teeth in the process. Damn. The dry cleaner was going to bitch about the blood on his fine wool pants come Monday morning.

In one continuous motion, Jack grabbed the guy by the hair, pulling him upright. Unibrow came surging up like a monolithic tidal wave, grabbed Jack's throat with both hands and shook him like a rat. Blood poured from the guy's mouth and the missing teeth made him look like a demented seven-year-old on steroids.

Jack bit his tongue a couple of times before he managed to seize his opponent's right elbow from underneath and turn rapidly to release the guy's hold. He followed that with a chop to the man's bull-like neck.

Uni rocked back on his heels like a drunk trying to look sober, and it was only quick thinking on Jack's part that he stepped away before Uni grabbed a leg and turned him over like a frigging turtle.

Mia used her long legs to kick Mullet-head in the jaw with full force while he was watching the stuffing being beaten out of Uni. He crashed onto the edge of the bed with a very surprised expression on his face.

"See what I mean, Jack?" she said, only slightly out of breath. "You're a crappy liar." She removed the .22 from her purse and got a solid two-handed grip on it. "And *everyone* knows it—" Weapon raised, she spun on Mullet-head who'd immediately staggered to his feet, his weapon aimed at her heart. "Would you *quit* pointing that thing at me? It's damn rude."

They stood there like cartoon characters. Four pissed off people, four weapons. Eight steady hands.

Who was going to yell chicken first?

"Tell you what, guys," Jack said, knowing the odds, and knowing he wouldn't risk Mia. Not even for his country. "Let's all just put our toys down and call it a draw, huh? Whaddya say?" His prime directive was to get this disk to HQ. More important was getting Mia out of the mix.

"Give us the computer disk," Mullet-head snarled, "and you can go."

Yeah, right. The good news was the ambassador apparently wasn't in on this. The bad news was they were standing here at gunpoint.

"If we only had the disk," Mia said, "we'd be happy to oblige. As it is…" She shrugged.

Jack glanced at Mia, noticed she suddenly looked shorter, and realized she'd kicked off her shoes. She wanted to be barefoot for the five-yard dash to the closed bedroom door. Only problem was, she'd get shot in the back before she made it. He gave her a warning look.

"Remember when we went to that cute cabin in the Poconos for the weekend last year?" Mia asked in a dreamy voice. Scary when she was standing there, feet braced a shoulder's-width apart, arms extended, and holding a fully loaded weapon aimed at a man's balls.

Cabin? Yeah, he remembered. They'd fought like two hellcats in a bag over her wanting to get married, and him wanting things just the way they were. Pissed, and with nowhere to run to, Mia had locked herself into the bathroom. And hadn't been able to unlock the door. Opting not to break it down at midnight, she'd had to...*climb out the window*.

No way. They were on the second floor. Snow was flurrying out there. They weren't dressed for the weather—

"Yeah," he warned. "You were stupid."

Her beautiful eyes widened. "Stupid?" she asked dangerously.

"Stop dickin' around," Mullet-head snarled, taking a step closer. "You two are pissing me off. Give us the disk. *Now*."

"Do you have a disk?" Jack asked Mia.

"Nope. You?"

"Na-ah."

"We don't have this disk you want. Sorry." Mia took a step back. Since both men were watching Jack with eyes like raptors, she took another. These two weren't likely to chase them down the stairs and through the house. Not in front of hundreds of witnesses. There were only two ways out. She preferred to do it through the nice warm house with lots of people around.

They could dump the disk and retrieve it later—

"Look," she said into the thick silence, "this is really freaking me out. Why don't you call the ambassador or his wife? They've both known us for years. They'll vouch for us."

"Don't know them. Don't care. I'm givin' you to three to hand it over. One. T—"

Lying bastard.

He shot Jack on two.

CHAPTER EIGHT

JACK FLEW BACKWARD, crashing into the wall behind Mia with such force his head bounced twice before he slid down to the floor in a boneless heap. Stunned, unable to catch his breath, he sprawled with his head on the wall and his body stretched out on the floor, beside the bathroom. What in the hell had just happened?

He blinked to clear his vision. Other than the screaming pain in the back of his head, his arm felt arctic cold and the breath was knocked out of him. He still couldn't figure out quite what had—oh, Christ! That hurt!

The pain from the bullet wound in his left shoulder suddenly hit and he gasped like a fish out of water with the shock of it. But the white-hot agony in his upper arm wasn't what concerned him.

Mia. Where the hell was Mia? Struggling to rise, he fell back, dizzy and still incapable of dragging in a lungful of air.

Then the fog in his brain lifted and he heard her

yelling. He smiled in brief celebration that she was all right, then rolled his head enough to see Mia and the two men. The men had their backs to him—apparently, they no longer considered him a threat. Thanks for the vote of confidence! He watched Mia's face as she berated them. She was on a tear.

And while she kept them occupied— Where was his own weapon?

"Low-life, lying pieces of crap! When you say you're going to count to three, you're supposed to count to three. Or maybe you can't count— Is that it?

"Shut up, lady."

She paid no attention. "Let me show you. One, two—" She closed her eyes and squeezed the trigger.

There was a pop followed by a shrill scream of agony. Jesus Christ! She'd blown out Mullet's knee cap!

Nobody was more surprised than Mia.

She'd never been a big fan of guns, though she'd been trained and coached on the range until she was a decent, if not always accurate shot. But as far as he knew, she'd never pulled the trigger on a human target. He looked at her with new respect.

"Oh my God," she said big eyed and stared at Mullet who—after catching sight of his own blood—grabbed his leg, which required him to drop his weapon. The gun skittered behind Jack as Mullet collapsed on the floor with a bellow in a tangle of bedspread and bright red blood.

"My bad!" she said unsympathetically. "I was never very good with firearms."

Jack had to get to Mia before the Unibrow got over his surprise and started shooting back. Ignoring vertigo and nausea, he pressed a hand over his own sticky wound and crawled to his pistol a few feet away. He tried to pick up the gun with his right. He couldn't get a good grip. Damn it to hell. He tried again. His hand was red, slippery with his own blood, his grip iffy. He scrubbed his palm on the carpet, got a better grip and staggered to his feet. When he'd started this little adventure it was to prove to Mia that they were made for each other. It wasn't supposed to be a dangerous assignment. Just a prelude to what he wanted to do and say later at his apartment.

"Stop moaning," Mia ordered the guy clutching his shattered kneecap. "You started this, remember? I always did find it hard to judge the amount of pressure to put on the trigger." Then she lifted her gun and focused on the wounded man's partner. "You better not make me nervous," she warned. "If I'm nervous, there's no telling what I might do and you already shot Jack and that doesn't exactly make me like you, you know.''

''Shut up!'' Uni yelled, his cheeks puffing in time with his angered breathing.

''Being rude is not going to improve my mood,'' she chided. ''I'm still not finished punishing you for shooting my fr—''

''Shut up!'' he tried again. ''Shut the hell up!'' Uni scratched his temple with the butt of his weapon in sheer frustration. Jack knew how the man felt.

Mia was having none of it. She continued to berate the guy as if the guns were mere props.

Unibrow tried to shut her up by talking over her. He'd shoot a man without provocation, but apparently was loathe to shoot a woman. Or so Jack hoped. *Keep him talking, sweetheart.*

Stealthily Jack walked up behind the man, then quickly struck him sharply on the back of the head with the butt of the pistol still clutched in his right hand. Unconscious, the man went down like a sack of potatoes.

''About time, I was running out of nonsense,'' Mia said briskly. ''What can I do to help?'' She talked a good game, but her skin was pearly white, her eyes worried, as she scanned his bloody arm without seeming to.

''Two choices,'' Jack told her, retrieving Uni's

weapon from his limp fingers then straightening with difficulty.

"The first one being I check that wound," Mia told him briskly. She pulled back the lapel of his jacket to see the damage and whistled. "Ow."

Jack gave her a lopsided smile. "Slight understatement, but yeah. We aren't hanging around here though. These two are going to wake up pretty soon. When they do we've got to be across town."

"First let me just find something to dam up the bleeding, okay?"

"No time. Come on."

She shook her head, already headed for the closet. "I'm not coming to identify your body in the morgue, Jack. Half a minute won't make any difference. Keep an eye on those two while I find something."

"Make it snappy."

She disappeared back into the closet. Jack glanced at the two lumps of lard on the floor. Not a lot of action from these two, although Uni looked as though he was thinking about waking up soon— "Get the lead out, sweetheart. Grab whatever it is you— Geez, not again! Bathroom. Now!"

The footsteps approaching were heavy, in motion, and *close*. Odds were, this time it was the good guys coming in response to the noise. And, by the sounds of it, excited party guests followed in hot pursuit.

This was not where they wanted to be seen, nor something they could be associated with. Time to split.

Jack grabbed Mia by the arm with his good hand and hauled her helter-skelter out of the closet, then whipped her into the bathroom. He slammed the door behind them, locking it just as he heard men's voices at the door to the bedroom.

Mullet was stretched across the doorway. His presence would give the arriving cavalry pause, at least for a bit of time.

"Your wish is my command." Jack raced to the sunken tub, clambered in, slipping on the slick, pale pink marble, and shoved aside the sheer, miles-long draperies concealing the window.

"I was kidding, Jack! Kidding. We're two stories up."

He grabbed her hand and hauled her in after him. Not the kind of romantic after-dinner soak he'd anticipated. He shoved open the window. Half the fairy fabric of the drapes fluttered out and drifted on the night breeze. The air coming in was arctic cold.

A shoulder slammed into the bathroom door with a loud *thud*. The lock was flimsy, wouldn't hold long. Another *thud*. A foot this time by the sound of it. Jack grabbed Mia by the waist and pushed her toward the window. She hooked a leg over the sill and slipped from view. He held his breath and hoped to God he wouldn't hear a thud as her body hit the patio below.

"There's a ledge about six feet under the window. What are you waiting for?" she growled, out of sight.

Indeed. Jack slung his legs over and dropped. He hated heights. Heights in the pitch-dark when it was snowing, and when he had a bullet in his shoulder, he hated even more.

Mia grabbed his hand as he joined her on the narrow, snow-dusted ledge. "Don't look down."

No problem.

Her fingers, gripping his tightly enough to cut off circulation, felt warm and steady and so damn right.

"Shuffle about ten feet to our left," she said, through chattering teeth. "There's a balcony over there. I think if we climb up—"

Suddenly a chunk of stone flew off the facade of the house right beside Jack's ear. Someone was firing at them. At least their assailant couldn't see them any better than they could see him.

But their assailant was standing inside a nice

warm room. Not balancing on tiptoes on a fourteen-inch ledge dusted with snow.

It was pitch-dark. Snow fell softly against his face. He pressed his back against the wall behind him and placed one foot firmly on the ledge before he picked up the other one. Mia was moving across their narrow balance beam at the speed of light.

"Not afraid of heights, are you?" Jack whispered as their feet slid in a strange kind of shuffle dance across the narrow ledge.

"Uh-uh. You?"

He swallowed hard. Not just yeah, but *hell* yeah. He managed to keep his tone even. "Can you see the balcony?"

"No, but I remember where it is from last time. How's the bleeding?"

Nice and warm. "Okay."

"Okay you're bleeding to death, or okay it's stopped?"

"Okay, can we please climb up that balcony and get inside?"

"Tell me if it gets bad. Don't lie to me ever again, Jack."

"I won't."

"Promise?"

"Yes."

Silence as they shuffled sideways several feet, the

only sound the crunch of their feet and their breathing. "Were you really in the system?" Mia asked very softly.

"Yes."

"Why didn't you just tell me all that before, Jack?"

"Because you were falling in love with the man you *believed* me to be. I didn't want to jeopardize that."

"You were afraid that I wouldn't accept who you really are?" She sighed. "Oh, Jack."

"Mia?"

"What?"

"Much as I want to finish this all-important conversation...have you noticed that we're precariously perched on an inch-wide piece of building twenty-five feet off the ground in the pitch freaking dark?"

There was a long pause. "The balcony isn't here."

"What? You said—"

"I think it's on the east side of the house. This must be the south."

Jack squeezed his eyes shut for a brief moment. "We have to go around a corner." It wasn't a question.

A chunk of the building fell with an ominous thud, to the ground far below them. Jack froze. The scrape of feet. Heavy breathing. He held his breath. Nope. Not his own breathing.

Crap.

Someone else was on the ledge with them.

CHAPTER NINE

MIA'S STOCKINGED FEET were numb with cold, but impending frostbite was the least of her problems. She cast a worried glance to her right where she could hear, but not see, Jack beside her. His breathing was labored. His footsteps unsteady.

This was completely insane. What were they *thinking* climbing out of the window like that? Jack was bleeding like a stuck pig, and neither of them was dressed appropriately for scaling the side of a house.

Snow began to blow around them in a blinding rush. Thick, fluffy blobs of icy white fell faster and faster.

To make it worse, there was at least one someone else on the ledge with them. Left hand on the rough, cold stone wall, Mia took small, shuffling sideways steps and wracked her brain for a solution to their dilemma.

In the snow-blanketed garden below them prowled the ambassador's security force, as yet unaware of the drama being played out directly above their heads. But they'd likely wise up soon. Then how long before they joined their pals up here on the roof?

Even if they *could* figure out a way to slide down a drainpipe, or swing down on a nonexistent vine, that would be a bad idea. Hard to look innocent and innocuous if they landed bleeding to death in the garden.

The solution would be to find a window—unlocked of course—and climb inside. Then they'd slip out a back way somehow.

While the answer seemed simple enough, Mia knew nothing in life was that simple. It was winter. Windows would not be left open on a night like this. Besides, nobody left windows unlocked anymore.

And the simple truth was, she was terrified Jack would bleed to death up here on the ledge while they went around and around the upper floor of the house like moons orbiting Jupiter.

When she'd pulled back his jacket to gauge the damage of the bullet wound she'd been alarmed at the amount of blood staining his nicely starched white shirt. She shied away from thinking about the hole in Jack that lurked behind that stain. He needed to be in a hospital, and he needed to be there *now*. Between climbing, teetering and balancing in the snow, she was certain his condition was deteriorating right along with the weather.

What to do?

A bullet gave answer to that question. There was no sound beyond a muffled *whoosh* from the silencer. The shot went wild, thank God, but the shooter, pinpointed by the muzzle flash, was too close for comfort.

They needed to haul ass. But to where? And how?

"Don't return fire," Jack warned in a low voice. "Our only advantage right now is they can't see us, while we have at least a vague sense of where they are." His fingers felt along the wall between them for her hand. "How're you holding up, sweetheart?"

He was close enough for Mia to feel the heat off his body and to smell the hot metallic scent of his blood.

"Been better." She paused as three more wild shots were fired in rapid succession. Terrifying in the darkness to see those ominous flashes, hear the whispered ricochet of a bullet pinging off the snow-covered roof. If this kept up, the ambassador's roof would be leaking come spring. "What are our options here, Jack?" she demanded urgently.

He grunted in pain. "Much as I'm enjoying our togetherness, I'd prefer to do it at my place. Let's not keep circling. So that leaves in, up or down. First option calls it. Speed it up though. This guy's going to be tripping over us PDQ.''

The first available option was up.

''I don't t-think so, Jack.'' Mia said through chattering teeth. She gripped the narrow metal bar of a ladder in one hand. The ladder was attached to the side of the house and went from where they were standing on the ledge…up. How far up, she had no idea. She cautiously felt down below the ledge with her foot, while hanging on for dear life. But there was no corresponding escape route snaking down to the ground below them. ''If we go on the roof there might not be a way down,'' she felt compelled to point out.

''Like there's a way *now?*'' he demanded.

''Yeah, fine. But in the movies, the idiot heroine always goes *up* when she should be running away.''

He chuckled and, despite her fear, it was good to hear him laugh. ''But the heroine always lives, doesn't she, darling?''

''Good point. But how will you manage with your shoulder?''

''I'll manage.''

A flurry of shots lit up the area. Mia could actually see the guy's face as he realigned the muzzle in the right direction.

Shouts from below. Slender flashlight beams aimed toward the facade of the house. Crisscrossing. Searching. Scanning. Not reaching this high. But people below were coming out of the house now. Voices. Shouting. The crunch of booted feet on gravel.

"Jesus," Jack hissed. "It's a three-ring circus down there. Fire escape ladder. Go. Go. *Go!*"

Mia went. She could practically feel Jack's hot breath on her feet as she climbed. His hand gripped the next bar before her feet left it.

She clambered up onto the flat roof, Jack a heartbeat behind her. His breath sounded ragged. She couldn't begin to imagine the pain he was enduring. Snow reflected a little light. Not much, but enough to see various dark shapes of household systems lying on the rooftop like the humps of prehistoric beasts. "Now what?" she whispered, rubbing her arms uselessly. God it was cold. The snow was falling faster now. Soft and icy on her face. "Jack?"

"Yeah. I heard you." He wasn't shivering, Mia noticed. That wasn't a good sign. "Hang on a sec."

He turned and kicked at the top of the ladder. He kicked again. Hard. And again. Harder. Once more, and the top of the ladder detached from its moorings with a screech. It didn't fall, but arced three feet away from the rooftop. No one was going to be coming up that way.

"Good thinking."

Jack staggered as he came back to her side. Mia wrapped her arm about his waist, her mouth dry with fear as she got more of his weight than she'd bargained for. She too staggered before she braced herself.

"Let's double back to the bedroom."

"What if the guy I shot is still there?"

"If he's stupid enough to still be hanging around, you can shoot him again. I have his weapon, remember?"

"Fine. Okay. Let's go." She didn't care where or how, just that she had to get Jack downstairs and to a hospital. If it meant spending the rest of her natural life in a jail cell convicted of espionage to accomplish that goal, so be it.

The noise of activities far below muffled their footsteps as did the snow. Their long legs were in sync as they ran back the way they'd come.

"About here?" Mia paused on the edge of the roof.

"Farther."

They ran. The roof, icy slick, made their progress dangerous and painstaking slow. The ground security forces were well behind them now, still searching the side of the building they'd been on moments before. Or possibly already on their way up to the roof. The bad guys who'd been a lot closer would find a way up here soon.

Heart in her throat, Mia saw the bathroom vent sticking up at the same time Jack did. "Bingo. Hold onto me for a sec—" When Jack grasped her arm with his good one, she leaned precariously over the side for a look.

She pulled herself upright. "The window's still open. It's about eight feet down. I think if we lower ourselves, we can stand on the frame and swing into the bathroom. Ready?"

"You are, aren't you?" he asked, his voice thick.

"Are what?"

"Ready," he repeated. "You're ready and rarin' to go."

"Uh, yeah," she said. "So what's the holdup?"

"Just one thing before we head back in."

"Jack," Mia shot a glance at the ground below. "Now really isn't the time for a chat."

"It's the perfect time for one of *our* chats, darling." He grinned, then winced as he shifted to take hold of her despite the wound in his shoulder.

"Jack…" She tossed another quick look behind them.

"Mia, marry me."

She almost got whiplash turning back to him. *"What?"*

"You heard me."

"You're proposing *now?*"

Jack stared at her and his heart kicked into a wild gallop. He'd been afraid of saying the words for so long and now that he'd said them, they felt...*right*. He loved her. He'd missed her every damn minute she'd been out of his life. Even the action was no fun without her.

But God only knew, he was braced for her to shoot him down in flames. He lost all feeling in his body as he prepared himself for the worst. What the hell could he say to convince her? How could he beg her to stay? What would *make* her stay? "I love you, Mia."

"Careful. I may fall off the roof."

"I'll dive right after you."

She stared at him for a long minute, brushing falling snow out of her eyes. "You're only asking because you think we're going to die and you won't have to go through with a wedding, aren't you?"

"No. I'm proposing now because I'm ready to live. I'm asking because without you, I might as well let that unibrow guy shoot me stone dead. I love you, darling, and God only knows I need you.

Hell, even the job is no fun without you beside me, keeping me on my toes.''

''You're serious.''

''Damn straight.''

He pulled her hard against him with the arm wrapped about her waist, then he crushed his mouth down on hers. His mouth was a liquid furnace. Hot, savage, hungry. A bolt of fire shot through her body as she stood up on her frozen toes to kiss him back with everything that was in her. Jack could take her from frozen to flashpoint in two-seconds flat.

He slid his hand up the back of her neck and tunneled his fingers through her damp hair. She wanted to curl into his warmth, stay in his arms forever—

''Jack,'' she murmured against his mouth, ''I love you—''

''How perfect is that?'' His voice was whisper soft as he nibbled her lower lip. Hungry little nips that caused her body to respond instinctively. Her hands tightened about his neck. Against her midriff she felt the hot seep of Jack's blood soaking through the thin silk of her dress.

''Just one more—''

''Stay right where you are,'' a rough voice said out of the darkness.

Mia froze, her mouth still locked with Jack's. The

muzzle of a pistol ground into her temple. Wouldn't you know it? He'd finally proposed and she was going to die before she could say yes.

She'd always known Jack would be the death of her.

CHAPTER TEN

"HAND OVER THE DISK, or I'll shoot the girl." The man's voice was thick and guttural. And horribly familiar. "This time I'm not gonna give you the courtesy of countin'."

"You're going down," Jack snarled. To *Mia*, not Uni. He hoped to God she got it, because before either she or the man with the gun at her head knew what was happening, Jack pushed Mia out of the way and spun around. In a lightning-fast move, he grabbed the guy's beefy right shoulder with his left, weakest, hand. Then Jack jerked Uni off his feet with the other arm around his thick neck and pulled him down to the snow-crusted rooftop.

They both went down hard. Jack saw sparkles as he fell on his bad shoulder. His wound screamed. Before the other man could recover, Jack straddled the bastard with his weapon in the man's face. Uni didn't make a peep.

Though he would have enjoyed putting a bullet into the guy, he settled for the alternate use of his weapon. Jack popped him one on the side of the head and the guy went limp beneath him for the second time that night.

A good thing since reinforcements were thundering across the flat rooftop like wildebeest on the Savannah. *"Go. Go. Go!"* Jack yelled to Mia.

He grabbed her by the arm. Damn it, what was taking her so long? "Brace yourself!" he shouted and swung her over the edge of the roof, still gripping her arm.

Mia bent her knees and then dropped over the side of the building. She dangled as she felt for the edge of the open window with her foot. She was grateful for how tightly Jack was gripping her wrist, and very glad she couldn't see the ground. Where the hell was that window? Her entire body swung like a slow-moving pendulum from side to side.

Side…to…side.

The skin around her wrist stretched painfully and she knew Jack was holding her full weight while lying prone on the very edge of the roof above her. This must be hurting him a hundred times worse than it was hurting her. Come on, damn it. Where was the—

There! She released the breath she'd been holding and brought both feet to rest on the solid frame of the window ledge. "Got it," she whispered up to Jack as she steadied herself on the precarious perch.

"Then get in and get out of my way— *Damn!*"

Mia heard the shots the same time Jack did, followed by heavy, muffled footsteps of several people running toward their position full speed, weapons blazing. Nice and subtle. *Not.*

"Move it, Jack! You're not getting out of marrying me this easily. Get down here!" With more haste than skill, Mia swung herself into the open window, then turned to lean out and help him.

His feet came in first, followed by his long body. With the propulsion of a guy being shot out of a cannon, he landed with more enthusiasm than finesse. His trajectory sent them crashing and sliding into the pale pink marble tub like beached whales. Arms and legs tangled.

But they were *alive.*

Jack looked up from his position of head smashed between her boobs. His face was sweaty, his skin parchment-pale, eyes shadowed with pain. But he grinned as he stroked a finger down her cheek. "Hello, darling. Come here often?"

Mia laughed, and boy, it felt good to laugh with Jack again. "Idiot. Come on. Let's get the hell out of here before *everyone* comes flying through that window."

They untangled their limbs and got out of the tub with some difficulty. Compared to their run across the rooftop under fire, this was a piece of cake. Mia closed the window firmly, locking it, while Jack went to scope out the bedroom.

Empty. Their friends had taken their toys and disappeared. There was a blossom of a bloodstain on the carpet right in front of the door. Mia shivered and averted her gaze.

She found a white shirt for Jack and helped him into it; his own shirt was soaked with dark red blood. The wound in his shoulder still seeped at an alarming rate, and he was sweating, while Mia still couldn't feel her extremities from the cold.

She tucked a small, folded hand towel against the wound, helped him button the shirt, then slipped his jacket back on.

"What's the plan?" she asked, slipping on the shoes she'd kicked off what seemed like days ago. She winced and worried her frozen toes would snap off.

"First we find a convenient bedroom to muss up—just in case we have to explain our absence. Preferably something on the other side of the house. Then we saunter downstairs as if nothing happened and walk out."

He talked a good game, but she wondered if he'd

be able to walk down the hall, let alone "saunter." Then she remembered that this was Jack Ryan, a man who wouldn't know the meaning of "quit."

"That easy?"

"You bet." He opened the door with a decidedly shaky hand. "Let's do it."

"I'm not going to have to carry you, am I?" she asked, trying not to show just how concerned she was.

He gave her a crooked smile. "Maybe over the threshold later."

Threshold. Wedding. Marriage.

She grinned at him. "Stay put," she told him casually. "I'll go find another room to muss and come back for you." She expected him to protest. It worried her even more when he *didn't*.

"Don't be long."

Mia flew down the landing. Hearing the chatter of party guests and the clinking of glasses from the floor below was surreal. She forced herself to slow her steps and go as far down the private corridor as her nerves could stand before opening a bedroom door. It only took a moment to rumple the bedspread and punch the pillows. Then she raced back down the corridor to where she'd left Jack.

She found him slumped in the chair near the door. He was clearly struggling to stay conscious, but he opened glassy eyes as she stepped in and closed the door behind her.

"Ready to rock?" she asked, helping him stand with difficulty.

"Call, Robert. Have him come upst—"

Oh, God. He wanted his driver. This was bad. Really bad. "Phone?"

"Inside p-pocket. Speed d—eigh—eighteen." He fell back into the chair and closed his eyes.

Mia knelt between his spread legs and patted his pockets looking for his cell phone. Her fingers were clumsy with panic, but she found the tiny phone, flipped it open and hit *1 8.*

It rang. And rang. And *rang.*

"As long as you're kneeling there..." He lifted one eyebrow.

Mia shook her head. "You're impossible."

"Insatiable," Jack licked dry lips. "Help me up." He slung his arm around her neck. "Whoa! Steady t-there."

Mia staggered on her high heels under his weight. "You outweigh me by eighty pounds, pal."

"All muscle."

"Yeah, between your ears." She wanted to distract him from what must be nearly mind-numbing pain. She kept him teasing as she guided him down the hall to the stairs.

"Is that any way to talk to your future husband?"

"Mom always said to bend a man's twig in the direction you want him to grow."

He chuckled. "Twig bending? Sounds pornographic."

"Then you should love it."

"Wanna see my twig?"

"It's *my* twig now, buster."

"True. My twig is your twig."

They made it down the stairs. Barely. Jack's hard head was the only thing keeping him upright. And they still had to get across the large room to the front door.

"And where have you two lovebirds been?" Sandy asked archly. She was standing right at the foot of the stairs, a finger of brandy in her glass and a plate of canapés in her other hand. "Where's that dance you promised me, you rat?"

"Rain check, beautiful," Jack gave her a sleepy grin. "I have to get my girl home before she turns into a pumpkin."

Sandy grinned. "Is your sweetie a little smashed?"

Mia gave the other woman a meaningful look and wrapped her arm more tightly around Jack's waist making sure his side was tucked against hers.

"Drunk on love, Sandy. I'll call you in a couple of days."

"One more dance before we go," Jack insisted, wrapping both arms around her. It took all Mia's strength to hold him up.

"We'll dance at home, honey." She refused to let him stay here where he could bleed to death on the polished parquet floor.

By the time they reached the front door, her dress was saturated with Jack's blood and her arms were screaming for mercy. Fortunately they looked the epitome of a romantic couple as they clung to each other wordlessly. Thank God no one stopped to talk.

"Don't you dare die on me, Jack Ryan," Mia growled as someone let the front door swing open in their wake. "Don't you *dare*." The door closed leaving the two of them standing under the portico. A limo, several yards away, flashed its lights.

Robert. Thank God.

"You're marrying me," she told Jack sternly. "I want the whole nine yards. Flowers, preacher, music, bunny hop, *everything*. Besides, I have about sixty-five years of flack to give you for this blind date from hell. So don't take the easy way—" He sagged against her. "Oh, thank God," Mia breathed a sigh of relief as Jack's driver stepped up and grabbed him from the other side. "I think he fainted."

"Passed out, darling. Passed out. Men don't faint, for God's sake. And I haven't," Jack muttered as Mia and his driver folded him into the back seat of the car. "You're going to remind me about tonight every year on our anniversary, aren't you?" Jack asked as the car flew down Massachusetts Avenue and away from Embassy Row.

"And twice on Sundays," Mia told him sweetly, cradling his head on her lap and brushing back his hair.

Jack sighed. "Good." Eyes closed, he stroked her leg. "I have candles at my place. And champagne on ice. I wanted to do the whole proposal thing right—"

So he'd known he was going to propose before their evening had even started. "Are you kidding?" she asked. "A proposal in the snow, with bullets flying and bad guys chasing us across rooftops? What could be more romantic than that?"

He smiled against her thigh as Robert stepped on the gas and headed for the hospital at illegal speeds. "I always knew you were my woman, Mia."

He rose up awkwardly to kiss her. Mia bent her head to meet him halfway. "And don't you forget it." Their lips met with aching tenderness.

"Gonna pass out now," Jack warned as his head dropped back to her lap and his eyes drifted shut. "Don' go, 'K? Love you...all my life."

"I love you, too, you impossible man. Rest now. I'll be right there when you wake up."

And she was. As Jack had known she would be.

HAL AND DAMNATION

Muriel Jensen

CHAPTER ONE

"HE'S INSUBORDINATE and subversive," Katarina Como told her father then cast a condemning look at the man beside her. In her usually quiet, even voice there was a slight quaver, left over from their recent argument. "His attitude is detrimental to the reputation of this establishment."

Hal Stratton laughed. "This is a restaurant," he countered with a sort of guy-to-guy charm her father seemed to buy, "not a military installation. Insubordinate and subversive?" He turned to her with amusement in his lazy dark blue eyes. "You're not Eva Peron, Kat. You're just the manager of Umberto's Tuscan Grille."

And that was it right there. She *hated* that he zeroed in on her weakness. She also hated that in a life filled with work, personal projects and little time for relationships, the only man who'd ever appealed to her physically was wrapped up in this tall, broad-shouldered megalomaniac. But her father seemed to like him and let him get away with one infraction after another despite her complaints.

Kat took a step toward her father's desk in the restaurant's cluttered office and pointed a finger at Hal. "See? Did you hear that? That's all I get from him day after day. He does nothing I ask…"

"Pardon me," Hal interrupted with calm courtesy, "but I always do what you ask."

"When you're good and ready," she retorted.

"Sometimes I have priorities you're unaware of."

"I've managed this restaurant for five years, and you've been a waiter here for two weeks. I think I'm more likely to know what should be done first."

"Now, Kat." Her father folded his hands on the desk and leaned toward her with a glance at Hal that asked for forgiveness. She knew she'd lost. "You two have got to learn to get along. You're a very good manager, and he's the best waiter we've ever had."

That, unfortunately, was true. Good waiters were a dime a dozen, but great waiters who provided the kind of hospitable service that brought patrons back again and again were few and far between. Hal Stratton had a gift. Trouble was, he also had a disdain for authority, particularly if it was female.

Kat folded her arms. "He is a good waiter," she

admitted, determined to make her point, "but he's not a team player. Tonight, he deliberately, physically…" She demonstrated by taking hold of Stratton's arm as he'd done to her earlier. "…stopped me from greeting Joey Percanto's table so that he could do it himself. He actually pulled me away, so that he could get ahead of me."

When her father seemed unimpressed with that major breach of etiquette, she dropped her hand from Hal's arm and went on in a carefully controlled voice. "Everyone who comes into this restaurant is greeted by family, and special customers are taken care of by us."

Her father nodded. It was a policy he'd established.

"But Joey likes Hal," he said, looking reluctantly into her eyes. "Hal served on him on your day off and Joey called to tell me that he wants to be served by him exclusively from now on."

Kat threw her hands up in despair, unable to stop the wellspring of her frustrations from bubbling up. "Then, why am I here? You offer the business to Giulio, who runs off to build boats in Maine, and I stay to work by your side year after year, but you don't offer it to me because I'm your daughter and not your son. And not only that—you won't even defend me from *waiters* who think they know more than I do!''

Then realizing they were getting into old family grievances, she turned to Hal with cool hauteur. ''Would you excuse us, please?'' she asked.

He bowed with grace and sarcasm. ''Of course, Your Highness. Excuse me, Mr. Como.''

Hal went back into the restaurant, and Kat faced her father with complete exasperation.

''The Monticello has offered me a generous salary,'' she said with the last shred of her patience, ''to run the place nights and weekends.'' The Monticello was a fine-dining restaurant with a wide menu and a staff of thirty-three.

''Kat...''

''You're making me give it serious thought, Dad. You know I love this place, but if you're going to stand by and do nothing while some smart-mouthed upstart ignores what I say—''

''Kat!'' Umberto Como stood and said with sudden asperity, ''Maybe you just say too much.''

She stared at him, cut to the quick. Fairness required that she acknowledge—to herself, at least— that he might be right. But it was his unwillingness to recognize her as a savvy, reliable partner in the business that made her feel undervalued and unappreciated.

She'd washed dishes in the restaurant since she was eight, had done prep and cleanup with her mother at ten years old and started waiting tables at fourteen.

Giulio, her younger brother, bussed tables when he was in high school, but participated in all the sports and, therefore, got afternoons and weekends off. He'd worked for spending money, but never had the love of the business that Kat developed early.

Still, when her father had begun to consider retirement, he'd offered Giulio the business. When Giulio had turned him down, Kat had suggested that she take over instead. She'd never forgotten her father's stunned expression. He'd stammered and evaded the question, but she'd gotten her answer when he put off retirement.

She'd decided then to make a last-ditch effort to prove her competence. Then, if he still refused to let her take over the restaurant, it would be time to move on.

So, perhaps she overcompensated for her father's inability to see her at the helm of Umberto's Tuscan Grille by obsessing over the staff's performance and appearance, but surely no one could blame her.

Except the new waiter, who considered her dictatorial.

She swallowed a painful lump in her throat. ''I

am trying to do the best job I can for you, Dad. We have a wonderful staff, but they have personal problems, too, and sometimes they have to be reminded of what…''

''Katarina.'' Her father came around the desk and wrapped her in his arms. ''You're the light of my life—you know that. Since Mama died and Giulio moved away, I wouldn't know what to do without you.''

Not because she could run the restaurant, but because the others weren't here. He loved her, she knew he did, but he was from an old-world family and mired in old-world prejudices about women.

''Please,'' he said heavily, ''don't talk about leaving.''

''Dad…''

''Kat, I have a lot on my mind right now.'' He held her at arm's length and smiled at her. ''You know we have Valentine's Day coming up and it's going to be big. I can't think about anything else right now. But, when it's over, we can talk about… maybe…possibly…turning things over to you and…you know…see how it goes.''

She almost fainted dead away. She couldn't have heard him correctly. He'd refused to talk about her taking over since Giulio left.

''What?'' she breathed.

"We'll see about it." He went back around the desk, probably already regretting that concession. She wanted a tape recorder, a notary, a witness!

"Dad, are you...?" she began, desperate to pin him down.

"We'll see about it," he said, a swipe of his hand in the air dismissing it for now. "Meanwhile, I need you to do something for me."

Still in shock, it took her a moment to process the words and respond. "Do something for you. Yes. What?"

"The new table linens and uniforms I ordered for the Ferreiras' anniversary party are lost somewhere between here and San Francisco."

"Oh, no." She knew he'd pulled out all the stops to put a fresh face on Umberto's for the Ferreiras. They'd invited many of their business and society friends, and he knew making a good impression on them could mean future business. And they could use it. Business had been steady, but *brisk* would be better.

"They've refilled the order," he said, "but I'd like you to pick it up."

She *was* having trouble with her ears. "What?" she asked. You mean...in *San Francisco?*"

He nodded.

"But, can't they overnight it?"

"They sent it Urgent Air last time and it's lost."

"But...Portland to San Francisco? Five hundred miles will take a whole day's driving. At least."

He nodded and smiled. "But much less time by plane."

She blinked at him. "You're sending me on a commercial flight to pick up...?"

She stopped when he shook his head. "Hal has a little Cessna."

She uttered a heartfelt groan.

CHAPTER TWO

HAL STRATTON sat on the corner of Umberto's desk after closing. He'd changed his apron for a leather jacket. Everyone else had left, but Umberto sat at his desk and in a chair near the desk sat Hal's captain, David Roth of the Portland Police Department.

"How did she take it?" Hal asked Umberto.

Umberto bounced a glance off him, then frowned and focused on the calendar on his desk. He flipped pages back and forth. "Well...not too badly."

"You told her why I'm here?"

"No."

Hal glanced at his captain, who was busy inspecting the crown molding in the old office.

"So you just told her to take a few days off then but didn't tell her why?"

Umberto gave him a pitying look. "Yeah. Right. You tell her to take a few days off and see where it gets you."

Umberto and Kat's relationship was difficult for Hal to understand. While the old man seemed to love his daughter a great deal, and relied on her managerial skills, he didn't appear to have much appreciation for her knowledge and experience, which were considerable. He also didn't have much to say about her bossy style, which was formidable—and annoying to an undercover cop accustomed to running operations his way.

Of course, she didn't know he was a cop, but he doubted her attitude would have been any different if she had. She was sure she knew everything.

"Berto, it's for her own safety." Hal pointed out the obvious. "If she knows one of your customers is planning to use the restaurant to get into the savings and loan next door, she'll want to help stop it. This is going down tomorrow night and she always stays late to prepare the deposit. What if he makes his move while she's still around?"

Umberto nodded emphatically. "I know all that. That's why I told her I'm sending her to San Francisco to pick up linens."

Hal thought about that a minute. "Okay. That's good. She didn't ask any questions?"

He didn't like the way the old man was avoiding his eyes. The way he looked at Roth, who also didn't look at Hal.

"She did complain about the drive taking eleven hours," Umberto said.

Roth finally cleared his throat and sat up in his chair, looking suddenly official. "That's why he told her that you're flying her down to San Francisco."

A long string of profanity sat on the tip of Hal's tongue. Only extensive training and long conditioning to remain calm under the most adverse circumstances held it back.

"What?" he asked flatly.

"You're going to take her away so that we can do our job," Roth said.

"*Our* job," Hal repeated with emphasis. "You came to *me* when Umberto told you he overheard Percanto planning to rob the savings and loan next door. I'm the one who set this up. I'm the one who's been shlepping plates for two weeks, brownnosing Percanto and planting bugs in the flowers so that we can collar him." As he piled up the details of his own case, his ability to view this sudden change of plans with calmness evaporated. "I know Berto is your friend, but I'll be damned if you're going to send me off as a baby-sitter to…"

"The plans are made," Roth said. Talk about dictatorial. Kat could take lessons from him. "I promised. Just pretend this is one of the private security jobs you do on your time off. You're off the precinct clock and Berto will pay you personally."

"She hates me," Hal added, desperate. "I doubt she'll even want to go with me."

"She'll go," Umberto assured him. "She'll do whatever's best for the restaurant."

"Captain," Hal pleaded. He couldn't believe this was happening. He'd handled this flawlessly and just when it was all about to come to fruition, they were sending him off with Evita?

Roth wasn't moved, but he did add with sincerity, "You're the best man for the job, Hal. And the most important element in this to Berto is Kat's safety. He let us set this up here on the promise that we'd keep her out of the way and protected. Your job in doing that is every bit as important as collaring Percanto."

Hal swallowed more profanity.

"There're Mariners tickets in it for you," Roth bargained.

Hal rolled his eyes. "It's February. There's no baseball in February."

"You can use my box every weekend this summer."

Well. Maybe that would help a little. The only thing he loved more than his work was baseball.

"I told her you'd call her tonight to make plans to pick her up." Umberto handed him a slip of paper with a telephone number on it.

Hal took it. "You two owe me big," he said.

"Yeah," Berto agreed.

When Hal got back to his apartment, he called Kat. "I understand I'm flying you to San Francisco," he said.

"You do have a pilot's license?" she asked.

Of course she would doubt him. "I do," he assured her.

"And you're actually a *good* pilot?"

"The government thought so. They trusted me with a sinfully expensive F-14."

She was quiet for a moment, then she sighed. "I haven't flown very much."

Did he detect a note of fear? Was she actually vulnerable to something? "Nothing to worry about," he said. "I have a very reliable little two-seater that I keep in excellent condition and I just had the engine overhauled. It's a short flight. I'll pick you up at eight. Where do you live?"

She gave him a northwest Portland address, then she asked with genuine interest, "How did you get an airplane? I mean...are tips really that good? Aren't they expensive to buy and maintain?"

Despite the deceit inherent in this trip, he could answer that honestly. "It was my dad's. He had a restaurant in Juneau. He flew for supplies all the time and I got my license when I was in college. I flew for the navy for a while, then when my parents moved to Florida, Dad gave me the plane.''

''Oh.'' She sounded surprised. ''Funny how there are certain people you don't think about having parents.''

He didn't know whether to be amused or insulted. ''Did you think I was conceived in a petri dish?''

It sounded as though she smothered a laugh. ''No, but I've come to think of you as some hybrid Robo Cop-waiter machine.''

He experienced an uncomfortable moment. Did she know? ''Robo Cop?''

''You do act all authoritative and armor-plated.''

''Hmm,'' he replied. ''I thought that was you.''

''Maybe we've been looking in a mirror. My place is above a coffee shop. I'll pick up coffee and scones, and be waiting in front at 8:00 a.m.''

''All right. See you then.''

IN HAL'S EXPERIENCE with his mother and his two sisters, women were seldom on time, but Kat was standing in front of the address she'd given him, two large paper cups in her hands, a brown paper bag balanced on top of them.

This was the first time he'd seen her in anything but the black and white that was the uniform of Umberto's Tuscan Grille. She wore jeans, a white roll-neck sweater, and a short black wool jacket. Her glossy dark hair was down and full rather than pulled back as she always wore it at work.

She was petite—something he seldom noticed on the job because of her personality. And she was very, very pretty. He felt suddenly a little off balance—as though the world had somehow changed overnight.

He got out of the car and came around to open her door. "Good morning," he said.

"Hi," she replied, looking at him as though he wasn't who she'd expected either. "Thank you." After she stepped in, he ran back around the car and climbed in behind the wheel. The interior, which usually smelled of fast food and a pine deodorizer, now had the fragrance of lilacs. Kat's fragrance.

The world tilted a little farther.

While he drove to Herrick Field, she removed the tab from the lid on his coffee and placed the cup in the holder. "I didn't know about cream and sugar, so I just got you a mocha. I hope that's all right."

That was a little sweet for his taste, but he couldn't fault her consideration in buying it. "Great. Thank you."

She told him about a small airfield not too far from the linen supplier. "I figure we can just pick up a cab and be there and back in an hour, if all goes well. I checked. It's well staffed and maintained.''

Trust her to check all details. But somehow, he had to make sure that all didn't go well. Her father didn't want her back for two days.

"Certainly we can fit lunch in there somewhere,'' he said.

"I'd like to be back for my shift tonight.'' She handed him a bite of a blueberry scone.

He popped it in his mouth. "I thought your father gave you the day off for this trip,'' he said after swallowing the scone.

"He did. But this shouldn't take more than a couple of hours. And if I don't come in, he'll be shorthanded and he's not as young as he used to be.''

"He's strong as a bull.''

He heard the little expelled breath that meant she was getting huffy. "I know you think you've learned everything about Umberto's in the two weeks you've been there, but he had a heart attack last year. It was just a small one, a sort of warning, but he's no longer strong as a bull, though he likes to think he is, and my job is to be there.''

"Pardon me, Your Highness,'' he said. There was no other way to respond to that tone. "I just thought it would be nice not to rush. If he gave you the day off, I'm sure he's brought someone in to cover for you."

That exhalation of air again. "And in what lifetime would you want to dally with me, Mr. Stratton?"

"Dally?" Now there was a word you didn't hear every day.

"Linger over," she relied. "Spend time with."

A very honest answer to that was right on the tip of his tongue. He didn't need to complicate an already tricky little trip, but what the hell. She had it coming. And it had been an undercurrent beneath the waves of conflict between them for two long weeks. He braked at a red light and was able to turn and look right into her eyes. "In any lifetime offered me, Miss Como."

He enjoyed her openmouthed expression of complete confusion. The light turned and he drove on.

"You don't like me," she reminded him.

"I don't like your presumption of superiority," he corrected, passing a small pickup burdened with lumber, "but that doesn't mean I'm not sexually attracted to you."

"Sexually att—" She said that on a gasp, then added, "You are not! You never have a kind word to say to me. And that cool courtesy isn't courtesy at all, it's disdain."

"It's disdain for your attitude," he corrected again, "not your appeal."

She said nothing for another five minutes, then he turned onto the airfield property. He pulled into a parking spot by the tiny terminal and coffee shop.

"Rest room's in there," he said, pointing to the coffee shop. "You look as though you need to splash water on your face. I'm going to check the plane." Then he pointed again to the yellow Cessna at the edge of the field. "Right there."

She studied him one speechless moment, then scrambled out of the car and headed for the coffee shop.

CHAPTER THREE

KAT WAS SHAKEN to her very femininity by Hal's admission. And that's just where she felt it—a little tremor where there'd been very little action in a long time. It was strangely exciting and a little alarming to experience a distinctly sexual reaction to a man she thought she despised, and who she'd been sure despised her.

She looked at her reflection in the age-spotted oval mirror above the sink in the ladies' room, teased by the notion that she attracted him. What was it about her? she wondered. Certainly not her brown hair—it was long and thick, but just...brown. Not the dark eyes—they were thickly lashed but not particularly wide or sparkling, and again...just brown.

Her body wasn't bad, but it was small with none of the voluptuousness men seemed to prefer. She'd been complimented on her smile acquired after two years of metal braces when she was a preteen, but she doubted she'd used it often enough lately for anyone to notice. Sad but true.

In fact, she'd been thinking a lot about where her life was going. She'd broken off an engagement last year when her fiancé had impregnated her best friend and left Kat's sense of self in tatters. To recover, she'd worked longer hours, weekends, painted her bathroom, learned to sew.

Her efforts to stay busy were a combination of a cowardly need to hide, and the conviction that she couldn't let what had happened destroy her faith in herself. Her mother had sewn, and she was the most womanly woman Kat knew, so Kat bought a machine and took a class.

But she'd turned out to be more adept at hiding than at sewing. She found any kind of fabric difficult to deal with, seams difficult to align, zippers and buttonholes impossible to accomplish, and once took a desperate trip to the E.R. with a sewing machine needle in her thumbnail.

But she couldn't hide forever; she knew that. She wanted a home and children, and though some women managed those successfully without husbands, she wanted a man in her life. She liked handholding, snuggling, sharing. She was a smart and capable woman who wouldn't be offended by the assistance of a smart and capable man.

But Hal Stratton?

There was that little tingle again at the very mention of his name.

She was going over the edge. That's all there was to it.

She brushed her hair, straightened her jacket and stepped back from the brink of attraction. He couldn't possibly be the man for her. With a family composed of determined and authoritative Italian males, she knew she needed something else. She had dreams of a gorgeous young Adonis wealthy enough and sufficiently besotted with her to set her up in her own restaurant on the coast and give her four little girls and a house overlooking the ocean.

God? Was that too much to ask?

Apparently. Because instead, He'd sent her a George Patton wanna-be with likely only a two-seater airplane to his name who probably lived on tips.

Well, she was stronger than this unexpected little burgeoning of desire. She squared her shoulders, set her jaw and headed for the plane.

HAL PREPARED for takeoff. At least, that's what she presumed he was doing. He wore a headset and talked to the tower while adjusting gauges, flipping switches, an occasional joke injected into the conversation suggesting a familiarity with the person he spoke to. The voice was female and Kat heard her ask if he was in pursuit of a bad guy.

"Not this time," he replied after a moment. Then

he added to Kat with a smiling side glance, "In another life, I was a skip tracer."

"That's tracking down suspects out on bail who don't make their court appointments, right?"

"Exactly."

He continued with the checklist. The powerful motor growled to life and made the small plane shudder. For one moment, she wondered what on earth she was doing with a handsome man in a small plane on a Wednesday morning when she should be home doing laundry because she had to be at work by eleven for the lunch rush.

Linens, she reminded herself. She was flying to San Francisco to pick up linens to make sure her father had them in time for the Ferreiras' party. That was an odd thing to do, but her father did odd things all the time, and she knew how eager he was to make a good impression on the couple and their society friends.

"Buckled up?" Hal asked, leaning forward to look at her seat belt.

"Yes," she replied, feeling as though his hand rather than his eyes had stroked across her stomach.

She had to think about other things.

Life and death seemed worth consideration as the little plane shuddered into the air and climbed toward an army of puffy clouds in a clear blue sky. Hal held the controls confidently, still talking to the tower. Then he finally leveled out, made a few adjustments to the intimidating panel of controls, thanked the tower and slipped off the earpiece and mike.

"Good day for flying," he said. "Weather's even good over the Siskiyous. That's a rare thing in February."

"Good." She made an effort to appear at ease. The principles of flight had never made sense to her, but then she was no scientist. Millions of people got safely to their destinations every day and she would, too. "You've flown this way before?"

"All the time. My sister lives in San Diego." He was quiet a moment, then asked with a smile, "This your first date in an airplane?"

"Date?" Her determination to remain sane was not going to be undermined by his in-your-face charm. "This is a business trip."

"Come on," he chided. "Only if we allow it to be. Let's make it a business trip that turned into a date. Let's go sightseeing, have dinner at the Top of the Mark, then stay overnight in the hotel."

It was naive to be disappointed in him for suggesting they get a room together, so she kept her feelings to herself.

"Stay over?" she asked coolly.

"So we can see the sights," he replied, "take in

a few clubs. It'd be criminal to travel this far with each other just for the tablecloths.''

''It's a business trip,'' she said again. ''My father wants those tablecloths back for the Ferreiras' party.''

''That's tomorrow night. We'll leave early in the morning and be home by lunch. Come on, Katarina. Don't you feel like dancing?''

She loved to dance, but she'd had no one to dance with in over eight months. She could almost see the lights turned down low, hear saxophones and drums thrumming in the shadows where couples clung together and moved lazily to the music.

But that wasn't her life, now. These days she worked until she dropped.

''No,'' she said stiffly. ''I feel like picking up our order and getting it home. I know you manage to charm everyone around you, but I'm impervious to you. I like to see substance and stability in a man and some respect for my opinion before I sleep with him.''

He smiled again. ''You're inviting me to sleep with you if I can show you substance and…?''

''No.'' He was trying to embarrass her and she refused to allow it. ''You said…''

''I said 'stay over.' But I could be talked into sleeping with you if that's what you want.''

If they hadn't been hanging thousands of feet

above the earth, she would have slapped him. But she didn't want to do anything to distract him. She was beside herself with frustration.

He reached a hand out to pat her knee in a curiously fraternal and affectionate gesture. "Relax, Kat. I'm teasing. I've been lusting after you for two weeks, but I respect your father and I wouldn't seduce you when he sent me to look out for you."

He'd said this was a short flight, but it was entirely possible she could go bananas before they were halfway to San Francisco.

"Just stop talking to me!" she ordered in a strangled voice.

He'd been *lusting* after her? There was that tingle. She pressed her knees together and folded her arms. "And my father sent you to transport me, not to look after me. I can take care of myself, and I assure you I'm in no danger of falling for your seduction."

"*Transport*," he said, "could have an entirely different…"

"Stop it!"

"Sure, Your Highness."

CHAPTER FOUR

THEY REACHED San Francisco by midmorning, its beautiful skyline glistening in the sun.

"If you were any fun," Hal teased Kat, "we'd leave the plane to be refueled overnight and find somewhere down there to have a good time and get to know each other."

"Why does that even occur to you?" she asked. "You've told me over and over again that I'm bossy and compulsive and no fun at all."

"But you could be if you'd just relax your grip on authority and see that the world goes on, even when you're not in charge."

She glanced at her watch. "Would you just get us down, please?"

"I'd like to wait for the airport, if you don't mind." His radio squawked, he pulled on his earphones, and there were spurts of conversation until they finally landed fifteen minutes later at the small airport on the north end of the city, just a quarter of a mile from the linen company.

The moment Kat stepped off the plane, she called them.

"What?" she demanded as someone apparently responded unfavorably to her announcement that she was on her way. "They were supposed to be ready. I've flown in from…yes, I appreciate that, but I have to…" She finally sighed, her shoulders sagging. It amazed him that she felt called upon to bear the weight of the world on them. "Fine," she said. "Two hours."

She stabbed the phone off and frowned at Hal. "They won't be ready for two hours. Two of the tablecloths got oil on them from a machine when they were being bundled, and they had to make two new monograms."

He caught her hand. It was time he took charge of the situation. "Good. Then we'll have lunch somewhere romantic, even if you refuse to have dinner with me."

He found a lone cabdriver near the terminal and gave him instructions.

"Somewhere romantic," the driver said to himself. "A man's idea of romantic, or a woman's?"

"Ah…" Hal considered that. "Well, a man's, I guess, because this is an unusually practical woman."

"I know just the place."

"Hal, we don't have time to be romantic," Kat insisted, "even *if* I wanted to be."

He frowned at her. "How much time do you think it takes? Romance is a look, a touch, secrets exchanged in a quiet corner."

She fell back against her seat with a groan, either tired of listening to him or deciding that arguing with him was hopeless. Either way, he lucked out.

The cabdriver deposited them in front of an English lodge-type building with a hanging sign proclaiming it The Royal Dragoon. On it was painted a man in military garb wielding a saber.

"Nothing says romance," Kat said coolly, "like a drawn sword."

He was beginning to wonder if his faith in cabdrivers had been misplaced when they were led into a large room decorated in the style of an old manor house, all columns and gilt, dark wood, leather, silver, copper and a fireplace.

Kat stopped in surprise, her determination to be uncooperative undermined by their surroundings. A waiter in livery guided them to a table by the fireplace where a real fire crackled behind an iron grate.

Hal pulled out a chair. Kat sat, still gawking.

"Wow," she said simply.

"I know," he agreed. "We live our everyday little drudgeries and forget sometimes that style and grace exist."

"We try to remind people of that at our restaurant," she said a little absently, studying the fireplace. When she looked at him again, she was focused once more, but seemed as though she'd relaxed just a little, less tense than the woman he'd flown with. "In an Italian way, of course. We're a little more raucous than the British."

He laughed at that. It was hard to think of her as raucous.

They ordered shrimp and angel-hair pasta in a light cream sauce.

"Salad's very fresh with interesting greens," she said when it came, poking into it with her fork.

"You don't have to critique the food," he said. "That's too much like work. We're on a date, remember? A romantic interlude."

"Hal, no matter how hard you try to make it otherwise," she disputed, "we're here on business."

"The linen company is business," he granted, "but they're not ready for us. This is two hours of time just for us." He leaned toward her over the table and smiled into her eyes. "It's that dallying we talked about earlier."

SHE WAS STARTLED by how much she wanted to believe that. Two hours just for her with a man intending to romance her. She even felt herself open to the idea, wanted to be receptive to whatever might happen. But playing coy wasn't in her nature; she had to be direct.

"You said you were attracted," she said, half-expecting him to now deny it.

Instead, he replied firmly, "Yes, I did. Attracted in every sense of the word."

"You never said anything before."

"You were always being a boss and never just a woman. It made it hard to approach you."

"I'm usually...all business."

He studied her now with a concentration that seemed to stop the breath in her lungs, slow the beat of her heart. "Why is that?" he asked. "When you're so beautiful and you have a body that would stop any man in his tracks? Has someone hurt you? Made you think it isn't safe to be who you really are?"

She opened her mouth to tell him her fiancé impregnated her best friend, but everyone had their problems and she preferred to suffer in private. She didn't want to share, but she didn't want to lose this moment.

She tossed her head. "I'm over it," she said.

"What about you? I suppose there are women everywhere who love your take-charge approach."

He shrugged. "I've been busy, too. Not a lot of time for myself. But I'd like to change that." He tilted his head and eyed her. "What are you doing on Valentine's Day?"

"Working. You?"

"I have it off," he said. His eyes played over her face. "Why don't I pick you up after work?"

She shook her head. "It'll be midnight before I'm finished."

"Midnight is good. The romancing hour."

She couldn't help a laugh. "I thought it was the witching hour."

"If you're a witch, maybe. If you're a romantic, it's the romancing hour."

The food arrived and they concentrated instead on idle conversation. Then the clock on the mantel struck two, and it was as though the two loud gongs brought Kat to her senses.

"We have to go," she said hurriedly, standing up and digging in her purse for her credit card. She'd never lost two and a half hours before. It was unsettling.

He stayed her hand, giving his card to the waiter when he came to see what they needed. She saw Hal's eyes question her sudden change of mood and didn't know how to tell him that as appealing as this sudden attraction was, she was afraid of it. She wasn't sure what had gone wrong with Dave, and he hadn't been half as threatening to her peace of mind as Hal.

"I'll get a cab," she said and hurried off.

HIS PLAN HAD BEEN to tell her that during refueling a problem had been found, but the "Everything's A-OK, Mr. Stratton," from a cheerful young man in coveralls who greeted them at the plane made that impossible.

He looked down at the mountaintops and the clouds as he flew home and thought he could tell her that Herrick Field wouldn't allow them to land because of a fuel spill or something, but that wouldn't work because they'd just be redirected to Portland International. They were going to be home for dinner if he didn't think fast.

If she'd been a little more open about how she felt at lunch, he might have talked her into coming back to his place when they reached Portland—for his own personal purposes as well as those of her father and his captain.

But she was determined to get the damned linens back.

He was mentally exploring other options to keep

her away from the restaurant until tomorrow when he heard the smallest break in the sound of the engine. It was an almost indiscernible flutter that didn't belong.

He sharpened his attention, scanning the controls while he listened. Altitude, speed looking good—whoa! In an instant, everything changed. Speed slowed considerably and he began to lose altitude.

Fear tried to rise in him, but he reminded himself that this wasn't an F-14. There wasn't much time to think at the speed of an F-14, but this was different. Instinctively he tried to figure out what was going wrong. He had plenty of fuel, so the sounds of fuel starvation didn't make sense.

He decided not to focus on what had gone wrong, but simply to look for someplace to land.

He felt Kat turn to him. "Something wrong?" she asked in a calm voice he was sure she'd had to work at.

"Yes," he replied honestly. "But nothing I can't control."

"Until we get to Portland?" she asked hopefully.

"No, until I get us down." He looked out the window, assessing his options. This wasn't the best place to go down. They were over the snow-covered Siskiyous, which extended from southern Oregon into northern California. They hadn't passed seven-thousand-foot Mount Ashland yet, so they hadn't crossed over the Oregon border.

The mountains were craggy and only small pockets of population existed in its cozy nooks and crannies.

She closed her eyes. "Oh, God. I left dirty laundry in the hamper, and I still owe thirty-two hundred dollars on my car."

He pulled back on the yoke as they descended, searching for a high meadow he knew was right around here somewhere. "Hold it together, Katarina," he encouraged.

"I *am* together!" she assured him in a very high voice. "And I'd like to stay that way, but I'm not going to, am I, if you crash this plane?"

"I said we were going down, I didn't say we were crashing."

"Going down means crashing!" she disputed. "Flying requires us to stay up!"

"We're going to fly down," he corrected calmly, hoping his faith in his ability to do that wasn't misplaced, "until we land."

She looked out her window. "On what? It's all mountaintops and...and..."

"There's a wide meadow coming up," he said, watching for it. "Right...there!" And there it was, snow-covered but wide and surrounded by small enough trees to stop them without killing them—hopefully.

"Hang on," he said.

"Can I do something?" she asked, her voice a shade shy of hysteria. "Give me something to do!"

"Trust me," he said. "That's something you can do. This is a task you can't take charge of, Kat. Just sit quietly and let me do it."

"If you kill me," she threatened, "I'll see that you're fired without severance pay!"

He ignored that nonsensical outburst and concentrated on getting the wheels down and easing onto the meadow, hoping the snow wasn't too deep.

It wasn't. He skated along the top of it, Kat making strangled little sounds as they pitched and rocked and headed for the trees.

"Trees!" she shrieked at him.

"They're going to stop us," he told her.

"Permanently?" she asked, holding on.

"You're supposed to be trusting."

"I am," she said, but she had a hand over her eyes.

TERROR WAS a new experience for Kat, but a corner of her mind not totally focused on whether she was going to live or die thought there was a weirdly stimulating excitement about it. She could feel her heart beating, her blood moving, her lungs expanding and contracting. She'd never felt so alive!

Then they were skating on the snow and speeding toward the trees at an alarming rate, Hal's knuckles white on the controls as he tried to steer toward a small opening.

She dropped her hand. If this was it, she wanted to see it coming to get her. She wanted to create the reality in her head that she was riding into it bravely, facing the unavoidable with a fearlessness she'd never had in life.

She regretted that now—that she'd worried so much about things. That she'd fretted about her father appreciating her business skills, when he'd always given her his love. That she'd harbored jealousy of Giulio. That she'd micromanaged Hal's performance at the restaurant because he'd resisted her efforts to control him and she needed so much to feel in control of *something*.

And now he'd claimed to have lusted after her for those two weeks, claimed she was beautiful.

There was that flutter! Even as they sailed out of control along the brink of death! The search and rescue crews were probably going to wonder why they found her body with a smile on her face.

The motor cut suddenly and there was an eerie silence as they sped along the snow. That was followed by snapping sounds as they reached the trees. Even without the motor, the noise was loud as they rushed into the woods like a stick run along a picket fence. Snow flew around them in spooky whooshes, and she closed her eyes when she heard tearing noises. She could only imagine as they spun around that a wing had snapped off.

They pitched and rocked and there was a sudden, vicious jolt. She got one glimpse of Hal's tense profile before blackness consumed her.

SHE FELT A HAND on her face. Through a weird mist that seemed to be part dream, part vision, her head hurt and she wasn't able to open her eyes. But she knew what that touch meant. Her Adonis had come at last. He probably wanted to make love to her, to give her their first daughter, and she couldn't even draw a good breath.

"Kat," she heard him say. He sounded a little desperate.

Eyes closed, she groped for his face. "I'm here," she said, her voice sounding frail, her breathing labored.

"Kat, wake up!" he demanded. He opened her jacket and unbuttoned the waistband of her jeans.

She smiled, loving that he was anxious for her. She wanted him. She struggled to open her eyes, to embrace him, but her eyes and her limbs refused to cooperate. "Take me," she said breathlessly. "Give me our daughter."

She heard a surprised voice reply, "Our daughter?"

He didn't know. Maybe men couldn't see into their futures like women could. "We're going to have four," she explained.

There was silence.

It couldn't be that he didn't want their daughters, she thought frowning, trying to will her eyes open. It had been ordained. She was *sure*.

"Kat, wake up," a firm voice said finally. "I'm sure if I take you up on your offer, you're going to take me before a judge and swear that you never made it."

She puzzled over that response as something cold was applied to her forehead and her cheek. The cold tore the gauzy half dream right out of her head and she opened her eyes to find herself looking into Hal Stratton's face as he wiped snow off her cheek with the sleeve of his sweater.

This obviously wasn't her dream life or her Adonis.

"Back to reality," she grumbled as he tried to rebutton her pants. She slapped his hand away and did it herself. "Or did we survive?"

"We survived." He put a diagnostic hand to her head. "How do you feel?"

She tried to assess that. "Okay, I think. A little headachey."

He nodded. "You hit your head on my shoulder when we lost the wing and spun around. Can you move your arms?"

She raised both and flexed them.

"Legs?"

There wasn't much room to move them but they didn't hurt except for the top of her right knee. She rubbed a hand over it. "Doesn't feel like anything's broken. Just banged my knee on something, I think."

"Good." He touched her cheek with a cautious index finger and she drew back when it hurt. "You're going to have a shiner," he said. "I'm sorry."

It would have been satisfying to hold him responsible for it, but unfortunately, not fair.

"I'll take a shiner over a toe tag," she replied. "Are you all right?"

"Yeah." He indicated the crunched radio under a smallish tree that had fallen neatly over the nose of the plane. "Radio isn't, though."

She looked around for her purse. "I've got a cell phone somewhere."

"I've got one, too. No signal."

She kept looking for the purse she'd tucked near her feet. "I've got one of those phones that works almost everywhere."

Hal considered pointing out the peaks and promontories all around that blocked reception, but he knew better than to argue with her. He sat back in his seat and waited until she'd found the small black leather pouch that had been hidden by a blanket and a backpack he kept in the back of the plane. They'd tumbled free during their wild turn.

"Ah, here we are!" she exclaimed with a triumphant smile, delving into her purse and holding up the phone. "Salvation!"

Salvation, he thought, was a pretty big word. He watched her punch out a number with the tip of her small index finger, then hold the phone up to her ear.

The smile turned to a frown almost instantly and she lowered the phone and studied it. She turned it off, then on again and stabbed in the number once more.

She lowered the phone with a dispirited pursing of her lips, hit a few keys, growled then tossed it back into her purse. "No signal," she said.

"That's what I said."

"Yeah, well you also said you were taking me to

San Francisco, then back. Unless you scheduled a stop on a mountaintop for sightseeing, I'm not sure I'm required to believe everything you tell me.''

He considered his police training a really good thing at the moment, because he wasn't sure his temper would have held without it. She was so gorgeous, and he was so attracted to her, he barely knew what to do with himself, but he'd about had it with the smart mouth and the fickle moods that made her stare longingly at him one moment and verbally claw at him the next. He'd like to understand what was behind that ambivalence.

"Look," he said. "We've got a problem here. It's not insurmountable, but it's going to require a little pulling together. Do you think you could stow the smart remarks until you have an audience that appreciates them?''

She bristled. "Don't get huffy with me! This is not my fault!''

''Well, it's not mine, either,'' he retorted. "I love this plane and I always keep it well maintained. I don't know what happened. Clogged fuel line, or something. But it shouldn't have. I just had it serviced. You might consider yourself lucky you were flying with someone with enough experience to get you down in sufficient good health so that you could yell at him!'' His voice had risen considerably at the end of that sentence and he paused to draw a breath and start again more quietly.

"Try to bear in mind that this isn't Umberto's and you're not in charge here. I am. And if I don't like the way you talk to me, I'll head off on my own and leave your pretty little backside right here."

"Who says you're in charge?" she asked after a brief shocked silence. The question was challenging, but her tone had an edge of restraint in it.

"Have you been lost in the mountains before?" he asked sharply.

"No," she replied.

"Then I'm in charge. I know what I'm doing."

"Oh. You've crashed here before?" She used that careful tone and her expression was bland but he still recognized the sass under it.

"No," he made himself reply quietly, "but I've hiked these mountains with my brother-in-law, Jack, and I had wilderness training in the military."

She sighed and wrapped her arms around herself. The cockpit was mercifully unbroken, but the outside air was well below freezing. "I'm sorry," she said. She sounded sincere. "I'm just a little...shaken."

He reached for the blanket that had tumbled out of the back and handed it to her. "That's understandable. Wrap this around you while I figure out just where we are and look for a trail out.''

She offered the blanket back to him. "If you're going outside,'' she said, pointing to the sweater he wore over a long-sleeved shirt, "you're going to need the blanket.''

He shook his head and grabbed the down jacket always stashed behind his seat. He'd used it a couple of times when the weather had changed during fall fishing trips with Jack.

"Take care of the blanket. We're going to need it tonight.''

He had to push hard to open the door and leaped down. Just before he closed the door again, he heard a muffled word of alarm come from the huddled bundle that was Kat.

"Tonight?''

CHAPTER FIVE

THOUGH TERROR had been a new experience for Kat, she hadn't really known what it meant until Hal slid down a snowy slope and disappeared from sight. She sat alone in the cockpit of the plane, holding the blanket tightly around her, and prayed that he'd meant to do that, that he hadn't fallen into some crevasse, never to be seen again. Because then, of course, neither would she.

But her concern for him wasn't entirely selfish. While she didn't really like him, she did find him gorgeous, and she had a grudging respect for him. Particularly since she'd learned a few things about him today she hadn't known before.

She hadn't known he'd served in the military, that he did family things like hike with his sister's husband, that he knew things about the outdoors she hadn't a clue about. She'd been a big-city-girl all her life, and the one and only time she'd been camping with a friend and her family the summer between her junior and senior year, she'd hated it. She never wanted an overnight experience more primitive than a room at a Hilton hotel and a short walk to the nearest Olive Garden restaurant.

Yet, here she was, faced with precisely what she hated.

And her cheeks flushed as this thought crossed her mind even though she was all alone—had all that stuff she'd said in that half dream after she'd banged her head been said aloud? Presumably that the hands she'd thought had been her Adonis's had been Hal's.

Had she actually asked him to…take her? To give her their first daughter?

"Oh, God," she said aloud, pulling the blanket up to cover her face. How could she possibly explain that? And after his smart remark about taking her up on her offer to sleep with him, did he think she was just reissuing the offer?

She felt happiness and relief when he reappeared suddenly over the lip of the mountain. Then remembering the questions she'd just asked herself, she felt embarrassment.

Fortunately for her, embarrassment wasn't as new to her as terror. She had a real working knowledge of it since her fiancé had married her best friend.

She leaned over to push open the door on his side of the plane as he approached. He swung inside with ease and closed the door, his cheeks red from the cold. He blew into his hands and rubbed them together.

"There's a trail right over that ridge," he said. He dug a map out of his backpack and filled half the cockpit with it when he opened it. He pointed in the middle of lines and squiggles that meant nothing to her.

"I'm pretty sure this is where we are. If I'm right, there's a little town called Nugget about five miles away. There's even a road to take us there."

"But no vehicle," she felt required to point out.

He folded up the map. "True. But hiking five miles on a road is preferable to even half a mile over this terrain."

"Can we make that by nightfall?" she asked, praying for an affirmative and two motel rooms.

He shook his head as he dipped it to look out the cracked windshield of the plane. He pointed to the sky and a dark mass of cloud moving fast. She hadn't even noticed it while lost in her own personal concerns.

"It's going to snow pretty soon," he predicted. "Doesn't look like a big system, but we don't want to get caught in it. If it stops by morning, we'll try it."

"We won't freeze overnight?" she asked worriedly.

"Of course not. We have body heat and a thermal blanket." He dug into a backpack behind his seat. "Not to mention a couple of energy bars, a few bottles of water, and a flask of brandy."

"Very civilized," she said. "I always thought the Victorians had the right idea about picnicking and camping. White tablecloths, china table service, candlesticks, the old Victrola." She was chattering, but she didn't seem to be able to stop herself. "Of course, your energy bars don't match their chicken and pork feasts, but we could pretend it's something more elegant. We can start with the brandy." He was watching her analytically. She was very aware of their confinement in this very small space and all the room the tension around her seemed to be taking up. She was going to choke on it. She didn't know what to do except keep talking. "Or, I guess it's more proper to end with the brandy. But if we're going to keep warm, we may have to have it before, during and after the…"

"Kat." The simple, quietly spoken sound of her name stopped her as effectively as if he'd shouted. He nodded. "Yes, I did hear you ask me to make love to you," he said. "I know you were in a mild state of delirium so I restrained myself, but I can't help but wonder where that came from. I mean, there was probably some basis in real desire if that's what came to you when your body was in turmoil."

She opened her mouth to dispute that, but he held up a hand and said amiably, "While that's a fascinating dilemma we really should explore—especially considering how *I* feel about *you*—we have more pressing problems at the moment. So don't lose it on me because you think it's impossible for a man to exercise self-control."

"I'm not going to lose it," she growled back at him, offended by the suggestion. "And I have no delusions about my sex appeal, believe me. I just remembered having that…dream." She shifted a little uncomfortably, but held his gaze. "And I didn't want you to think *you* were under any pressure because I'm your boss."

"I don't," he assured her with unflattering swiftness. Then he added with a superior lift of an eyebrow. "And I thought we'd settled the hierarchy here. You're not my boss this trip." Then he laughed wickedly. "Not that that'd discourage me, anyway. It has an interesting, late-night-movie sort of appeal. If you want to dismiss what you said as the words in a dream, that's okay for now. But we'll have to follow them to the source of their inspiration when this is over."

Then, mercifully, he dug a small silver flask out of his backpack and offered it to her. One small sip had an immediate warming, therapeutic effect. "I have four energy bars," he said. "We'll split one for lunch, one for dinner, then save the other two for the hike to Nugget."

That made sense to her.

After they'd sipped at the brandy, he put it back in the pack and rummaged around in the back, looking for something to put between the seats to turn the buckets into a bench. The arms folded back, he said, and if he could fit a box or something between them, they could stretch their legs.

She thought that sounded like a worthwhile plan. As he worked, she dug a notebook out of her purse. She kept it there for notes to herself about things she had to do at the restaurant, supplies she needed for projects at home or any good idea she was afraid she'd forget.

Her heart ached at the knowledge that her father would be nearly hysterical with worry when she didn't arrive home this afternoon. He'd probably call the linen company himself and they'd tell him she'd been there and gone. He'd undoubtedly call the airport afterward and they wouldn't be able to tell him anything either. Just that they'd been lost somewhere.

He would be pacing the restaurant, alternately praying and swearing in Italian. She couldn't help but wonder if he'd wish then that he'd let her take over the restaurant.

Then she dismissed that thought as petty and made some notes to herself about what she had to do when she got home.

"Keeping a journal of the experience?" Hal asked, pushing a long narrow box forward between the seats. *Seawolf Rubber Boat* was printed in bright green letters on the side of the box.

"I suppose if you'd carried skis instead of a rubber boat," she teased, "we'd have crashed into the water."

He sent her a look that was only slightly amused as he raised the aisle arms of both seats and fitted the box in tightly. "We didn't crash, we landed—granted it was a little dramatic, but it was a landing."

"Right. I forgot. No, I'm not keeping a journal—I'm making notes to remind myself of what I have to do when I get home."

"Mmm." He stood, leaning an elbow on the edge of each seat back. "I'm sorry your first airplane date isn't going better."

"It's a business trip."

"You haven't forgotten The Royal Dragoon, have you?"

She shrugged noncommittally.

He looked into her eyes. "Stretch your legs out," he directed, "and see if that's more comfortable."

She did as he asked. "It is," she said, arching her back against something pressing into the small of it. "Just the door handle jabbing into me." She reached for her purse, tucked it behind her, and leaned back again. "There," she said, wriggling against it, testing it. "That's better. If we just had a way to make coffee, life would be good."

"We'll just have to live on the memory of what you bought us this morning."

They sat upright in their seats, using the box as a table as they shared an energy bar for lunch and half a bottle of water.

AS DARKNESS FELL, Hal watched her slip into a pensive mood. That worried him a little. So far she'd been either critical and combative, or supportive and helpful. But until now she hadn't lapsed into the fatalistic hopelessness this kind of situation could inspire.

"What?" he asked, rooting through his backpack for the extra socks he always carried.

She blinked at him and almost smiled. "What? Are you asking me what's wrong?"

He grinned back, finding the socks. "I know. Silly question under the circumstances. But I've seen you completely reorganize a banquet when the refrigeration died. It should have been a disaster, but you raided several supermarkets, and not only succeeded in providing an eclectic and completely unorthodox buffet instead, but pulled it off as a triumph. You're not usually one to look defeated."

"I'm just worried about how my father's going to feel when he thinks I'm lost. That *we're* lost."

He sat down in his seat and handed her the socks. "Put these on over your shoes. If your feet are warm, you feel warmer all over. And put your scarf over your head. That'll help, too." His parents didn't worry about him, because though he loved them dearly, they led a busy life in Florida and he sometimes went months without calling. But he knew Umberto kept close tabs on Kat. He'd be destroyed if he thought he'd lost her. "I'm sorry. We'll have to make it up to him when we get home."

Of course, he knew that Umberto wouldn't be looking for them until tomorrow. He was trusting Hal to keep her out of the way while they caught

Percanto in the act of breaking into the savings and loan.

He felt a little guilty now about that deceit, but this didn't seem like a good time to tell her they'd been plotting against her to keep her safe.

"I grew up at his side—literally," she said, a faint smile on her face as she apparently thought back. "When Giulio and I were toddlers, we were set up in playpens in the restaurant kitchen, and when I was still really small I started working with my mother. My father would be in and out checking on the kitchen all day. Giulio escaped a lot of that because he was a boy and athletic, but I'm not sure my father would know what to do if he looked up in the restaurant and didn't see me there."

Hal nodded. "I've watched you work. You can do anything."

"I've covered everybody's shift at one time or another." She sighed, a look of grim acceptance on her face. "But my father's convinced I can't run the place. He thinks it'd die if I took over. He'd rather keep working, than turn it over to me."

"He knows how consuming it is." Hal said. "Maybe he knows if you took over, it wouldn't leave you time for a life."

"He had one."

"Because he had your mother and you."

She thought about that and sighed again. "That's true. But all kinds of people live their dreams and find a way to have a personal life as well. I know I could do that, too, if I wanted to."

He'd seen no suggestion of her having a life outside the restaurant in the two weeks he'd been there. "Why don't you want to?" he asked.

She looked startled by the question. "I never said I didn't want to. In fact...I tried." She waggled her head from side to side in a gesture of reluctance. He remembered that she'd almost shared something of her past at The Royal Dragoon, then changed her mind. She said unhappily, "I was engaged to be married last year to a lawyer who came into the restaurant all the time at lunch. After we got engaged, my best friend was suffering through a breakup, and Dave and I double-dated with Cassie and one of his partners. But it was Dave Cassie was attracted to, and apparently the feeling was mutual because about a month before my wedding, she told me she was pregnant."

"Dave's baby," he guessed.

"Right."

"I'm sorry. But you're smart enough to know that there's a broken heart in everybody's life at one time or another."

She nodded. "Of course, I do. But I'm a little…"
She groped for the right word.

"Reluctant to trust?" he suggested.

"No."

"Afraid to get hurt again?"

"No."

He grinned. "Ticked off?"

"That's it." She laughed. "I felt used, abused
and betrayed for a while, but I'm getting over it. So
a life would be nice, but I'm sure I can have one
and run the restaurant, too."

"I believe it. Can't you ask your brother to talk
to your father?"

"I don't want to put him in the middle. He's doing what makes him happy, and I don't want to
upset that for him."

"That's very generous, considering."

"Yeah, well, on good days I'm generous. On bad
ones, I'm jealous and resentful and feel like I used
to when we were teens and he used to get to go play
football on weekends while I made salad and
washed dishes." She took a breath, then said with
a sincere smile. "But he grew up into a very nice
man who loves water and boats, and I love that he's
happy in Maine."

Apparently done with her reminiscences, she

looked into his eyes. "You must have had a similar background if your father had a restaurant, too."

He had. "Very similar, except that my father was in partnership with a friend, and there were my sisters and me and two kids from the other family to fill in the same way you did. I got a job as a camp counselor in college to get away from the kitchen, one of my sisters went right into nursing school and the other got married. But, you apparently never wanted to escape."

"No," she agreed. "I love the work. But if my father wants to keep working, it may be time for me to strike out on my own."

"Would you stay in Portland?"

"I'd love to have a restaurant on the coast. Seaside, or Cannon Beach, maybe."

He could relate to either location. "They're both great places in their own way."

She smiled as she apparently focused on her dream. "I'd live on the cove in Seaside in a grove of trees."

"With your husband and four little girls," he said, remembering that moment after the plane had run through the trees, lost the right wing, then finally stopped. He'd had to practically pry his own fingers off the yoke, then turned to see her unconscious. He'd felt major panic until she'd told him in a quiet, dreamy voice to take her, to give her their first daughter.

She looked momentarily uncomfortable, then angled her chin and tossed her hair. "And a black Labrador for the backyard, and a tabby cat for the swing on the front porch."

He could see it all in his mind. Three of the girls roughhousing with the dog, and the quiet one on the swing with the cat. Every family had a quiet one.

"A big swing set in the back," he said, gate-crashing her dream, "and window boxes in the front. With pansies?"

"Geraniums would last longer." She closed her eyes and leaned her head back. "A picnic table and a barbecue in a gazebo-sort-of-thing because you can never trust the weather."

"A van in the garage."

"Right."

"A French nanny?" he suggested with a straight face.

Even with her eyes closed, she knew he was teasing. She smiled. "No nanny. I'll be there when the girls come home from school."

"Who'll be overseeing the restaurant?"

"I will." She smiled again. "I'll be a formidable force whose power remains even when she's away. And that'll work as long as I don't hire a waiter who ignores everything I say and does what he damn well pleases.''

''Not very subtle, Kat. If a customer likes me waiting on him, I should be able to wait on him.''

''Mr. Percanto liked *me* before you came,'' she said, opening her eyes and rolling her head along the back of the seat until she could look at him. ''I just resented him asking for the smart-mouth waiter who was giving me a lot of grief when I'd been standing on my head to make sure his table had everything he needed.''

Hal suspected that Percanto was as aware as everyone else of her eaglelike attention to everything that went on at Umberto's. It was entirely possible he'd asked for Hal to wait on his table because Hal was new and Percanto thought he might be too focused on doing a good job to overhear anything suspicious or notice anything suspect.

''It's a guy thing,'' Hal replied lightly. ''I'm sure it's nothing to feel sensitive about. I probably remind him of his son or something.''

She folded her arms and said a little grudgingly, ''You are a good waiter. You're just not the kind of employee who's easy to manage.''

''Some people just aren't manageable.''

''Then they should have jobs where they don't disrupt a well-oiled system.''

He couldn't help but smile at that. She was serious, and probably wouldn't like his amused reaction.

"You have an exceptionally fine and devoted staff. You don't have to be watching every move to get a good performance out of them, and from what I've observed, you seem to know that. You leave them alone. But *I'm* a different story."

"Because you never cooperate."

"You never give me a chance. You're telling me what to do every single moment, then telling me what I've done wrong even before I've done anything at all."

"I am not."

"You are. I think it's just an excuse to spend time with me," he said with a grin. "You can't very well flirt when other people are within earshot, so you grumble at me instead."

She gasped indignantly and grew so rigid that had he been able to get the plane in the air, she could have served as the other wing.

"That's ridiculous!" she accused. "You're smart-mouthed and contentious."

"And yet you keep asking me to take you."

"That was a dream!"

"Fed by something in your subconscious."

"I...I..." she stammered. "I thought you were

my…'' She sighed and put a hand to her forehead, obviously unwilling to share what was on her mind, but needing to disabuse him of the idea that she had feelings for him. "I dream about a man. When I was unconscious, he came to me, and when you touched me, I thought you were him. That's all."

"Are you sure I'm not him?" he asked.

"Yes!" she replied firmly.

He'd have taken issue with that, but the sky began to spit snow. It would be dark by midafternoon, so if he was going to make them comfortable for the night, he should do it now.

"Explain me to your journal," he said, pointing to the book still on her lap, "while I see what happened to the flashlight and a few other amenities when we came down."

CHAPTER SIX

GOD, HE WAS AGGRAVATING, Kat thought. But she'd have hated to be alone out here, so she could put up with him. And he wasn't entirely wrong in his conclusion. She had considered him handsome and competent when he'd first arrived, but he'd seemed completely uninterested in her and that had been demoralizing.

So she'd tried to talk to him in a personable way about providing attentive service to their patrons while still making sure that each course was promptly cleared away. That way the table could be turned over several times in an evening.

He'd told her in a very superior way that where he'd learned to wait tables, customers weren't rushed along, but allowed to relax and enjoy their meals so that they'd return. She'd resented his attitude and gotten superior in return. After that they'd argued over everything every chance they got. Until she'd dragged him into her father's office yesterday and been as good as told that her father intended to do nothing about it. That the fault was probably hers.

It had surprised her. Her father usually supported her decisions and opinions regarding the staff. But it was different with Hal Stratton. She wondered if her father saw in him the son he'd wanted in Giulio.

She was suddenly very tired. She snuggled under the blanket and closed her eyes.

When she woke up, an emergency light hung from the ceiling of the plane, and in its eerie light, she saw snow swirling against the windshield. The temperature inside the cabin had fallen considerably, and she noticed that Hal's jacket had been thrown on top of the blanket covering her.

Hal's seat was empty and she heard no movement from the back of the plane. She wondered idly if he'd simply decided she was too cross and too much trouble and had just left her to try to make it to town on his own. She felt one moment of stark panic.

Then she came to her senses. He'd have never taken off in the dark, and he wouldn't have left his jacket. The gesture would have been chivalrous but fatal.

"Hal?" she called.

"Yeah?" came instantly from the back of the plane.

"What are you doing?" She held her watch up to the light and saw that it was just after 8:00 p.m. There'd be a good ten or twelve hours until daylight. Great. And she was confined in a tiny space with a man who was convinced she had the hots for him.

And she did.

The sound of Hal's voice in response to her call filled her with comfort and relief. His calm management of all this made Dave seem like PeeWee Herman.

The truth of her feelings for him came down on her in a swirl of confusion like the snow beyond the windshield. It occurred to her that this realization was a really weird thing to have happen to her in a crashed plane on a mountaintop—that is, a *landed* plane on a mountaintop.

This couldn't have happened in the civilized atmosphere of the restaurant when she could have had a little space to think, could have had some connection to the real world, one in which she would know her feelings were irrational.

No. It had to come to her in the rarified atmosphere of the cockpit of a light plane from which there was no escape—at the moment, at least. A place disconnected from reality. A tiny space suddenly heavy with her awareness.

"I WAS JUST CHECKING what we've got." Hal stopped right behind the seats, feeling as though the sudden tension was a wall he had to break through. "I was hoping I'd find packaged jerky left over from a previous trip, but no such luck."

He wondered if his challenge to Kat about her feelings for him had created this environment. It had been a shot in the dark, but perhaps a valid one. Either that, or this tension had been created by his own libido confined in such close quarters with the woman he'd longed to possess for two weeks.

She held up his jacket. Her cheeks were pink from sleep, though she was shivering.

"You found a hat," she said, noticing the Navy watch cap he also kept in his backpack.

"Another thing I always carry in the plane along with the extra socks."

He had to get firm about their situation, put things in a practical perspective so that she didn't panic on him—and so that he could remember that this was a really bad time for romance.

"We're going to have to share the jacket and the blanket if we're going to stay warm," he said, putting his backpack with the water and energy bars in it at the base of her seat. "Are you up for that?" Give her a challenge. That would put her on her mettle.

"If you can stand being that close to the dragon who's always yelling at you," she replied. Her voice was even, but her eyes looked wary. It was interesting to speculate over whether it was him or herself she didn't trust.

"I don't like the yelling." He put the jacket on, but didn't zip it, then he climbed into his seat, putting his legs on her side of the cabin. "But I've grown rather fond of the dragon." He gestured her to him. "Just climb over the box and stretch out on it until you're lying in my arms."

"Here comes the dragon lady," she quipped, doing as he asked.

He opened the jacket and drew her in against him, then closed it as much as possible over her. Next, he pulled the blanket on top of them.

He knew instantly that this was going to be torturous. Unfortunately, he didn't have an alternative. But she was all soft and fragrant and—for the first time in their acquaintance—amenable and pliant.

"Is my elbow in your ribs?" she asked.

"Can't feel it through my sweater."

"My weight's going to crush you eventually."

"No, it won't."

"Will you tell me if it does?"

"When you land on the floor," he teased, "you'll know you got too heavy. Try to sleep a while longer. I'll wake you later for another half an energy bar and some water." He reached over his head to turn off the light.

He didn't expect to be able to sleep—and he was right. On one level, there was something curiously calming about having her lying in his arms, doing as he asked without argument.

But he felt her tension for several moments, a sharp reminder of his own. He withstood it stoically, pretending a distance from the whole situation that he didn't feel at all. Then there was a sudden inclination of her body weight against him, as though she'd finally relaxed. Her breathing evened out and he guessed she'd fallen asleep again.

He lay awake, wondering what was happening at home. It was hard to believe that dinner was still being served at Umberto's. Someone would be clearing a table for the next seating, and someone else would be serving dessert and coffee to some diners who were still lingering.

Berto and Roth would be in Berto's office, making last-minute plans. According to what Hal had overheard at Percanto's table, he intended to pay his bill then return later, probably to break into the basement through which he could reach the savings and loan next door.

Gordie Hoffman, who often ate with Percanto,

was an old safecracker. Hal could only conclude the rest of the plan involved applying Gordie's small explosives skills to the safe. That involved the not-very-subtle but usually dependable use of plastique.

Then they'd probably leave the way they'd come in. At which point Roth and Hal's fellow detectives would be waiting for them.

He felt his adrenaline stir at the thought of grabbing Percanto and his men when they climbed back into the restaurant. After the familiar but sometimes backbreaking work of waiting tables in a busy restaurant, Hal thought he deserved that.

But here he was in the dark, frigid night in a downed plane with a beautiful woman sprawled on top of him, apparently perfectly contented. He smiled thinly at the thought that the guys might disagree with him over who had the better part of the deal.

He thought ahead to what would happen to him if he married this woman and had four daughters and a beach house on the north coast. He'd have to give up thoughts of an advanced career in law enforcement. He'd be able to find a job, certainly, but police work in a small coastal community wouldn't provide him with the kind of experience that fueled advancement in the ranks.

And that would be all right. He preferred the beat

cop work right now, anyway. Life in a quiet little town still had undercurrents that made police work interesting. Mayberry existed only in fiction.

He was just beginning to drift off when Kat shifted her weight and hitched a leg up along his. When the confining seats stopped her from moving farther, she lowered it again, her knee sliding down his leg.

One would think that with layers of clothing between them, he wouldn't feel her breasts against his chest, her arm wrapping cozily around his waist, her knee moving along his thigh, her womanhood right over the part of him that resisted all his efforts to settle down.

God. He was going to have to jump out and roll in the snow.

KAT DREAMED of Adonis again. She was pressed close to him and he was stroking her cheek, whispering her name.

She couldn't see him in the darkness, so she followed the sound of his voice to his lips. She put hers to his and kissed him for coming back to her, for keeping her dreams of him alive, for promising her their future with the restaurant and the house on the beach and the four little girls.

"I love you," she whispered to him, kissing his

mouth, then rubbing her lips along his jaw, nibbling there where the line was so firm.

"Katarina," he said in a heavy voice, taking a handful of her hair and tipping her head back. "It's me!"

Her eyelids fluttered open and she saw Hal's face. Another revelation setting over her and became truth. Adonis and Hal—they were one and the same.

"I know," she said, kissing him again, leaning into him with passion and purpose.

When she pulled back, he was frowning and trying to read her eyes, wondering, she guessed, just how serious she was.

"Kat," he said, combing her hair out of her face with his fingers. "I just wanted to give you half an energy bar and..."

"I'm filled with energy," she said, moving her fingertips along his jaw, feeling the prickly surface of stubble, the sturdy bone underneath. "I'm overflowing with energy." Then she braced herself against him to reach up and kiss his lips.

He caught her hand and dodged her lips. "Kat, you're playing with fire here. I'd like nothing better than to..."

"Then just do it," she interrupted, running her index finger of her free hand along his lips. "You're the man I want."

"No, I'm not," he denied, grasping that hand, too, and tucking it between them. "You hated me only last night. You're just scared and tired and…"

"I want you, and I think I'm falling in love with you."

"Stop saying that."

"I'm just coming to understand it," she said, her playful mood pushed aside by heartfelt sincerity. "I was attracted to you from the beginning. Only you didn't seem to even notice me, so I…I think I began to behave in a way you couldn't miss. You couldn't ignore your employer, or so I thought. So I found fault with everything…" She talked quickly, afraid she wasn't going to be able to make him understand.

But he nodded, his expression unreadable. "I know. I resisted everything you asked me to do for the same reason. I knew it'd bring you back to yell at me again. I think we both need counseling." Then he smiled and she could see in his eyes that she was winning. "Or," he said softly, "we need to make love."

He freed her hands and she threw them around him and kissed him soundly. He pulled her back from him for one serious moment.

"But I have to warn you that whatever decisions you make in this kind of situation might seem right because your reality is altered right now. There's a good chance you might regret it in the morning.''

She had to ask. "Will *you* regret it?"

He gave her a look that melted all concern. "Not if I live for all eternity. I'm falling in love with you, too."

CHAPTER SEVEN

THAT DECLARATION deserved another kiss. Then she looked around them with a very practical concern. There was barely room to move.

"Can we make love right here?" she asked. "Or is there more room in the back?"

"We can put the blanket on the floor behind the seats," he replied, then added as practically, "Leave your jacket and your socks on."

When they were stripped of boots and jeans, Hal took his jacket off and wrapped Kat in it, then drew her with him to the blanket. They lay side by side on it in the tight space behind the seats.

"I wish I could carry you to a bed in a suite at the Ritz Carleton," he said, holding her closer with a slightly chilly hand to her hip. "This is just a step up from the back seat of a car."

She didn't feel that way at all. "It only matters to me that it's happening," she said, exploring his back and down the crenellated line of his spine. "And when we tell our children how we fell in love," she said, "it'll make a very dramatic story. How the date from hell turned into a heavenly experience." Then she realized what she'd said and waited for his horrified reaction. She'd made him the center of her dreams. Now he knew just what that meant.

He took it with surprising calm and acceptance. "I'd say we keep the details to ourselves, but I suppose four daughters will want details as they grow up."

"I'll be discreet."

"I'd appreciate that."

He kissed her with silencing determination, then showed her in delicious detail that though he'd made her life as difficult as possible in the restaurant, he had it within his power to make it sublime right here. With his lips and fingertips, he explored every inch of her exposed to him, then drew up her sweater and planted kisses on her midriff as he reached under her to unfasten her bra. He nipped and kissed her breasts, then worked his way down again.

Feeling as though the temperature had gone up thirty degrees in the cabin of the plane, she took advantage of his distraction to run her hands up under his sweater and his shirt to find and trace the line of his ribs and pectoral muscles.

"Warm enough?" he asked, kissing her throat. "I see gooseflesh."

"That's not the cold," she whispered back, moving her hands around him to stroke his tightly muscled backside. "That's your touch."

And then, as though to prove that he had the power to alter the inside of her body as well as the outside, he dipped a fingertip inside her.

Everything within her rioted. Her heartbeat sped up, her blood warmed, her lungs worked double time.

Suddenly desperately needy, she closed her hand over him and felt his immediate response. Moments later, he entered her in one sure stroke that brought a small cry from her.

"Katarina!" he said anxiously, about to withdraw.

But she held him to her, struggling to catch her breath. "No," she tried to explain. "That wasn't pain. It was…discovery. Wonderful discovery."

KAT TIGHTENED around him, drawing him deeper. Though he'd always been a very sexual being, he'd never been particularly sentimental about it. He'd taken great pleasure in sex, done his best to give great pleasure and accepted it as a great restorer of physical and emotional balance.

But being inside Kat made him feel as if he'd climbed an evolutionary step. The man he was when connected to her was better than the man he was alone. And it was too affecting to be a temporary thing. He'd be different forever. Impatience receded. Appreciation of the moment—of everything life offered—grew.

He loved her slowly, lengthily, warming her with his body while ignoring the cold himself.

When he finally collapsed atop her, she tried to wrap his jacket around him, then when that didn't work, she wanted to pull it off and give it to him. "You're freezing," she said, her small hand rubbing his thigh.

He pushed off her, handed her her jeans and pulled on his own. Then they climbed back onto the seats to stretch out as they'd done before, taking the energy bar and the half bottle of water with them.

After they'd eaten, he held her tightly to him, loving that she had her arms and legs wrapped around him, claiming possession.

"Wow," she whispered.

"Yeah," he agreed. "To think we've been fighting when we could have been making love."

Through the lingering, mellow afterglow, he thought he should tell her that her father had asked him to keep her away from the restaurant tonight, that though the crash had been accidental, the subterfuge that had put them on his plane had been planned.

But she clung to him with an adoration he couldn't bring himself to risk losing. And if he and Berto played their cards right, she might never suspect she'd been tricked, might be led to believe that her father had simply stayed late at the restaurant in her absence, heard the sound of someone in the basement and called the police.

Yes. He liked that scenario better.

"I'm going to hate leaving here," she said lazily, burrowing her nose into his throat.

He squeezed her to him. "So am I. But when we get home we'll work on getting you that restaurant and house on the beach and those four little girls."

"I hope we've got number one already," she said, heaving a deep, sleepy sigh.

He felt a pinch of guilt at the possibility that they'd conceived their first child in the middle of a lie—even if it had been told for Kat's own good.

Then he put it out of his mind, his body and his heart still sated with love and satisfaction. He closed his eyes.

BRIGHT SUN woke him the following morning. He'd drifted in and out of sleep all night, felt Kat squirm and huddle closer when she'd dislodged the blanket. And he'd sat up in alarm when she'd cried out in the darkness.

"What?" he'd demanded, unable to see her though he could feel her weight on top of him.

"Hal?" she asked, sounding surprised. She groped in the dark and stuck her finger in his eye.

"Ouch." He laughed, catching her hand. "What's the matter?"

The silence was heavy for a moment. "I thought I dreamed you," she said finally.

He put the palm of her hand to his lips and kissed it. "No, you didn't. I'm here." Then he pulled her back into his chest. "Was I a bad dream?"

She held tightly to him. "No. You were very real, but I was sure when I woke up that you wouldn't be. That's always the way it is. But...tonight. Wow," she whispered and drifted off again.

He was real all right. Not straight with her, but real. He could only hope all had gone well with Percanto and that was all behind them. Then a small detail occurred to him.

At some point, he was going to have to explain to her that he was a cop.

Well. He'd worry about that when they got home.

In the light of day, that fact raised its bothersome head again. He forced it aside as he shouldered the backpack and helped Kat out of the plane. The air was frigid though the sun was bright, and he knew the trek to town would be sufficiently strenuous that they'd warm up on the way.

"Stay right behind me," he told her, "until we get to the trail."

"You're sure we can't bring the linens?"

"They weigh a ton. We'll send someone for them later."

"Are there bears up here?" she asked.

"Not sure," he replied. "I've seen cougar."

"You're kidding!"

"They live here. We're the ones trespassing."

"If we see one, I'm explaining that you're the one who crashed the plane."

"I can see the kind of supportive wife you're going to be."

He heard her ringing laugh, the sound appropriate to the crisp, clear day.

THE MORNING was glorious and still, tall, snow-shouldered pines lining the road with dense forests behind them. The air was sharp and sweet, filled with the smells of pine and the freshness of winter.

Once Kat and Hal reached the road, they walked side by side, Kat torn between enjoying the moment and worrying about her father's state of mind because she didn't come home last night. She couldn't wait to reach a telephone and call him.

Hal, probably aware of her concern, tried to distract her by asking her what sort of restaurant she wanted her own to be.

"A family place, I think," she replied, focusing on her dream, "with breakfast and lunch—traditional fare and some trendy stuff for the health-conscious. Then at dinner it'll turn into an intimate little café with steaks and seafood and...Hal!"

She stopped in her tracks, unable to believe her eyes. Staring back at her from the side of the road was a cougar about the size of a St. Bernard. It had a fawn-colored coat with a white chest and muzzle and black tips on its ears. And eyes that were not at all catlike. They were large and intelligent and focused closely on her.

"Stay absolutely still," Hal said softly. "And try to make yourself look bigger."

"What?" she demanded in a whisper.

"She's just analyzing which one of you is tougher. Move slowly, but raise your jacket over your head."

"Can't I just assure her that *she* is tougher?" Her voice sounded close to hysterical as she did as he asked.

Hal, who'd been slowly sliding his backpack

down his arm as he spoke, said gently, "Don't panic. So far she's just interested."

And as he said that, the cougar took several graceful, powerful steps toward her.

It was all Kat could do not to scream and run.

Hal quickly put himself between her and the cougar, and reached a hand inside his backpack, shouting at the animal and taking an aggressive step forward.

The cougar sniffed the air, stiffened suddenly in a gesture Kat was sure meant attack, then ran off into the underbrush and disappeared.

Kat fell forward against Hal's back and simply stood there as the sound of a motor approaching broke the quiet. Apparently the cougar had heard it before it was audible to them.

Hal turned to wrap her in his arms, her heart thundering in her breast. "I was almost breakfast for a cougar!" she exclaimed with a half laugh.

"I promise I wouldn't have let her eat you," he said, handing her their precious half-filled bottle of water.

She took a swig, wishing it was gin. "I hope not. That would have been hard for you to explain to my father."

A blue, midsized American car with a government emblem on the door pulled up in front of them.

"Oh, Hal!" she said, putting the cap back on the bottle. "Rescue!"

A deputy sheriff climbed out of the car and Kat took a step toward him, excited and relieved at the sight of another human being. Then she noted with plummeting spirits that his gun was drawn.

Hal caught her arm and drew her back to him as the deputy approached, the sight of the gun changing the mood of the morning even more effectively than the presence of the cougar had.

"Good morning," Hal said, taking a step forward. "Our small plane crashed yesterday on the high meadow." He pointed in that direction. "We…"

"Put your hands up where I can see them!" the deputy barked at Hal. He looked very young. He was thin and pale and had an air of uneasiness about him that was contagious. He widened his stance and nervously waved the gun. Then he added for Kat's benefit, "Both of you!"

"But, we…" Kat began, unable to believe that now that they finally had help, he was holding them at gunpoint.

Kat saw Hal comply and followed his example.

Her throat was dry and the panic she'd held at bay since yesterday demanded release. Some rescue.

"We're on a freight errand from Portland," Hal told the deputy calmly, "to pick up linens in San Francisco. We had a fuel line problem and went down just before the snow. We decided to wait for sunshine to make our way to Nugget."

"Nugget isn't even on the map," the deputy said. "How do you know where it is if you're from Portland going to San Francisco? In a plane, yet."

"I fish near here in the fall," Hal replied. "What's the problem? We were just…"

"Drop the backpack," the deputy ordered.

Hal lowered his arm and eased the pack to the ground.

"That wouldn't be full of Darla Montrose's Harry Potter books, now would it?" the deputy asked, pulling the pack toward him and holding the gun on them as he opened it.

Kat looked at Hal in bewilderment. He appeared equally confused.

"'Cause we took a call not half an hour ago that two teens cleaned out her whole shelf of J. K. Rowling, stuffed the books into a pair of backpacks, and ran away. Planning to sell them in Bolen, are you, where they don't even have a bookstore?"

As he spoke, the deputy pulled out a wallet, a

checkbook, a flashlight, and a copy of the current Patrick Larkin novel.

"Rowling didn't write that one," Hal pointed out as the deputy perused it suspiciously. "And the young lady might be mistaken for a teenager, but do I look like one?"

The deputy looked up into Hal's face, and Kat saw the fear in his eyes. He apparently hadn't been a deputy long enough to acquire the authoritative presence that could intimidate a large opponent.

"Darla was pretty panicked," he said. "Told the sheriff they held a gun on her. Might have mistaken you for younger."

"Okay," Hal conceded, "but if Darla What's-her-name is in Nugget, and we were running away, wouldn't we be heading away from town instead of toward it?"

The deputy didn't seem to be listening. He looked up from the pack with a self-satisfied expression and produced a metal object that caught the sun and gleamed. A gun!

Kat's mouth fell open. She looked at Hal.

"I have a permit for that," he told the deputy. "I always carry it when I travel."

Kat closed her mouth. That sounded logical. She couldn't imagine why a waiter needed a gun, but she remembered him reaching into his backpack when the cougar approached her. She was sure if the cougar had decided to taste her, she'd have been glad he had it.

The deputy, however, seemed determined to put a criminal spin on it. It apparently confirmed his worst suspicions about who was responsible for the theft of Darla Montrose's Harry Potter books.

He tucked Hal's gun in his belt as she'd seen cowboys do in western movies, and gestured Hal toward the pack with his own gun. "You're just making it all up. Put your stuff back in it and get in the car," he said.

As Hal complied, the deputy made a call on his radio.

"I'm coming in with the two that stole Darla's books. Yeah. Well, I got the backpack, but no books. They either stashed them somewhere, or handed them off to an accomplice."

Kat concluded that she had to be losing it because she wanted desperately to laugh. He made it sound as though plutonium had been stolen.

"Got a gun, too," the deputy went on. "Claims to have a permit. No, they were on foot. Said their plane crashed on Wilson's Meadow. Right. I'm on my way in."

The deputy handcuffed them, ushered them into the back seat behind the protective screen, then climbed into the front and drove off with a screech of tires and a dangerous slip in the snow. But he regained control and drove toward town.

"We could leave this part out of the story we tell the kids," Kat said, holding up her cuffed hands. "In fact, I'm not dating you anymore. I've spent twenty-seven years without crashing in a plane, attracting a cougar and getting arrested."

"We haven't been arrested," Hal said with a smile, taking her cuffed hands in his. "We're just invited for questioning."

"At gunpoint."

"Newbies are always a little overzealous. He probably has dreams of making the big collar."

"Collar?" she asked.

"Arrest," he replied. Then when she seemed surprised he knew law-enforcement jargon, he shook his head at her. "Don't you ever watch *NYPD Blue*? *Law & Order*?"

She didn't, and she had other things on her mind anyway. "Why do you carry a gun?"

"It's a good idea in the wilderness."

"We were going from Portland to San Francisco."

"I've had a permit since I was in the Navy. And travel can be unpredictable. Or is that too much of an understatement given the circumstances?"

CHAPTER EIGHT

AND IT'S HARD being a cop without one, Hal thought.

He almost said the words aloud, but Kat was already upset. And when you were riding in the cage of a sheriff's car wasn't the time to find out you'd been lied to.

When they arrived at the Gold County Sheriff's Office, Hal discovered to his surprise that he had found Mayberry. It wasn't on the Oregon Coast, but in the California mountains.

The office was one big room with two barred jail cells in the back, one of them occupied by an alcoholic, judging by the smell of cheap whiskey that filled the room.

A big man with a thick shock of gray hair and a wide, ruddy face sat behind a desk. He looked up when the young deputy moved them toward him. Hal saw the sheriff look them over, his expression changing from pleased victory to frowning concern.

"Darla said they were teenagers," the sheriff said

to the deputy as he pulled up chairs for them near his desk. "A boy with a ring in his eyebrow and a girl that looked pregnant." The sheriff's eyes went to Kat's stomach, disguised by Hal's jacket.

She opened the jacket so that he could see her small, belted waist and flat stomach in a pair of jeans.

"The ring could have been removed," the deputy said, looking not at all discouraged, "and the pregnancy could be a disguise. And here's the topper." He placed the gun on the sheriff's desk. "I think the whole plane thing is a cover-up."

The sheriff shook his head. "Weather service plane reported seeing a downed plane on Wilson's Meadow."

He looked at the gun, then into Hal's face. Hal could see that the sheriff was a smart man. This was a small town, but he'd just bet he kept its security tight as a drum and nobody messed with him.

"Deputy Daggatt here says you have a permit for this," the sheriff said. "So you won't mind if we just check that out."

"Not at all," Hal replied. He only hoped that his cover remained intact when the sheriff finished the gun permit check. "And you can check Herrick Field right outside of Portland where I filed a flight plan to San Francisco. Left 8:42 a.m. yesterday." He rattled off his plane's ID number.

The sheriff wrote it down. He asked a lot of basic questions, then smiled at them. "Daggat'll get you coffee and a couple of the bakery's butter horns."

"Sheriff..." Daggatt began to complain, then at a look from the sheriff, took off out the door.

The sheriff pointed to the second cell. "You two have a seat in there for a while and I'll check you out. It's the most comfortable place to wait. Leave the door open."

"Sheriff." Kat remained in her chair. "Could I use your phone to call my father in Portland? I'm afraid he's beside himself with worry because he expected us home last night, and I was unable to get a signal to use my cell phone."

"Of course, you can." The sheriff smiled. "But not just yet. I'm waiting on a call. Won't be very long."

Hal and Kat walked into the cell and sat in the middle of a cot covered in a blue chenille blanket. It was surprisingly comfortable.

Kat grinned at Hal and gave him a look under her lashes that revved his pulse. "It's a good thing you're such a great lover," she whispered, "because this is by far the worst date I've ever had. I could probably get on Jay Leno's worst date segment. This is one for the *Guinness Book of—*"

He cut her off with a kiss. He couldn't believe her sense of humor remained intact after all she'd endured in the past twenty-six hours.

"I'll make this up to you," he promised, guilt riding him with spurs. "When we get home we'll take a long weekend in Seaside to rest and recover. And we'll look around for the right spot for your restaurant."

She leaned into him with a surprisingly contented sigh. "It'll be a while before I can seriously look for a place. I have to prepare my father, see about getting financing. I have a little saved, but not..."

"I have a small inheritance from my grand-mother," he interrupted, "sitting in the bank doing nothing. You can have it."

"What?" Her eyes widened in astonishment. "Ha-al!" she said. "I couldn't. I mean, you must have dreams you want to realize? What if I failed? What if I lost it all?"

She didn't seem capable of failure. "I can't imag-ine that happening," he said, "but if you did, we'd just try again."

"I want you to have your dreams, too," she in-sisted. "The long weekend is a good idea, but we'll talk about what to do. I want to know what's in your heart.''

"My dreams are modest, actually," he said. "Find a warm, loving woman, get married, have sons…"

"Sons?" she asked worriedly. "You didn't tell me you wanted sons."

"I've adjusted that part of the dream to daughters," he assured her.

She smiled with startling brightness. "You know, with your experience in a restaurant added to my experience in the business, I'll bet we could have a dynamite place! Would you want to be partners in a restaurant?"

Before he could reply, Daggatt arrived with their coffees and Danishes, glowering as he delivered them, clearly not pleased with the sheriff's doubts about their guilt.

Then the telephone rang on the sheriff's desk, and he picked it up. "Hey, cupcake, how are you?" he asked. Then after listening a moment, he said, "I know you're having a party, but Grandpa's busy today. Grandma and I are coming down Saturday, though, to take you someplace really special, okay? Okay, sweetheart. Be a good girl. I'll see you then."

He hung up the phone, then turned it on his desk

so that it faced the chair in front of it. He beckoned to Kat.

"Sorry for the delay. My granddaughter's birthday is today and I didn't want her to think I forgot her. Made her mom promise to let her call me as soon as she got home from her ballet lessons. Maybe some day the taxpayers will agree to give us two lines in here."

Kat and Hal exchanged a smile over the sheriff's obvious weakness for his granddaughter, and then Kat went to his desk to make her call.

She dialed her father's home first, presuming he'd be there at this hour, but when there was no answer, she called the restaurant. She was surprised when an unfamiliar voice answered with a simple, "Roth!"

"Ah...hello? Captain...Roth?" she asked, wondering what he was doing there before opening. "It's Kat."

"Oh." There was noisy throat clearing, then a hastily mumbled, "Let me get your father."

Then her father's robust voice said, "Umberto's Tuscan Grille."

"Dad!" she exclaimed. "It's me!"

"Hi, Kat," he replied cheerfully—and without a suggestion of the angst she'd been so sure he'd be suffering. "How are you? Did you get the linens?"

Did you get the linens? She was struck speechless. "Dad." She got that out, then tried to imagine what could account for his complete lack of surprise at the sound of her voice, at his complete lack of emotion at the discovery that she was alive.

Was it possible that her usually detail-obsessed father hadn't called her at home to make sure she'd picked up the linens and delivered them to the restaurant? But how could he not have known when the linens hadn't been there this morning for tonight's party?

"I'm calling you from California," she said, feeling as though she had to paint him a picture of what had happened. "Hal's plane crashed in the mountains and we had to stay in it overnight. Then we were walking to town…"

"Plane crashed," he repeated in a shocked tone that had a strange ring to it, as though he didn't quite know how to react. "Are you all right? Is Hal okay?"

"We're both fine," she replied in mild annoyance. "But I can't believe that these linens were so important to you that you sent me by plane to get them, then didn't even notice when they weren't there. And you didn't even notice that I hadn't come home!"

"Kat…" He began, then stammered, "I…we…ah…

Ferreira's party will go fabulously, even with the old linens.''

''What?'' she demanded. ''Well, if you don't care about the new linens, weren't you even worried about what had happened to your daughter and your favorite waiter?!''

She was losing it; she could hear it in her own voice. She'd remained fairly levelheaded under difficult conditions, but not even having been missed was more than she could take.

Suddenly, Hal took the phone from her and rubbed her back gently while he spoke to her father.

''Mr. Como,'' he said with a strained little smile in her direction. ''It's Hal.''

''HAL!'' the old man exclaimed. ''You were shining her on about the place crash to keep her overnight, right? You didn't really crash the plane?''

''Not deliberately, no,'' he said, thinking that was an honest reply that wouldn't give him away to her. ''We had a fuel line problem. But your daughter's fine. We'll get to an airport and take a commercial flight home. Maybe you should have the linens shipped after all.'' This part of the conversation would be trickier. ''Was last night very busy?'' He fished carefully while Kat paced the office, clearly in an emotional snit.

"We got him!" Berto said triumphantly. "And his safecracking buddy! I may even get a reward from the savings and loan for helping foil a robbery. Though, hell, I'd be happy if they just send the staff here every day to have lunch!"

The sheriff, while pretending to give him privacy, sent the occasional questioning look his way.

"Well, I'm happy to hear it went well," he said carefully.

"But now Kat's upset because I wasn't worried about the two of you!" Berto groaned. "She doesn't know I wasn't expecting you back last night, so she thinks I'm an unfeeling father."

"No, of course not," he said with a smile in Kat's direction, "I'll try to explain that to her."

"What?" Berto demanded. "Explain what?"

"I appreciate your confidence in me, Mr. Como," Hal said, the answer for Kat's benefit not quite aligned to Berto's question.

"I have no idea what you're talking about," Berto said, "but if you can stop her from thinking I'm a horrible father, I owe you big. Let me know when to pick you up at the airport."

"Yes. Okay. I'll call you as soon as we know what time we're arriving."

They went back to the cell and their Danishes and coffee.

"I don't understand," she said sitting beside him on the cot. "This whole thing has been strange from the beginning. I can't believe I was missing overnight and he wasn't even concerned!"

"That's because you were with me," Hal said. He waggled his eyebrows wickedly. "He said he knew there's been something between us since I first came to work, and he just thought we'd finally acted on it."

She looked as though she might believe that, then she shook her head. "No, no. He knows me! He knows I'd never leave a job unfinished. He sent me to get linens! I'd have delivered them to the restaurant, and then made love with you."

He had to smile at that because he knew that was true. He was going to have to tell her the truth, he admitted grimly to himself. He couldn't have her thinking her father hadn't even noticed she was missing.

"Although, maybe that's why Captain Roth was there," she speculated. "Because Dad called to report us missing." She enjoyed that thought for a moment, then shook her head on it. "No. He'd have responded to hearing my voice. Instead, he just sounded...uncomfortable."

He was sure both he and Berto would pay a high

price for the collusion, but certainly she'd understand.

Hal was putting the words together in his mind to explain when the sheriff walked up to stand in the open cell doorway, a sheet of paper in his hand.

"Just got this faxed reply about your gun permit," he said to Hal with a wave of the paper. "Why didn't you tell me you were a cop?"

CHAPTER NINE

GREAT. SO MUCH for his cover holding now that the collar was made. And so much for his determination—finally—to be honest with Kat.

He heard her intake of breath and her high-pitched, "What?"

The sheriff was taken aback by her surprise.

"You didn't know your boyfriend was a highly decorated member of the Portland P.D.?" he asked.

She looked at Hal as though he'd just murdered Emeril Legasse. "No, I didn't," she answered.

"Says here he's been a detective for three years—burglary division. Under Captain David Roth."

"Roth?" she repeated questioningly. Then, her brows forming a vee, she turned on him. "That's why he was at the restaurant just now!" she said, her voice trembling. "What's going on?"

Before he could answer her, she seemed to have a sudden revelation, judging by the widening of her eyes. "Something was going on at the restaurant," she said, murder in her eye, "and my father didn't miss me last night because *he didn't expect me back!* He sent me off with you because... because..." She didn't seem able to find a reason.

He was so deep in it now, there was little point in pretending she was wrong.

"To keep you out of the way," he replied, "so you didn't get hurt."

He expected her to turn on him in full fury. Instead she went to the cell door, planted a hand in the middle of the sheriff's chest and pushed until he was out of the cell. Next, she closed the door, as though that gave them some kind of privacy. Then she turned on him.

"Keep me out of whose way?" she demanded.

He opened his mouth to begin an explanation when she raised one hand in a STOP gesture and said, "Wait! You're not a waiter, you're a police detective?"

He had a sense of the world collapsing under his feet. Or, at least, the future they'd been planning.

"Yes," he replied intrepidly.

"And you've been lying to me for two weeks?"

"I'd put it differently than that, but yes."

Her anger seemed to radiate off her. Her cheeks were pink, her eyes combustible. "Go on with your explanation. Keep me out of whose way?"

He told her about her father overhearing Percanto's plan to break into the savings and loan from the restaurant, his call to Roth, and Roth assigning Hal to work undercover to get the details of when and how.

"That's why I kept beating you to Percanto's table," he said. "Your father didn't want you involved, and he knew that if you knew what was going on, you'd want to stop him yourself, or help stop him, or something equally dangerous. And because I was someone new, we figured Percanto would be less guarded around me. And Percanto was more comfortable with me. He probably thought I wasn't paying attention. Because I was new he probably thought I'd be more focused on doing a good job and earning a big tip than listening to his conversations."

She rolled her eyes. "Oh, of course. Keep silly Katarina out of danger. Let her do all the things that are really life-threatening like making the weekly schedule, or telling the chef his expensive addition to the menu isn't selling, or bussing tables when the busboy *ignores* the schedule and takes Friday night off anyway! But send her out of town with a phony on a wild-goose chase when something important happens. And why don't you crash her in a plane for good measure in the middle of a snowstorm. But, goodness, please keep her out of danger!''

''The plane crash was an accident,'' he said simply. ''I wouldn't frighten you like that on purpose.''

''No,'' she said, her glance poisonous as it raked over him. ''You'd just lie to me and tell me you were falling in love with me, make plans with me and make love to me in order to keep me out of the way so I don't get hurt! Why don't you just put a gun to my heart?!''

''Kat, I'm sorry.'' He was doing his best to be reasonable. ''Okay, maybe your father didn't handle it well, but his heart was in the right place. He wanted you safe. Certainly you're aware that he loves you very much…''

''I'll deal with him when I get home,'' she snapped at him. ''But you're the one who carried out his plan! You're the one who lied to…''

''Kat!'' He had to shout to be heard because her voice had risen considerably. ''A cop doesn't go undercover to prevent a crime and then tell people who he is!''

''I wasn't *people,* I was…me!'' she shouted at him. ''Maybe my father thinks I'm incapable of behaving like a businesswoman, but you knew me two weeks before he asked you to take me out of the way. Why didn't you stand up for me?''

"Because I knew you to have precisely the traits he was afraid would get you in trouble,'' he replied, getting to his feet to stand toe-to-toe with her. He was sorry that he hadn't told her the truth before the sheriff spilled it, but he'd be damned if he'd let her accuse him of motives he didn't have. "You keep tabs on everything that's going on, and if you don't like the way it's going, you have to get involved, fix it or change it. Every detail of everything has to be the way you want it to be. And while that's admirable in a manager, it isn't ideal in a woman with people who care about her. You think of yourself as the restaurant, the business, and you would likely not think twice about putting yourself on the line for it. But your father thinks of you as his little girl, and I think of you as…'' She wasn't going to like this, but he was beyond caring. "I think of you as mine—not inferior, not subservient, but not ever to be left to fend for yourself as long as I draw breath. So be offended all to hell about that if you like, but you should know that now if we're planning a future together. I'm sorry your feelings are hurt, but I'm not sorry that when my boss came down on Percanto last night, and Percanto drew his gun, that you were nowhere around.''

They were now glowering at each other, her chin stuck out pugnaciously, his hands in his pockets so he didn't shake her.

"Go to hell," she said in a furious undertone.

"Thanks." He nodded. "I'm already there."

KAT LET HERSELF out of the cell and went to the sheriff's desk, intending to make it clear that she wanted out of there now.

Having heard the entire argument, he seemed well aware of her mood and warded her off with a slip of paper. "Seems the young couple who stole Darla's books were arrested in a Jeep that went off the road several miles out of town, littering the snow with stolen books. So the two of you are free to go with my apologies."

"Great!" She wasn't even worried about how she was going to leave Nugget, she was just relieved to know this hideous experience was almost over.

"My secretary's going to drive the two of you to Medford where we've booked you a 2:17 flight to Portland. All you have to do when you get there is pay for the tickets. You can do that?"

"Yes," Hal answered.

"Thank you, Sheriff," Kat added.

"Least I can do. Sorry about your…mishap."

She wasn't sure if he meant the plane or Hal.

"It's never safe to judge somebody else's intentions," he said with a paternal smile. "Or you'd still be in jail instead of heading home. Things aren't always the way they look."

She thanked him for his help, but ignored his philosophy.

"Call your father and tell him when to expect you," he said, turning the phone her way again.

THE SHERIFF'S SECRETARY was a plump blonde in her middle to late thirties who talked about her children all the way to Medford. Kat sat in the front passenger seat and Hal sat in the back, the atmosphere between them as cold as last night had been.

Kat felt a jolt at that thought. The truth was, last night hadn't been cold at all. They'd kept physically warm in their little cocoon and then they'd discovered love and it had warmed their hearts.

She felt a sudden and violent sense of loss and abandonment. For the space of a few hours, it had looked as though all her dreams would be fulfilled— the restaurant, the house on the beach, the four little girls. And then it had all been ripped away at the realization that she'd simply been a pawn in an undercover operation.

How melodramatic.

She did her best to ignore Hal while they waited

in the tiny terminal for the plane that would take them home. He paid for their tickets, then came back to her with two cups of coffee and two bagels, handing her one of each.

She accepted hers with a stiff thank-you, going immediately back to her *Vogue* magazine.

With a sigh of exasperation, he took the magazine from her and put it aside. "How long are you going to keep this up?" he asked impatiently, "because I'm getting tired of it."

She tried to slap him with a look. "Keep it up?" she repeated, her voice strained by the effort not to holler. "Like it's some kind of pose? Well, it isn't! I'm completely disgusted with you and your lies, so the best thing you can do for both of us is just *leave me alone.*"

If she'd expected that little speech to inspire guilt and self-recrimination in him, she was sadly mistaken.

"Oh, grow up, Katarina," he said, looking not at all remorseful. "Your father's first thought was to protect you, but all you can think about is your own insecurities. So he's a little misguided about your abilities. He's a little old-world, but he's not malicious. He probably just thinks a woman should have other things on her mind twenty-four hours a day but business."

She glowered at him. "Considering the luck I've had with the men in my life, I'll just devote my future to the business. It's more rewarding."

"Well, poor you. You'll recall that I didn't impregnate your best friend. All I did was follow through with a plan to keep you out of danger. And you know damn well everything that happened between us was as true as it gets, even though you thought I was a waiter instead of a cop. You just don't like that the woman who has to control everything was manipulated by someone else—even if it was for her own good."

"A lie is a lie," she said judiciously. "There's no way around that."

"Please," he said with a roll of his eyes. "You told me you were falling in love with me, and yet this is how you react to an effort to keep you safe? I guess you could say that you lied to me, too."

"It's not the same thing!"

"You just said a lie is a lie."

She had to walk away from him before she reclaimed her magazine and beat him with it.

There were enough vacant seats on the plane for them to sit separately, and she didn't see him again until they disembarked.

Her father waited for them at the gate and wrapped her in his arms. She wanted to shout at him, too, but she was suddenly too empty of emotion. She felt as though she could sleep for a week.

Her father looked from her face to Hal's grim expression and said without hesitation, "Sending you away was all my idea. Hal didn't want to do it, but I insisted and Roth made him. So if you want to be mad at anyone, you should be mad at me."

"Oh, I am," she told him. "I'm giving you one month's notice, Dad. I'm leaving the restaurant." To Hal, she added, "And when we drop you off, I never want to see you again."

"Fine with me," he said.

CHAPTER TEN

IT WASN'T FINE with him at all, Hal thought as he stood on the sidewalk in front of the precinct and shook Berto's hand. But he knew Kat was feeling betrayed and nothing he could say would reach her. He had to bide his time.

"I'm sorry," Berto said, clapping him apologetically on the shoulder. "I didn't mean to put you in the middle. I was just so grateful you were around to look out for her."

"I was happy to do it for you, Berto," Hal said, giving him a quick embrace. "Maybe given a little time she'll change her mind."

Berto tried to give him a plain white envelope. He pushed it back at him.

"But it was a private job for me," he insisted. "You lost your plane, and I know how she can be. Please take it."

Hal shook his head, his heart filled with memories of those hours in the darkness in the cockpit of his plane. "And *I* know how she can be. So, I can't take it."

He glanced toward the car as he said that and saw her set profile looking determinedly straight ahead, clearly not even tempted to get a last look at him before she rode out of his life. He experienced an anxious moment as he realized that her stubbornness could win out in this case.

Then he took a little comfort in the fact that he'd written the book on stubborn. It had always gotten him in trouble as a child, but had stood him in good stead as a cop. He just hoped he was right to think it would help in dealing with a woman.

THE SQUAD ROOM was a busy place as he walked in, but Roth waved him to his office before Hal could head for his desk. The office was small and cluttered, a double frame of Roth's wife and two sons, also police officers, catching Hal's attention from the top of a file cabinet.

Roth pointed him to a chair. "Sorry about your plane," he said. "And sorry about…the whole thing with Katarina. Berto tells me she's angry at all of us."

Hal nodded. "Me, particularly. But it was the right thing to do. So, it all went down all right?"

Roth nodded. "It did. But we've got a loose end."

Hal sat up and frowned. "What's that?"

"We thought Percanto would hide out in the men's room or something, so Berto would lock up and go home without realizing he was still there. So we planted Mark White as a late customer, and had him order dessert after closing so Percanto would be able to hide out."

"And?"

"Percanto left, big as you please. I saw him get into his car and drive away."

"But you caught him."

"Right. He came back around 1:00 a.m., pulled around the back and got in through the alley door that leads to both the kitchen and the basement."

Hal finally understood the problem. "So... somebody let him in."

"Right."

"Who stays that late?"

"Nobody. Berto says they're all gone by midnight. I saw the chef, his assistant and the kid that runs the dishwasher all leave out the front door."

"You think somebody came back to let him in?"

"I didn't see anybody but him come back."

"Then...somebody deliberately left the side door open before they left."

Roth nodded. "Percanto had an accomplice inside, but he's not giving him up. I checked backgrounds and...I have a thought."

"And a plan?"

"You're the department's bright boy. I want you to come up with that."

IT WAS VALENTINE'S DAY, the day after Kat's return home, and there were several large parties scheduled for dinner. Though usually a night for intimate celebrations, the grille's patrons this evening also included a single women's group that met regularly there, a large Italian family that celebrated everything together and a motley collection of younger men who went to the gym across the street, then met at Umberto's for drinks and antipasto.

Kat put on a red woolen dress with long sleeves, a vee neck, fitted waist and a flirty flared skirt. She had to will herself not to burst into sobs as she brushed her hair. She caught it back in an old-fashioned but romantic French twist and fixed it tightly in place with pins. She attributed the tears in her eyes to the tightness of her hairstyle.

She went into the restaurant through the kitchen, remembering from the reservations book that the restaurant would already be full.

Marco, the chef, and Joseph, his assistant, looked

up from their frantic pace to whistle and catcall. Johnny, a high school senior who did dishes, just stared.

"Thank you, thank you," she said, pretending to take bows as she hurried through the kitchen. "How's it going?"

"Everything under control," Marco replied. "At least, for now. But you know how quickly that can change."

The moment the words were out of his mouth, the door from the dining room burst open and a young waitress stood in the doorway, her eyes wide and horrified. "An old lady," she said on a gasp, "just fell into the dessert cart, and…and…"

Kat turned to Marco. "Keep your prophesies to yourself from now on," she said, and donned an apron to hurry out and tackle the mess.

Her father was already there, supporting the little old lady to a bench in the small vestibule where he helped her lie down. Her husband, a wiry but little man, followed in their wake.

"Is she all right?" Kat asked, detouring around the mess on the edge of the floor and going to the bench.

"I think so," her father said, taking his jacket off and placing it under the woman's head. She was tiny and frail-looking, but the epitome of fashion in a beaded red dress that unfortunately now was marked with tiramisu, torta, chocolate mousse with grappa and cookie crumbs. Her white hair was short and fine, and Kat could see a purpling bruise on the pink scalp underneath. "But I've called 9-1-1, just to be sure."

"It's our anniversary," the woman said as her husband hovered near her head. He knelt beside her with great effort and held her hand. "Fifty-six years," she said. "And don't worry, Morton, I'm not going to die on you. We're going on that cruise and nothing is going to get you out of it. It's just a bump on the head."

Morton held two fingers up in front of her face. "How many fingers am I holding up, Lucy?"

"I don't know," she replied with a laugh. "My glasses are somewhere in the tiramisu. Oh, dear. I was raised never to make a scene, but look at what I've done."

"I thought it was very gracefully executed," Umberto said. "I saw you from across the room, and thought you intended to ride the dessert cart like a skateboard."

The woman giggled.

"Does anything hurt?" Kat asked, dabbing at the mess on the woman's dress with a towel she'd picked up on the way out of the kitchen. "Arms and legs okay?"

"Arms and legs always feel as though someone's hammering them from the inside." She grinned at Kat. "But they don't feel any worse than usual." She frowned suddenly. "I just got a little dizzy when I got up to go to the ladies'. I skipped lunch, so I'd have a good appetite for tonight, and that probably wasn't wise."

"The doctor told you," her husband scolded, "that with all your medications, you have to eat—"

"I know, Morton. I know," she interrupted. She smiled at Kat. "He nags me, and I should yell at him, but life's too short."

Morton turned to Kat and said with a frown. "She's just recovering from a tough round of chemo, and this cruise was going to be our celebration."

"I am going on this cruise," Lucy said with great determination, "if I have to go as ballast. Now, someone help me sit up."

Umberto put an arm around her back to steady her, and Kat took one of Lucy's arms while Morton took the other. She looked good, Kat thought. Her cheeks were pink, her eyes a little unfocused, but that was because of her glasses. Sure that she was steady, Kat ran back to the dessert cart and found the glasses on the floor near the mess, remarkably unharmed. She wiped them off with a clean towel and hurried back with them.

When the ambulance arrived, Lucy was looking well, except for her ruined dress, and entertaining the crowd that had gathered around her with amusing anecdotes about her long marriage to Morton and their seven children.

The paramedics insisted on taking her to the hospital for a more thorough examination, but told a very worried Morton that her pulse and blood pressure were fine.

"You have to call when you leave the hospital," Umberto said, "and let us know how you are. We expect you back tomorrow night for dinner on us."

Lucy's eyes brimmed. "You know the best part about living a long time?"

"What's that?" Kat asked.

"You get to add lovely people to your life, year after year. I'm so sorry about your dessert cart," she said as the paramedics put her on a gurney.

"Don't give it another thought," Kat said.

"We'll see you tomorrow night for that dinner," Lucy said as they wheeled her away. Morton followed, looking awkward carrying her red satin purse.

Kat hugged her father.

"What's that for?" he asked.

"Because you took such good care of her," she replied, wiping a spot of frosting off her father's sleeve, and off of her own, too. Lucy's accident was a reminder that there was more to a place where people gathered than the prescribed service offered there. There was kindness, humanity, caring.

Her father accepted her praise with a modest nod. Then he asked worriedly, "Is there more dessert in the freezer?"

"We just have cookies in the freezer," she replied. "But I'll run to the market for ice cream. We can offer two scoops for the price of one for Valentine's Day."

"Go."

Kat returned with several sinful, sumptuous flavors. Meanwhile, her father had cleaned off the dessert cart and tidied up the room. Once they resumed control of the evening, everything went as well as could be expected on a night crowded with reservations.

As Kat hostessed, bussed, helped in the kitchen, she thought about Lucy and Morton and how devoted they seemed to one another. After all those years, seven children and a bout with cancer—that had probably been almost as hard on Morton as on Lucy—their love shone brightly.

She felt small for getting angry at her father and Hal. She was still annoyed by what they'd done, but they had been guided—or misguided—by love and concern for her.

Hal hadn't called or stopped by today. Of course, she'd told him she never wanted to see him again, so that shouldn't be a surprise. She wondered if she called him after all the cruel things she'd said, whether he'd want to talk to her. He'd offered to pick her up at midnight on Valentine's Day, but that was before she'd banished him from her life.

Meanwhile, couples throughout the restaurant were toasting each other with wine, gazing into each other's eyes, sharing the two-scoops dessert. She worked through the evening with a smile hiding a fear that she'd never know that kind of devotion for herself.

Work was safer than love, so she'd dedicated herself to it in the hope that all the rules and procedures she'd established would fill the void. But nothing could replace love. Lucy knew that.

Kat did, too, actually. She'd just hated to concede to its demands. It wasn't orderly and couldn't be made to do what she wanted it to do. The only control she had was choosing whether or not she would give her love to someone.

That was another truth that came down on her

with all the subtlety of a frying pan upside the head. It staggered her, made her ears ring, mixed up everything in her brain until she had to reconsider what she'd thought she knew. Life had been teaching her things for several days now, and she was beginning to wonder if she was going to survive the lessons.

Love wasn't something dropped down between two people that they could accept or reject as if it was present. It was something created by two hearts and two souls seeking to come together. It could be added to, subtracted from, molded to become something that could be comfortably shared.

She found herself desperately eager to share that new knowledge with Hal. Maybe she wouldn't wait until morning. Maybe she'd just have to share it now.

But she didn't know where he lived. She wondered how Captain Roth would feel about being awakened in the middle of the night to give her Hal's address.

There was no time to think about that as the evening began to wind down and couples left arm in arm, still looking into each other's eyes, leaving little doubt about the balance of their plans for the evening.

The big cleanup and resetting of tables for tomorrow's lunch began. Kat took time to put fresh water in all the bud vases to help the red roses her father had ordered survive as long as possible.

Then she helped bus tables, gathered up tablecloths for the laundry, and reset them with the red-and-white-checked tablecloths they used for lunch. She wondered with a suddenly amused and wiser smile when the tablecloths would arrive from Nugget.

She was wiping off chairs when the telephone rang and her father went to the desk to answer it. He held his hand over the receiver and announced happily, ''Lucy's fine! She's on her way home. They'll be here at seven tomorrow night!''

Kat cheered.

It was after midnight before everything was ready for tomorrow. She'd said good-night to her father and taken over his office to count the night's take and prepare the deposit. It had been a big night and she didn't want to leave it until tomorrow.

Besides, she wanted to telephone Hal and she needed a little time to build up the courage.

Marco and Johnny called their goodbyes through the half-open door as they left. Joseph, as the sous chef, stayed to prep for tomorrow's lunch.

She had the deposit in the bank bag, and had a sudden, simple inspiration to check the phone book for Hal's phone number when Joseph appeared in the office doorway.

She looked up to bid him good-night but stopped, the words stuck in her throat. He was tall and slender, with a long serious face and a gift for pastry that was almost divine. But he was holding a gun on her.

She had a sudden memory of Deputy Daggatt pointing a gun at her and Hal. Man! Did she suddenly look like everyone's idea of a criminal?

He had to be kidding. That was it. She smiled. "Joseph, if you want a raise, you have to take it up with my—"

She stopped abruptly when he walked into the office and stopped directly in front of her desk, the gun aimed right between her eyes. She changed her mind. He wasn't kidding.

"That's right, Katarina," he said. "Best to be quiet. Even for the woman who always knows what to say about everything. Well, you can't do anything about this, so just give me the bag and keep still."

She couldn't believe this was happening. Joseph baked cakes for staff birthdays, came in early on big nights, stayed late without complaint, stood in for Marco on the occasional Monday when the chef had been out too late the night before.

She kept her hand on the money bag. What accounted for this aberrant behavior? "Are you in trouble, Joseph? Can I help you?"

He made a scornful sound. "That'd be an over-simplification." He held out his hand. "Just give me the bag, Kat, or I'll have to take it. I don't have any choice."

"I don't understand," she said, still holding it.

"This is a gun!" he shrieked at her. "What don't you understand?" Then he drew a breath and went on more quietly. "Tina's a gambler, you know that." Tina was his wife. "She borrowed from a Burnside loan shark and when we couldn't pay it back, I told Percanto, thinking maybe he could lend us something to satisfy the loan shark."

What was wrong with her, she wondered, not for the first time, that she hadn't known Percanto was anything but a nice old man?

"He lent me the money on the condition that I leave the side door of the restaurant open for him so he could get into the basement, then into the savings and loan."

She nodded, her mouth open in surprise. She hadn't imagined there'd been an accomplice.

"Well. When he gets out, he's going to think I ratted him out. I paid the loan shark, but I'm using that money…" he pointed the gun at the bag "…to get me and Tina as far away from here as possible."

"Joseph, that's crazy. The police had planted a detective here who heard everything. He's the reason the deal went bad, and Percanto knows that. He can't blame you."

"But even though I did what I was supposed to, he didn't get the money from next door, so he's going to want me to repay what he gave me, and I can't!" He was growing more and more desperate as he spoke.

"But if Percanto's business is shady loans," she asked, puzzled, "why would he risk federal prison by trying to rob a savings and loan?"

Joseph shrugged. "Something to do with a loan of his own, I think. The higher up the food chain you get, the nastier they are. Now, Kat. I'm not going to ask you again!"

"Joseph, calm down," she said, getting to her feet. He braced his stance and pulled back the hammer.

Afraid she was a dead woman, she closed her eyes and thought back to the crashed plane and the long hours she'd spent curled into Hal's chest.

"I love you, Hal," she whispered, feeling that was a good thought to go out on.

She opened her eyes abruptly when she was jostled back against her desk during a sudden commotion. Hal was grappling with Joseph, Captain

Roth and Kat's father standing behind him as though waiting to see if they were needed.

But Hal pinned Joseph to the floor in a remarkably efficient move, then cuffed him. Two officers appeared to take Joseph away.

"Wait!" Kat pleaded for him. "He didn't mean me any harm. He..."

Hal waved them away. "We heard everything," he said, taking her by the shoulders. "Are you all right?"

"His wife gambled all their—"

Hal gave her a small shake. "I heard all that. I want to know if you're all right."

Her father stepped up beside Hal. "I'm going right down to the station to put in a good word for him, maybe put up bail, see what I can do to help. Now, please. Answer Hal's question."

Kat smiled and wrapped her arms around her father. "I'm fine. He was just desperate. I'm sure he wouldn't have hurt me."

"He was holding a gun on you," Hal disputed. "And the next time someone wants your money or your life, give them the damned money!"

"We slaved for that money!" she argued, fully expecting argument in return. That seemed to be the kind of relationship they had.

"Yeah, well, now I'm a slave to my love for

you," Hal said quietly, his eyes assuring her he meant every word. "So think twice about your safety from now on."

While she stared at Hal in surprise, her father kissed her cheek. "I'm gone. See you in the morning." He turned to shake hands with Hal. "Thank you, Son. Again, you came through for me."

"Sure. I'll see you in the morning, too. We have things to talk about," he said, giving Kat a meaningful look that held a promise she couldn't quite understand.

Her father and the captain left and Kat stood alone in the office with the man she'd been so sure would never want to see her again. Yet, here he was. Because it was his job? That last declaration hadn't sounded like it, but she'd just been held at gunpoint—again! Her brain was unraveling. In this state of mind, what did *she* know?

"I don't understand," she said simply.

He nodded, his manner suddenly professional. Oh, no.

"We figured out that somebody left a door open for Percanto, but when Percanto wouldn't roll on him, we had to figure out who it was. Joseph, with his wife's problem, was the logical choice."

"But, how did you know about her?"

"We picked up the guy she owes money to a

couple of weeks ago on an assault charge, and got his list of 'clients.' She owes him big time.''

''And again...'' she said in a softly scolding tone because she really wasn't up to being angry, ''you didn't tell me.''

''You weren't speaking to me.'' He caught her arms and drew her toward him. His eyes ran over her face in a warm sweep that brought about that cursed tingle. It made it hard for her to think. ''So, I thought if I used you for bait, rather than sent you away to someplace safe, you'd like that.''

She had to smile. She had that coming.

He laughed and wrapped his arms around her. ''You were safe every minute. I've been here since you arrived. Hot dress, I might add.'' He held her away to look at her.

She wrapped her arms around his neck and drew him back to her, the love in his eyes destroying all her doubts. ''It's Valentine's Day.''

Didn't he know it. He'd been watching her heart-shaped little backside in the red dress all evening long. ''Then...will you be mine?''

She kissed his mouth with slow, lingering promise. ''I thought I already was.''

''I want your lips to tell me.''

So she kissed him again.

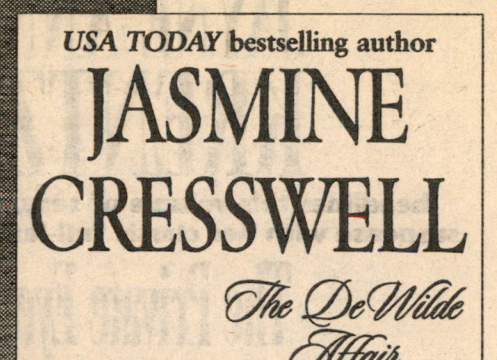
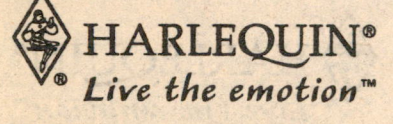

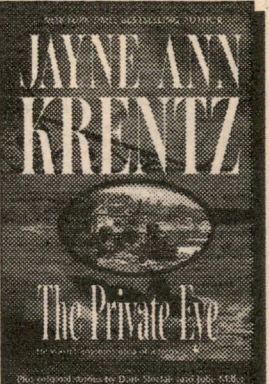
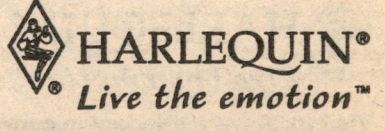

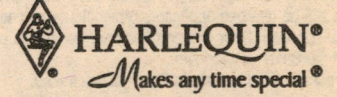

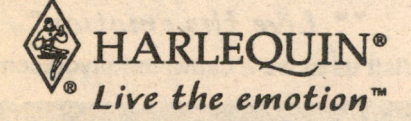